ABOUT THE AUTHOR

Lisa Stone lives in England and has three children. She has always been a writer from when she was at school, with her poems and articles featured in the school magazine. In her teens she began writing short stories, a few radio plays and novels. She finally made it into the bestseller charts with *Damaged* in 2007 which she wrote under the pseudonym Cathy Glass. Since then she has had 27 books published, many of which have become international bestsellers.

CATHY GLASS BOOKS

LISA STONE

THE DARKNESS WITHIN

avon.

This novel is entirely a work of fiction.
The names, characters and incidents portrayed in it are
the work of the author's imagination. Any resemblance to
actual persons, living or dead, events or localities is
entirely coincidental.

Avon
A division of HarperCollins*Publishers*
1 London Bridge Street,
London SE1 9GF

www.harpercollins.co.uk

This Paperback Edition 2017
1

A catalogue record for this book is available from the British Library

ISBN-13: 978-0-00-824884-0

Typeset in Bembo by Palimpsest Book Production Ltd, Falkirk, Stirlingshire
Printed and bound in the United States of America by LSC Communications

Find out more about HarperCollins and the environment at
www.harpercollins.co.uk/green

Acknowledgements: A big thank you to my editor, Phoebe; my literary agent, Andrew; my copy-editor, Alice Wood, and all the team at Avon, HarperCollins.

Chapter One

It was always worse when he'd had a beer or two. That Feeling. Hot, urgent and raw, tearing through him. Making him restless, argumentative. Angry. It was as though something or someone took control of him, forcing him to act badly, to be nasty and cruel. It happened when someone had a go at him, took the piss or said something he didn't like.

The feeling was there at other times too, Shane had to admit, but it was worse when he'd had a drink. It didn't take much; just a few beers. He wasn't an alcoholic, but it lowered his guard enough to allow his anger to come to the surface.

It was because of his childhood, Rosie said. They'd moved in together four months ago, and on the whole she was sympathetic. In some respects, she was too understanding for her own good. She was a good person and he liked her, even told her he loved her when she asked.

But why didn't she realize that the kinder and more understanding she became, the easier it was for him to overstep the mark?

It almost incited him to do it. Yet she continued to be understanding despite what he did to her: hitting her, making her scream, cry out and beg for mercy. Afterwards he knew that it wasn't the gentlemanly way to act, but when he was angry and out of control he didn't care a fuck for the gentlemanly way.

Anger, resentment, the feeling that he wasn't good enough brewed together in an unwholesome concoction and made him act as he did. He sensed that others felt he was inferior to them; that he was uneducated, stupid, and fair game to laugh at. That was the worst feeling – that they were laughing at him, especially when it was someone he knew taking the piss. It made him so angry that he couldn't be held responsible for his actions. This had got him into trouble many times and then recently he'd smashed a bottle and glassed his best mate, Kevin, which had put him in prison. They'd been drinking and telling jokes and Kevin had told one which he hadn't immediately grasped. Kevin had laughed and called him a dickhead. The others had laughed too, which didn't help, but he expected more from Kevin, being his best mate. Then before he realized what he was doing he'd smashed the top off a bottle and had ground it in Kevin's face.

He looked at Rosie now, cowering in the corner of the bedroom, the one that was theirs since he'd moved in. Why she'd let him move in he wasn't sure, but he was pleased she had. It was kind of her, but then Rosie was kind. He could admit that even now when she'd got on his nerves and made him hit her. Had she been a horrible bitch, a slag, like his mother, he could have better justified hitting her. He'd gone to his mother's house first on his release from prison but she hadn't wanted him. No surprise there; she'd never wanted him, not even as a baby. The shrink he'd seen in prison had said his mother could be part of his problem – his anger stemmed from her lack of nurturing and ultimate rejection of him. But it couldn't be helped. No one was perfect; not his mother or even Rosie for all her kindness and forgiveness.

The bedroom had been decorated in pale pink when he'd first moved in. 'Yuck,' he'd said to her when he'd first seen it, and she'd laughed.

'Jesus!' he'd exclaimed as he'd looked at her collection of china dolls in period costumes arranged on a small satin-covered chair. 'Dolls in my bedroom! What do you take me for? A nancy boy?'

He'd told her the dolls would have to go, but she hadn't understood to begin with because they were still there for another two days. Then he'd got angry that she hadn't done as he'd told her and he'd thrown the dolls and the chair across the room.

He might even have thrown Rosie, but he wasn't sure. He'd been in a really bad temper at the time. What normal bloke has dolls in his bedroom? He'd asked her nicely to remove them, and he'd had a couple of beers that night when he'd hit her so he couldn't be held entirely responsible for his actions. Perhaps on another day when he'd been in a better mood he might simply have asked her again to remove them. In any event, the dolls and the frilly chair had gone, together with the flowery duvet cover and the matching pillowcases. She'd heard him the first time when he'd told her to get rid of those, and together they'd chosen plain white.

He liked white, it was pure and virginal, which made him feel good and think happy thoughts. The only problem with white – as it turned out – was that it showed every mark, and the bloodstains never completely disappeared. Even when Rosie scrubbed the stains over and over again and used bleach, the blood spots greyed but were still faintly visible. Once white was damaged it was spoiled for ever.

Now he saw her gaze shift to the fresh spots of blood on the duvet cover. 'Sorry,' she said, her voice quivering. 'It'll wash out.'

'No, it won't,' he said. 'You've ruined it.'

'I'm sorry,' she said again. Seeing her cowering in the corner, apologizing with her face covered with blood, reignited his anger. He felt nearly as hot and uncomfortable as when he'd discovered that all the beer had gone from the fridge. He'd only had a few bottles and had been expecting to find more. It was a Saturday night for fuck's sake, and if a bloke couldn't have a few drinks on a Saturday, what was the world coming to?

It was Rosie's job to shop, to buy what they needed and restock what they were low on. But she hadn't bought more beer or vodka because of some silly discussion they'd had after the last time he'd hit her about him drinking less. He couldn't remember agreeing to that, it seemed highly unlikely, so he'd been bitterly disappointed at the lack of alcohol. He'd been anticipating a pleasant Saturday evening in with Rosie – a few beers, a takeaway, and then sex. He liked having sex with Rosie but she'd ruined it all. When he asked where the beer and vodka were she reminded him of his promise. It was the wrong thing to say; his disappointment had exploded into anger and he'd hit her. He hadn't meant to split her lip and send splatters of blood across the white duvet cover. It had just happened.

He appreciated that she wanted space now. After they'd argued and he'd hit her she usually needed time alone to wash her face, clean up the flat and change her clothes, so that when he returned all evidence of their disagreement had gone. She would cover the bruising on her face with make-up and all traces of blood would vanish. He didn't like any reminders of what he'd done.

'We're out of beer,' he said. 'I'll go and buy some. Do you want anything?' He was feeling a bit better now.

She shook her head.

'OK. Won't be long,' he said jovially and left.

Chapter Two

'Fuck! It's raining,' Shane said as he stepped out of the block of flats. He didn't like the rain. Getting wet reminded him of when his mother had left him for a whole night in a bath of cold water, because he'd said something bad.

Rosie's car was parked by the kerb. It was their car now. He used it whenever he wished. She'd given him the keys to the car and her flat when he'd come out of prison and moved in. She was good like that, he had to admit. He really shouldn't have hit her so hard, but he'd make it up to her. He'd buy her some of her favourite chocolate, he decided as he opened the car door and tucked himself in. That would please her and make it OK. Arguments upset him and reminded him of his childhood, so a few beers for him and some chocolate for her and their evening would be back on track.

As he started the car and then switched on the windscreen wipers, he briefly wondered if he might be over the legal drink-drive limit. He'd had three premium-strength beers. Was that enough to do it? He doubted it. But just to be on the safe side he wouldn't drive into town, he'd go to the hypermarket instead, which was along a less-used route. The police wouldn't be patrolling out there, stopping and randomly breathalyzing motorists; they'd have more pressing matters to attend to in town on a Saturday night. It was a bit further to drive but better to be safe than sorry. He didn't want another spell in prison. He'd already spent too much time inside and wasn't going back there any time soon, not now his life was good and things were looking up. He liked living with Rosie in her nice flat and driving her car. It made him feel normal, someone, like others he knew. That was one of the reasons he hadn't told her he'd already lost his licence for driving while under the influence of drugs and alcohol. He wanted to be able to hold his head proud, and then perhaps his mother would be proud of him too.

The only fly in the ointment was the age and model of Rosie's car. It was old and small. He was a big chap and had to stoop to get in, and he could never get the driver's seat comfortable. His head nearly touched the roof. It was a car designed for a woman or the elderly, not a man. To feel really proud a bloke needed a new car that reflected him – big and powerful – and a dark colour, not light blue. This wasn't at all good for his image. He didn't mean to sound ungrateful but it just wasn't right for him, and the car was well past its use-by date. Not that Rosie minded. She loved her car, treasured it, and when he'd told her they should buy a new one, she'd said she couldn't afford it, which had niggled him. Surely having a decent powerful car was a priority, but he supposed that was women for you. They'd rather buy clothes or a handbag. But he'd work on her and persuade her. She'd see he was right in the end.

At least the engine wasn't completely fucked, he thought as he accelerated. She still had some power in her, probably because she hadn't done many miles. It took her a while to get up to speed but with his foot firmly down, she understood and responded. He did this a lot when he was alone in the car – pushed her to the limit. Once he'd done it with Rosie in the passenger seat, when he'd dropped her off at work. He'd put his foot down hard, making the tyres screech and the engine squeal, and the car hadn't been the only one to protest! 'Treat Betsy kindly, she's getting old,' Rosie had said. He'd laughed scornfully. Betsy! He referred to cars as 'she' but to give it a name was pathetic.

He'd laughed loudly, perhaps a bit harshly, but had eased his foot off the throttle. Not so much from any desire to treat Betsy kindly – cars, like women, needed to be worked – but because he'd been doing seventy in a thirty and there was a speed camera ahead. So he'd slowed to the limit. If he was caught on camera, they'd discover he was banned from driving, and that would ruin everything.

After that he never thrashed Betsy in the town or where there was any chance of being caught. He drove steadily, within the speed limit, and while not exactly courteous to other road users he made sure he kept his rage under control and didn't draw attention to himself by getting out and thumping anyone.

Thankfully there was no need for all that polite constraint nonsense now. The road he was on didn't have speed cameras so he could thrash Betsy to bits if he wished. And Rosie wasn't with him to protest so everyone was happy. It gave him pleasure, a thrill; the ultimate blow job as she sucked up the road. He'd done it before on this stretch when he'd been alone. Race her, press her to the limit and see what she could do. He was a racing-car driver, the best in his field, zooming around the track. A Formula One driver leading the way and well ahead of the others in the Grand Prix. He could picture it, see the crowds waving and cheering, the look of admiration on their faces as he flashed past, skilfully taking another bend with the minimum drop in speed, the smallest deceleration required to keep him on the track and in the lead. You couldn't let up if you wanted to stay ahead of the rest. Sometimes he swerved to avoid an oncoming car. Idiots! Didn't they know he was in the race? The number one leader. Admired, respected and revered by men and women alike.

He swerved again, narrowly missing another oncoming car. 'Get out the fucking way, you prick,' he yelled, sounding his horn, and cursing their existence for slowing him up.

The road was poorly lit and the rain didn't help; driving on full beam, he was still forced to slow to take the next bend, which was a bummer. He really would have to talk to Rosie again about getting a new car, with better roadholding. He would explain that the new models were safer as they were lower and gripped the road better. Safer for them both to drive. That was the way to tackle it – women appreciated and understood talk of safety, not powerful engines. He felt very clever for having thought of the best way to approach Rosie about the idea. Perceptive, intuitive, that's what he was, and it made him feel smart and proud.

The windscreen wipers continued their relentless journey back and forth as he pictured himself in his new car. A black one, large, big wheels, with presence and a hint of mystery. He would have liked blacked-out windows but they were illegal now, so he'd have to settle for the darkest tint that was available. Yes, he could see himself at the wheel of that large powerful black car. He'd start visiting garages on Monday while Rosie was at work and test-drive what he liked the look of. The salesman would be so grateful when he showed interest in a decent car and then struck a deal.

Headlights came towards him. What the fuck! Was someone trying to overtake? No – it was a wide vehicle, he realized too late as he slammed on the brakes and pulled the wheel hard left to try to get out of its way. A delivery lorry. A fucking delivery lorry! He felt the whiplash in his neck at the exact moment he heard the crunch of metal and the sound of shattering glass. In a split second, almost simultaneously, the wipers stilled, his headlights went out and he felt as though he was flying through the air, up and over and then down.

'Fuck!' he cried as the car landed on its roof and the pain shot through him. 'Fuck you!' Then his world went very dark and silent as he blacked out.

Chapter Three

The lorry came to an abrupt halt, stopping as quickly as it could on the wet road. 'Jesus!' the driver exclaimed, his heart racing. He felt hot and cold at once. There was no way he could have avoided him. The other bloke was driving like a madman. It wasn't his fault, he told himself.

He had broken out in a sweat and his hands shook as he cut the engine. 'Jesus,' he said again, and opened the cab door to survey the damage. 'I hope the silly bugger's all right.'

His legs felt unsteady as he climbed out and then stood in the rain and examined the damage to the offside wing of his lorry. It wasn't much but that didn't mean the car had escaped as lightly. The lorry was far more robust and built of stronger stuff. He looked down the road to where he'd hit the car, or rather it had hit him. There was a significant difference – he wasn't responsible for the impact.

But there was nothing to be seen on the dark and wet road, apart from something that could have been glass glinting in the light of his headlamps. There was no sign of the vehicle.

A car came towards him from the opposite direction. It was going slowly, the driver proceeding with caution, just as one should on this narrow slippery road. It came to a halt and he went over. The woman driving peered at him through her window and then lowered it a little.

'Have you broken down?' she asked.

'No. I've been involved in an accident. Just now,' he said anxiously, nodding down the road to where it had happened.

'Are you OK?'.

'A bit shaken,' he admitted. 'He was driving like a maniac.'

'Not that small Fiat?'

'It might have been.'

'It overtook me back there. Blaring its horn, flashing its lights. I'm not surprised it's been involved in an accident. He nearly killed me.'

The lorry driver began to feel a little better knowing that someone else had been subjected to the driver's dangerous manoeuvres. 'I've no idea where the car is now,' he said, frowning. 'There's some damage to my lorry but I can't see the car. I'm going to fetch my torch from the cab and take a look.'

'Perhaps he's driven off?' the woman suggested, opening her car door.

'Perhaps,' he said. But he doubted it, not from the strength of the impact. And if he wasn't mistaken he thought he might have caught sight of the car in his wing mirror just after it had hit him, spiralling towards the edge of the road. He couldn't be sure though, since it had all happened so quickly and in the dark and the rain.

Without being asked, the woman got out and offered to help him look. He thanked her and she switched on her hazard warning lights, pulled up the hood on her coat, and went with him to his lorry. He took his torch and anorak from the cab and slipped on his jacket. With the torch held in front he led the way past the lorry in the direction the car had been going. Further up the road they came across a pile of broken glass and a piece of chrome almost certainly from a car's bumper. But there was no sign of the car. He swept the torch around, scanning as far as the beam fell, left, right and in front. A car came from the direction of the hypermarket, slowed and pulled over. Lowering his window, the driver asked. 'What's up? You OK, mate?'

'There's been an accident,' he said. 'Did you pass a small car just now? Possibly a Fiat?'

'No,' the man said, and glanced at the woman seated beside him. She shook her head.

'I think it could be in the ditch,' the lorry driver said.

The man immediately got out and joined in their search, while his wife stayed in the car. The torch beam shone brightly into the dark, sweeping through the drizzle to the bare trees and grassy banks which flanked the ditches either side of the road. The three of them moved forward in silence, watching and listening, the air quiet, save for the sound of their shoes on the tarmac and the rain dripping from the trees. Then, further up the road, the beam fell on the outline of something more solid, something partially raised and sticking out above the ditch.

'Over there!' the lorry driver cried, and the three of them ran to the spot.

'Jesus!' he gasped.

'Bloody hell,' the man said.

'I'll call an ambulance,' the woman said, taking out her phone.

The car was completely upside down in the ditch, fitting in so exactly it was almost as if it had been made for it. The doors and windows were compacted against the sides of the bank; only the underneath of the car and the bottom of the doors were visible. It was as though the car had been turned upside down and then dropped in directly from above to fit in so precisely, the lorry driver thought. And in a way it had, for the impact had flipped it over and sent it flying to land squarely in the ditch.

'There's no way we can get into that,' the man said, and the lorry driver nodded.

As the woman spoke on her phone, giving details of their location to the emergency services, the man from the car began knocking on the metal of the upturned car and calling, 'Anyone in there? Can you hear me?'

But there was no reply.

'I suppose he could have been thrown clear,' the lorry driver said.

'It's possible,' the man from the car agreed. Together they began walking slowly up the road, peering where the torch beam shone – on either side of the road, into the ditches and up the bank, but there was no sign of anybody, dead or alive.

Other vehicles began joining the slow-moving queues forming in both directions from the hypermarket. Some of the drivers wound down their windows and asked what had happened, and, their curiosity satisfied, continued around the lorry and parked cars, driving over the glass which crackled like ice. The two men, having found nothing, returned to the woman, who said the emergency services were on their way. The men began tapping on the metal of the upturned car, calling out, 'Anyone in there? Help is coming.' Just for a moment they thought they might have heard something, possibly a groan, but then another car passed and sirens sounded in the distance, after which they heard nothing further from the wrecked vehicle.

Police, ambulance, and fire tenders arrived within minutes of each other and the officers immediately took control. The police closed off the road in both directions and rerouted the traffic. Portable spot lamps flooded the scene and the fire crew quickly established that there was one male in the vehicle, then set about cutting him free. Sparks flew as they worked and the man and the woman who'd stopped to help told the officers what they knew, which wasn't a lot as neither had actually witnessed the accident. However, the woman did tell them about the driver who'd overtaken her on a blind bend, and the police officer included it in his notes. Once she and the man had given their statements and contact details, they were allowed to leave.

The lorry driver meanwhile was in a patrol car giving his statement. The police had already completed an initial safety check of his lorry and had found nothing untoward. They'd also looked at his driving licence and insurance, breathalyzed him, and checked his mobile phone, all of which they said was now standard practice at the scene of a road traffic accident. Everything had been in order and the last call he'd made had been before he'd left the hypermarket. As he finished making his statement, they saw the fire crew finally cut the driver free from the now backless car. They laid him on the waiting stretcher where the paramedics took over. An oxygen mask was placed over his mouth and nose and a line ran from his arm to a bottle held up by one of the paramedics. As they prepared to load the stretcher into the ambulance, the lorry driver turned to the officer beside him and asked, 'Do you think you could find out how he is?'

'I'll see what I can do,' he replied helpfully.

The driver watched through the windscreen as the officer went over and spoke to two of his colleagues. It had stopped raining now but a damp mist hung over the scene. They talked and nodded and at one point smiled. The ambulance sped away, its siren wailing and light flashing.

'He's got a broken leg and arm and a head injury,' the officer said on his return. 'They'll know more once he's at the hospital, but it seems he's lucky to be alive.' He paused, then added, 'He's known to us. He's already lost his licence and there's alcohol in his blood.'

The lorry driver let out a sigh of relief. He was very sorry that the accident had happened at all, but it could have been a lot worse. Supposing there'd been a seriously injured woman or child in the car – or even someone killed? He'd never have forgiven himself.

Chapter Four

Rosie had almost stopped shaking now. She'd had to force herself to appear calm. Shane would be back at any moment – indeed she had expected him sooner – and he hated to see her crying and trembling. She looked silly, pathetic, he always said, like a scared-shitless rabbit. It reignited his anger if he saw her in a state.

'Surely you're not scared of me!' he would say, and she'd tell him she wasn't, trying to keep her voice steady to belie how frightened she truly was. Of course she wasn't scared of him. She loved him. While this was true some of the time, those moments were now few and far between. Even when she wasn't in fear of him she was on her guard, walking on eggshells, constantly making sure she didn't upset or disappoint him. It was hard work keeping him happy and the strain was taking its toll, so much so that she wasn't sure what was worse: being attacked or anticipating it. Life was so confusing now, especially when he apologized and told her how much he loved her and that it would never happen again.

When did her life become this difficult? She knew the answer. A week after he moved in.

Rosie had wiped the blood from her face and cleaned the vomit from the floor, scrubbing the carpet with disinfectant until the smell of sick had gone. She often vomited after he attacked her; she thought it was from shock and the pain of being punched in the stomach. She never used to be sick – not before. She'd been very healthy and happy back then, before he'd moved in. But now even thinking about his anger and what he might do to her caused her stomach to contract and the bile to rise to her throat.

Shane liked everything to be back to normal with no trace of 'their fight' when he returned, so she'd also changed out of her blood- and vomit-splashed clothes. They were in the washing machine. The duvet cover would go in once the first load had finished, and she'd already put a fresh cover on the bed. The only sign of their fight now was her swollen lip. She'd managed to stop the bleeding by pressing a wet tissue on the cut, and make-up had covered the redness and bruising around her mouth and on her cheek, but it couldn't hide the swelling. In fact, if anything, it accentuated it.

Had she really deserved the beating? she wondered as she examined her face again in the bathroom mirror. Was it really always her fault? Did she provoke him beyond reason as he accused her of doing? She honestly didn't know. So much of her life had changed in the last six months that she barely recognized herself any more. Work colleagues and her mother had noticed the change in her too and had commented. Her mother, aware of Shane's past, had never liked him and refused to have him in her house, saying he was a 'bad lot' and that a leopard never changed its spots. Her friends, even her best friend Eva at work, had never met Shane because she no longer went out socially. Shane didn't like it. Rosie wished she could have confided in Eva or her mother. They might have been able to offer a fresh perspective and make some suggestions on how to help, but she knew that was out of the question. Shane had told her plenty of times that if she went blubbering to anyone he'd have to kill her, and she believed him.

The doorbell rang, making her start. Shane? Why didn't he use his key? Had he lost it? Quickly checking her appearance in the mirror again she glanced around the living room, making sure everything was back to normal, then gingerly went into the hall and opened the front door. Two uniformed police officers stood side by side.

'Rosie Jones?' the woman police officer asked.

Rosie nodded, a sinking feeling hitting the pit of her stomach. Shane had promised to keep out of trouble.

'I'm PC Linda Simpson and this is my colleague PC Tim Marshall. I believe you own a car with the registration number BA06 FYS?'

Rosie's mouth went dry and her legs began to tremble. 'Yes. Why?'

'I'm afraid there's been an accident. May we come in?'

Rosie stared at them, not fully understanding. She'd been expecting Shane and now this? 'What sort of accident?'

'I think it would be better if we came in to explain,' Linda said.

Rosie moved aside to let them in.

'In here?' the policewoman asked, nodding to the living room.

'Yes,' Rosie said, and followed them in.

She sat on the sofa and Linda sat beside her, while Tim took the single armchair: Shane's chair. She saw them glancing around. Were they looking for something? Her lip began throbbing.

'Your car was involved in an accident earlier tonight along Bells Lane,' Linda said, turning slightly so she could look at Rosie. 'A person called Shane Smith was driving. Do you know him?'

Rosie nodded. 'He's my boyfriend. He lives here.'

'I'm sorry, he's injured and is being treated at St Mary's Hospital,' Linda continued. 'He has a nasty head injury but it isn't thought to be life-threatening, so he's been quite lucky considering the state of the car. You'll be able to find out how he is later.' Rosie nodded. 'You knew Shane was driving your car? You gave him permission to do so?'

'Yes,' Rosie said, her voice unsteady. 'He has a key.'

Linda touched her arm, concerned. 'Are you OK, love? You're very pale. Can I get you a drink of water?'

'No, I'll be all right.'

'He's been well looked after,' Linda reassured her. 'But I'm afraid the car's a write-off. He seems to have escaped with some broken bones and a head injury, but it could have been a lot worse. Do you mind if I ask you a few questions?'

'No,' Rosie said. PC Tim Marshall took out his notepad and pen.

'How long have you known Shane?'

'Not long. He went to my school for a while.' Rosie tried to keep her voice steady. 'But I hadn't seen him for years.'

'And how long has he been living here?'

'Four months.'

'So you hadn't been in touch with him before you became a couple and moved in together?'

'No,' Rosie confirmed. 'I met him by chance and he had nowhere to live.'

'Where was he before he came here, do you know?' Linda looked at her carefully.

'He was in prison, for something he didn't do,' Rosie said, and saw the look the police exchanged. Her cheeks burned.

'So he came straight here then after his release?' Linda asked.

'He went to his mother's first but she didn't want him there.'

Linda nodded. 'Did he tell you why he was in prison?'

'No. He didn't like talking about it. He wanted to put it behind him and make a fresh start.'

'It was for GBH – grievous bodily harm. Were you aware he'd lost his driving licence for drink-driving offences? Shane wasn't allowed to drive.'

'Oh,' Rosie said, genuinely shocked. 'I didn't know.'

'To allow someone to drive your vehicle if they are banned is a criminal offence,' Tim added.

'I'm sorry, I didn't know,' Rosie said again. 'I put him on my insurance,' she added, hoping this would make it better.

'Driving while banned invalidates any insurance I'm afraid,' Linda said. 'They won't be paying for your car.'

Rosie looked at her. 'Will they keep Shane in hospital tonight?' she asked.

'For quite a few nights,' Tim said, glancing up from writing. 'He had to be cut from the wreckage.'

'Thank you,' Rosie said politely.

She saw them exchange another pointed glance and realized it wasn't the reaction they would have expected, but she was a bit overwhelmed at present and struggling to take everything in.

'That's a nasty cut on your lip,' Linda said.

'I fell,' Rosie said, her hand going nervously to her mouth.

'Tonight?' Linda asked.

'Yes.'

Linda held her gaze. 'Look love, I'll be honest with you. Shane broke the terms of his probation by not informing his probation officer where he was living. Added to which, he was driving while banned, over the legal limit of alcohol in his blood and in a manner likely to cause harm to other road users. As soon as he's out of hospital he'll be returning to prison.'

'Oh, I see,' Rosie said. 'I didn't realize.'

'No. I take it he didn't involve you in his criminal activities? He hasn't been arriving home with expensive items, for example? Items he can't provide receipts for?'

'No, not as far as I know. You can have a look around if you like.'

'Thank you.' Tim was already on his feet.

'So Shane won't be home tonight?' she asked, still trying to come to terms with it.

'No. You can phone the hospital now if you want and see how he is.'

'I will,' Rosie said. 'After you've had a look around.'

She watched as Linda joined Tim and they went first into the bedroom. The flat was only small and Rosie could hear them moving across the floorboards, opening and closing the wardrobe doors, and then the drawers. There was nothing to see in there apart from the wet patch on the carpet smelling of disinfectant. She'd no idea what they were searching for and frankly she didn't care. Shane wasn't coming home tonight and she was starting to feel relieved. They came out of the bedroom and searched the bathroom and then had to pass through the living room to enter the kitchen. She heard them open and close the cupboard doors.

'You're very good doing your washing on a Saturday evening,' Linda called.

'Yes,' she said quietly.

She heard the stainless-steel bin ping as one of the officers opened and closed it. They would have seen the bloody tissues she'd used to wipe her bleeding nose and mouth. And very likely the duvet cover in the laundry basket waiting to go in the wash. They came out and Linda returned to sit beside her while Tim remained standing.

'Is there anything you want to tell us about Shane?' Linda asked, encouraging confidentiality.

Rosie shook her head. Linda looked at her for a moment longer then sighed.

'OK, love. I'm going to give you the number for the Domestic Violence Unit anyway,' she said, taking a card from her pocket and handing it to her. 'You can just phone for a chat if you wish. You don't have to give your name.'

Rosie gave a small nod but didn't look at the card.

'We'll leave you to it then. Phone us if you need to. We can see ourselves out.'

Rosie stayed where she was as they left. She was still struggling to come to terms with what had happened and wondering what she should do for the best. Phone her mother? Phone the hospital? Speak to the Domestic Violence Unit, or change the locks? Possibly all of them, but in which order? Suddenly her life had changed in a way she could never have foreseen, and while she was sorry Shane had had an accident it had opened up an escape route. A huge weight lifted from her shoulders. There were decisions to be made and opportunities to be taken, and a light now shone at the end of what had been a very dark tunnel. She needed to galvanize herself into action. The washing machine bleeped as it finished its cycle and she stood to unload it. Once she'd sorted out the washing she'd start packing Shane's belongings. And although she wasn't a religious person, she said a silent thank-you to someone out there, grateful that she had been given this chance.

Chapter Five

The Reverend Andrew Wilson was going about his normal early-morning duties. He'd let Mitsy, their old Labrador, out for a run, had taken his wife and son up a cup of tea and now set out across the Maybury village green to unlock his eighteenth-century church, St Stephen's. Mitsy had followed him as usual, circling playfully at his feet, despite her age. Dressed casually but wearing his clerical collar he walked swiftly across the damp grass, still wet from the rain of the night before. At 8 a.m. on a weekday he didn't expect to see many of the villagers out; the commuters had already left for the station in the neighbouring town, so he tended to see the same few faces: the milkman who also delivered groceries, the paperboy finishing his round before going to college, and two dog-walkers. They all greeted him as usual with a warm, pleasant but slightly formal, 'Good morning, Reverend,' and he replied using their first names. He knew most of the villagers in his parish by name and he liked the village way of life. His previous parish had been in a deprived inner city which he'd initially believed was his calling. He'd done his best for five years and then asked to be moved, saying he felt he could no longer meet the challenges with everything else that was going on in his life. The bishop had been very understanding, and three months later he and his family had arrived here.

Unlocking the outer door, Andrew left Mitsy sitting obediently in the vestibule as he unlocked the second door and went into the main body of the church. He savoured the welcoming aroma of well-oiled oak, candle smoke, and the slightly musky damp of the solid stone walls. It was reassuring and comforting; a reminder of age and endurance. The church had stood here for nearly 300 years and would remain long after he had left this earth. That he was merely passing through and part of a bigger plan helped nudge his considerable worries into a slightly better perspective.

Facing the altar, he stood at the end of the aisle and crossed himself, then went to a box on the wall and switched on the lights and heating. Mrs Tremain, much-respected chairperson of the parish council, would arrive punctually at nine o'clock as she did most mornings to say a prayer in memory of her dear departed husband, and she didn't like to be cold. Then at ten o'clock his darling wife, Liz, would lead the Bible study class while he went about his many duties in the parish. He would return to lock the church at nightfall as he did every evening apart from Sunday when he held Evensong. It was a pity the church couldn't remain open twenty-four hours as it had in previous times – offering shelter and warmth to the needy – but vandals and thieves had put a stop to that some years before when they'd stolen the silver candlesticks from the altar and smashed a stained-glass window.

Andrew went up the aisle to the little altar with its white cloths, simple wooden cross, Bible, and candles in steel holders. Lowering his head he began his usual silent prayers, thanking the Lord for all that He had blessed them with, remembering those less fortunate and those living in famine and war-torn countries. He asked for guidance to make decisions wisely, and then mentioned by name parishioners who needed some extra help: Mr and Mrs James, whose son had been injured while serving in the army abroad; Mrs King's husband, who was recovering from stomach surgery; Mr and Mrs Watson, who had just moved into a nursing home and whom he would visit later that afternoon; and last but not least his own son, Jacob. He always felt slightly uncomfortable, almost guilty, asking for help for his own, but he was sure the good Lord understood why it had become absolutely necessary. He wouldn't have asked had it not been essential. *Forgive me Lord for asking again but if it is your will . . .* He struggled now; his prayer needed to be answered even if it wasn't the Lord's will. He was desperate and his wife was desperate too, and if he was honest they were both struggling with their faith, as they were being tested as never before. When life went well it was easy to have faith, he acknowledged, but when it went badly, really badly, and you stood to lose your only child, it was surely enough to shake the faith of even the most devout and ardent of believers?

'Please don't test me further in this way,' he said as part of his prayers. 'Anything but this. Not my son.' As he spoke, the small inner voice of God reminded him that He had sacrificed His only son for the sake of humanity, which wasn't what Andrew wanted to hear at all. He finished praying by thanking the Lord again and then asking that this day be the one.

Uncharacteristically, Mitsy began frantically scratching at the church door. Crossing himself, Andrew turned from the altar just as the door flew open and his wife Elizabeth ran in, without her coat and out of breath.

'What is it?' he asked, panic-stricken, and fearing the worst news possible.

'They've found a donor!' she cried. 'It looks a good match. We have to leave now. Come on! I've left Jacob getting up. We'll phone and cancel our appointments from the car. Be quick.'

Mitsy barked as though sharing this good news, and as Andrew hurried after his wife he thanked the good Lord for answering his prayers, and promised he'd never ask for anything for himself again.

★ ★ ★

Upstairs in the rectory Jacob had managed to wash and partially dress himself and was now sitting on the edge of his bed trying to catch his breath. Stick-thin, pale, permanently exhausted, and out of breath even with the minimal exertion, he'd been off work sick for nearly a year. At 23, having left university with a degree in business studies, he'd been six months into his first job when illness had struck, and a range of symptoms were eventually diagnosed as congenital heart disease. His heart began failing fast and he and his parents were told that a heart transplant was his only hope. While he didn't have the strength of faith his parents had, he did believe in something – a deity? He too now said a short prayer of thanks before texting the good news to his long-term girlfriend, Eloise.

His parents arrived in his room together. He couldn't remember a time when they'd looked so relieved and happy. While his mother helped him finish dressing his father checked his bag, which had been packed since he'd been put on the transplant list, ready and waiting for the call. Downstairs they shut Mitsy in the kitchen with food and water (a neighbour would take her out later) and barely thirty minutes after receiving the call they were on their way, overjoyed, but not forgetting that another family had lost a loved one to make this happen.

Chapter Six

At the transplant centre a specialist team of doctors and nurses was now assembling as two operating theatres were being prepared, one to remove the donor heart and the other to implant it into the recipient. It was unusual for the donor and recipient to live so close – just twenty miles apart. The transplant programme stretched nationwide and organs often had to be transported miles and at great speed when a donor was matched with a recipient at the other end of the country, although neither the donor's next of kin nor the recipient of the heart would be aware of this. Their details were confidential and would be kept secret unless they both wanted to know who the other person was. Sometimes the recipient wanted to thank the donor's next of kin, and if they agreed they were sensitively put in contact with each other, but this was unusual, and often resulted in a heart-warming story in the press or on the news.

It wasn't just the heart that was being removed. The donor's family had given consent for all of his body to be used, so as well as his heart going to Jacob, the kidneys, liver, lungs, pancreas, intestine, corneas, skin, nerves, veins, tendons and even the bones from his legs were going to benefit others.

When Jacob arrived at the transplant centre with his parents they were shown to a single room where nurses weighed and measured him, checked his temperature and blood pressure before listening to his chest to make sure he was well enough to undergo surgery. He confirmed he hadn't had anything to eat that morning; they then took a blood sample and gave him a pot for a urine sample. The anaesthetist arrived, explained what he would be doing and asked him if he'd ever had a bad reaction to an anaesthetic before. He hadn't – the only surgery he'd had in the past was a tonsillectomy at the age of six. The two surgeons leading the team arrived shortly after and the atmosphere in the room became electric – joyous, with a sense of occasion. They went over the procedure again with Jacob and his parents and reassured them that all would be well. It was a good tissue match, they said, and they would gown up now and see him later. Before prepping began, Jacob's parents had to say goodbye. 'We'll be here when you wake,' his father told him.

'And I'll phone Eloise,' his mother said, knowing that

it could be a few days before he was out of intensive care and could receive visitors.

One of the nurses gently showed them out, reminding them that Jacob was in very good hands – the best. She suggested they went into the city and had some lunch to pass the time as it would be at least four hours before there was any news. She would call as soon as Jacob was out of theatre. They thanked her, but before they left they made a detour to the hospital's little chapel, where they asked the dear Lord to watch over Jacob and the donor family who had given so generously and were now grieving over their loss.

Chapter Seven

After the transplant and following usual practice, Jacob was taken directly to the intensive care unit where he was kept sedated, connected to a ventilator to help with his breathing, and given a drip passing fluids and medication into his arm. As with the other transplant patients, doctors and nurses monitored him around the clock until he was stable enough to be removed from the ventilator and brought out of the drug-induced coma.

As Jacob rose up through the layers of consciousness, he began swearing and cursing at the nurses, saying things he wouldn't have done when fully awake. He told one nurse to 'fuck off' and another that he'd like to 'give her one', before trying to grab her breast.

'That's not very nice coming from a vicar's son,' she joked, aware it wasn't the patient talking but the cocktail of drugs – particularly potent after a transplant.

As soon as he was fully conscious Jacob returned to his normal self and, still slightly confused, asked politely, 'Where am I?'

'You're in hospital, Jacob,' the nurse said. 'You've had your transplant and everything is fine. We're moving you to a different ward soon and your family will be in to see you again later.'

Relieved, he thanked the nurse and then fell into a more natural sleep. The next time he woke, his parents and Eloise were at his bedside, his mother, holding one hand and Eloise the other, while his father stood at the foot of his bed, smiling. The glow from the ceiling light caught his hair, circling his head like a halo, and just for a moment Jacob thought he'd died and was in heaven. After a few seconds, reality hit him, and he remembered what had happened.

Jacob's recovery continued well and after a few days he was allowed out of bed to go to the toilet, and from then on he was encouraged to walk a little each day. He was very weak to begin with but the doctor and nurses told him that was only to be expected. In addition to undergoing major surgery he'd been weak in the months prior to the operation when his own heart had been failing. He'd only been able to take a few steps before he was out of breath and feeling dizzy, and going to the gym had become a distant memory. But that would change once he was deemed well enough to embark on the supervised cardiac rehabilitation programme run by a physiotherapist in the hospital gym. He was looking forward to gaining some muscle strength and getting fit again.

His chest hurt whenever he moved, coughed or cleared his throat but that was normal too. The surgeon explained that he'd had to cut through his sternum to operate and it was now held together by wires, which Jacob could feel clicking slightly when he moved. It would take six weeks for that bone to heal, during which time, it had been emphasized, he mustn't put it under any stress, which included not lifting anything heavier than a litre of milk. No pushing, pulling, twisting, or driving, as turning the steering wheel put pressure on the sternum. What would happen if he did exert pressure on it Jacob didn't want to know. He was already having unsettling dreams about being stitched together like Frankenstein's monster. The less he was told about what they'd actually done in the operating room or the details of what could go wrong, the better.

He was allowed home three weeks later and it wasn't a moment too soon. Alone in the single hospital room and with only his parents and Eloise allowed to visit – to minimize the risk of infection – Jacob had developed cabin fever, and knew he was becoming tetchy and short-tempered. To have been holed up for much longer would have driven him mad. For the first week he would have to return to the hospital every day for a check-up, then once a week, then every other week, and then once a month for the first year. After that, assuming he stayed well, his appointments would be every three months for two years and then every six months for the rest of his life. If he had any health concerns he had to return to the hospital immediately. But as he said goodbye to the nurses, thanking them again for all they'd done, returning to the hospital was the last thing on his mind. He was about to enter the world again and with a new heart in place, he intended to live life to the full.

His parents carried his case and bags to the car and he sat in the rear, as his mother took the front passenger seat and his father drove. He put his earbuds in straightaway. He wasn't being rude but they'd exhausted conversation during his long stay in hospital and they really didn't have anything left to say to each other.

His mother held his bag of medication protectively on her lap and it wasn't long before she was sorting through it, reading the instructions on the huge assortment of boxes and bottles. She'd put herself in charge of his medication and had told him she'd bought Dosette boxes. As soon as they were home she'd put the pills he needed for the week into the boxes so none would get missed or taken twice. It had been drummed into them how important it was for him to take the tablets as directed and at the correct times. There were plenty to take: two types of immunosuppressants, antibiotics, blood-pressure-lowering drugs, diuretics, aspirin, anticoagulants, painkillers, and those were only the ones he could remember. Doses of some of them would decrease and even stop over time but he'd have to take immunosuppressants for the rest of his life. If he didn't take them his immune system would recognize his heart was not his, label it as a harmful invader and attack and destroy it as if it was a virus.

His mother would also be looking after his appointment card for the time being, and the printed handouts containing the lists of post-operative dos and don'ts. They had seen the dietician together and while much of the advice had been common sense – eat low-fat foods, limit cholesterol, salt and sugar intake – others were more specifically for transplant patients: fresh produce had to be washed well before cooking or serving as the bacteria and viruses it harboured could be transmitted to the transplant patient, whose resistance was lowered by the immunosuppressant drugs, rendering them more susceptible to infection. His potassium intake had to be managed, as did his fluid and calorie intake. The dietician had said that his new heart would be put under strain if he carried extra weight, but he'd been fit and healthy in the past so there was no reason why he wouldn't be again. There'd been so much talk about his new heart that what had once been an innate organ like any other body part had become a living entity in its own right, and he was starting to resent the time and attention it demanded.

But what Jacob hated the thought of most were the biopsies he'd have to have once a week for the next six weeks. He'd already had two and couldn't stand the thought of more. He had to lie on the operating table while they gave him a local anaesthetic, cut a hole in his neck and pushed a wire down the vein and into his heart to cut out a small piece. It was then sent to the lab and examined for signs of tissue rejection. 'Transplants aren't for the faint-hearted,' his surgeon had said. Arsehole!

It was a little after 3 p.m. and as Jacob gazed out of the side window listening to his music he suddenly realized he was very hungry and craving meat, which was a first. Since meeting Eloise at university he'd become a vegetarian as she was, although he still ate fish, cheese and eggs. But right now, after all that healthy eating in the hospital, he was craving meat: a rump steak or a rack of ribs, rarely cooked red meat that he could sink his teeth into.

'What's for dinner, Mum?' he asked, removing an earbud so he could hear her reply.

She turned to face him. 'I've made a vegetarian cottage pie,' she said, pleased he was regaining his appetite. This dish had become one of his favourites and she'd put time and effort into making it. 'Eloise is coming as soon as she can dismiss her class.' Eloise was a primary-school teacher at a school not far from where she lived with her parents – about an hour away.

'Any chance of some meat?' Jacob asked. 'I really fancy some tonight.'

'Well, yes, if that's what you prefer,' his mother said, surprised. 'I've got some steak in the freezer. I'll take it out as soon as we get home.'

'Count me in,' his father said chummily, glancing at his son in the rear-view mirror. Neither of them were vegetarians except when Eloise joined them for a meal. Jacob knew that given a choice his father would much rather have meat than Quorn or soya beans any day. He threw him a conspiratorial wink in the mirror.

'Oh Jesus!' Jacob exclaimed as the rectory came into view. A large *Welcome Home* bunting was draped across the front of the house and bunches of balloons festooned the porch. 'Did you have to?'

'It was your mother's idea,' his father said, ignoring the blasphemy. They only used Jesus Christ's name with reverence.

'We can soon take it down,' Elizabeth said, feeling a little hurt. She'd wanted everything to be perfect for his homecoming. 'I thought you'd like it.'

'Suit yourself,' he said with a shrug.

Clearly they were going to have to continue to make allowances during his convalescence. It was almost impossible to imagine how frustrating it must be for a lad of Jacob's age to have to deal with chronic illness and then a major operation. But at least now he was home, and with time, patience and understanding, nature would do the rest. Allow at least six months, the surgeon had said, then gradually life will return to normal.

Chapter Eight

Mitsy, having heard the car draw up, was now barking furiously on the other side of the front door.

'She'll be pleased to see you,' Jacob's father said as he finished parking.

'But remember not to let her lick your face,' his mother warned. 'And to wash your hands after stroking her.'

Jacob nodded. More guidelines from the dos and don'ts list to reduce the risk of infection.

His parents carried his bags into the house and Mitsy was immediately at his feet, panting and wagging her tail excitedly. Jacob automatically bent to stroke her and as he did so felt a sharp jabbing pain in his chest. He straightened. It was his own fault; he'd been warned to avoid sudden movements until his breastbone was fully healed. Leaving the dog, he went over and sat in one of the armchairs by the fireside. Another *Welcome Home* banner hung from the mantelpiece with more bunches of balloons either side. They'd certainly gone to town, he thought, and with a niggle of guilt wondered if he shouldn't have been more grateful. His mother was now in the kitchen sorting out his medication. She meant well.

'I'll take these to your room,' his father said, picking up his case and rucksack.

Jacob stifled a sigh of frustration, resenting his dependence on them. He watched the fire for a few moments, unsure of what he should be doing now he was home. It felt strange, after all those weeks in hospital. 'I'm going to my room for a while,' he said at last.

'Yes, of course,' his mother said, stepping in from the kitchen. 'You're bound to feel tired to begin with. I'll bring up your tablets. Would you like a snack and a drink to see you through to dinner?'

'Just a drink,' he replied, heaving himself to his feet.

'Tea, fruit juice, milk? What would you like?'

'A beer,' he replied.

She laughed; they both knew he was joking for he wasn't allowed alcohol, as it would reduce the effectiveness of his medication. 'Just as well you weren't a drinker,' she said. 'At least you won't miss that.'

Upstairs, he found his father unpacking his case.

'Leave that, Dad, I can do it,' he said.

His father hesitated. 'OK, but don't overdo it, son. You know what the doctor said.'

'I won't.'

They looked at each other awkwardly for a moment, not knowing quite what to say or do, then his father cleared his throat. 'Well, if you're all right for a couple of hours I've got some parish business to attend to.'

'Yes. Go. Do what you normally do. Mum's here if I need anything. But I must start doing things for myself again.'

'I know, son. But not too much all at once.'

Jacob nodded and watched him go, then looked around his room before easing himself onto the bed. Almost immediately a tap sounded on the door and his mother appeared, carrying a tray with a mug of tea, a glass of water and his pills in a small plastic pot given to them by the hospital. 'You look comfortable,' she said, coming over and placing the tea on his bedside cabinet. She held out the glass of water and pot of pills as if she expected him to take them while she waited.

'Put them on there,' he said a little brusquely, nodding to his bedside cabinet.

She did as he said. 'Don't forget to take them.'

'I won't.' He yawned.

'I'll leave you to rest then,' she said, and left.

He wasn't physically tired as she thought – more exhausted from the narrow strip his life had become. He needed some space and time to himself, and he needed to establish some ground rules. He'd been washed, dressed and even taken to the toilet by nurses in the early days. Continuously examined by doctors who discussed him as though he was theirs, so that he felt his body was no longer his own. Everyone seemed to have a claim on it and knew more about it than he did. And all the advice about his recovery, although necessary and well meant, had become suffocating, as was being constantly fussed over, not only by the nurses but by his parents and Eloise. Some blokes might have enjoyed all the attention but he didn't; it had reduced him to a childlike dependency, humiliating and degrading. It would be a sharp learning curve before his parents and Eloise saw him as an independent bloke again, if he'd ever been one, which he was starting to doubt.

He'd had too much time to think in hospital; indeed there hadn't been much else to do. He'd spent hours, days thinking about his life – the years before his illness. Gradually he'd come to see that he'd never carved out an identity, a will, a personality of his own. He'd always toed the line, done as he was told and what was expected of him. He'd worked hard at school, learnt to play the organ so he could help out in church, been polite to his father's parishioners, and had tolerated the down-and-outs and misfits who'd arrived regularly at their door in the city looking for help and a handout. Even as a teenager he hadn't rebelled. In fact he'd been a bit of a mummy's boy. And away at university he could only remember one instance of drunk and loutish behaviour, before he'd joined the Christian Union and met Eloise.

Eloise was a nice girl; kind, well-mannered and polite. His parents had taken an immediate liking to her and were soon treating her like the daughter they'd never had.

Jacob was looking forward to seeing her again tonight and hopefully having sex – the first time since he couldn't remember when – sometime before he'd become really ill. When he stayed the night at her house her parents gave them a double room, but when she stayed with him his mother showed her to the guest room. They then had to wait until his parents were asleep before he could creep along the landing and into Eloise's room to make love to her. Although he apologized for his parents' Victorian and prudish attitude, he had to admit that the secret risqué nature of their liaison added to his enjoyment.

Tonight, however, there was an additional hurdle to be overcome. The list of dos and don'ts included post-operative sex with the warning that his breastbone mustn't be put under any pressure until it was fully healed, which ruled out the missionary position – the one they usually used. After some thought Jacob decided that the best way – perhaps the only way – would be for her to sit astride him as he lay on his bed. And as he pictured this, the conservative, rather prim Eloise bouncing up and down on his erect penis, it caused it to come to life. A very good sign, he thought, for one of the possible side effects of his medication was impotence, which would require more pills and be yet another blow to his manhood.

He must have dozed, for he woke with a start to the sound of his mother tapping on his bedroom door again. 'Eloise is here. There's no rush. I've made her a cup of tea.'

'I'll be right down,' he called, easing himself off the

bed and into an upright position. It always took a few minutes after a sleep or a nap for his muscles and brain to start working again; he assumed it was the tablets.

He used the bathroom, combed his hair and checked his face in the mirror before carefully making his way downstairs. Before he'd become ill he'd taken the stairs two or three at a time, but now, aware of what a fall could mean, he made his descent slowly using the hand-rail. He resented that he had to approach everything with caution and trepidation but for the time being it was unavoidable. As he entered the living room Mitsy ran to him again, panting and wagging her tail, asking to be made a fuss of. Jacob ignored her and crossed instead to Eloise.

'Good to see you home,' she said warmly. She knew not to throw her arms around him until his chest was fully healed, so instead she smiled and looked up into his eyes, waiting for him to slip his arm around her as he'd done in the hospital. But he didn't – he briefly kissed her cheek and then sat in one of the fireside chairs. Elizabeth had come into the living room in time to see her son's dismissive greeting and the look of disappointment on Eloise's face.

'Let's draw up this chair so the two of you can sit together,' she said, pulling the matching armchair from the other side of the hearth.

Eloise flashed her a smile of gratitude as together they positioned it as close as it would go to Jacob's chair and Eloise sat down.

'Do you want anything, Jacob?' Elizabeth asked. He shook his head. 'Eloise, another tea?'

'No thank you.'

'I'll be in the kitchen if you need me. Dinner won't be long. We'll eat just as soon as Andrew returns.'

Eloise smiled and thanked her again, then turned to Jacob. He was gazing into the fire that danced in the magnificent inglenook fireplace, part of the original house and now only lit on special occasions or when they had guests staying.

'So how are you?' she asked him after a moment.

'Fine,' he said without taking his eyes from the fire. 'How are you?'

'I'm good, thank you, but it's not me who's had the heart transplant.' She gave a small nervous laugh. 'Pleased to be home at last?'

'Of course.'

'How's the pain today?'

He shrugged. 'I just take the tablets if I need them.'

She moved a little closer and rested her hand gently on his arm as she had done for hours and hours in the hospital. 'How are you feeling in yourself?' she asked, aware he had been feeling low at times.

He shifted, finding her intensity uncomfortable. 'OK,' he said. She seemed to expect more but that was the trouble with women – they expected you to expose yourself, pour out your feelings and vulnerabilities as they did.

There was silence as the fire crackled.

'I left the teaching assistant to dismiss my class so I could leave early,' she said, making conversation.

'Good,' he said, which seemed to please her. She smiled and, taking his hand in hers, kissed it tenderly.

'I've missed you so much,' she said.

'I've missed you too,' he agreed. This was clearly the right thing to say for she beamed at him and kissed his hand again.

Thankfully his father arrived to save him from further conversation. Eloise and he greeted each other with a warm embrace and cheek kisses as they always did. He asked her how she was and how her journey had been and then he went to wash and change, ready for dinner.

Conversation over dinner became easier as he didn't have to talk much at all. Eloise and her parents did all the talking and he appeared to have been excused, he assumed on the grounds of health. They chattered away non-stop about day-to-day trivia, small talk about nothing in particular, which they seemed to thrive on. He didn't know how they managed it. All that polite tattle that filled the gaps between eating and seemed to bind them together. Had he ever been part of it? He supposed he must have been, although he couldn't remember doing it with the enthusiasm they did. He felt like a visitor or alien from another planet as they prattled on, Eloise about the changes in the school curriculum and how it would impact on her teaching and the class's learning, and his father about the village bypass. He was on the committee and had attended a meeting in the village hall that afternoon – lots of fogies trying to feel important. And as for his mother, she managed to create a storyline out of collecting him from the hospital which he really didn't appreciate. He frowned. Perhaps he was jealous? Was he envious that they could share this warm comradeship of conversation that eluded him? He'd be the first to admit that he didn't have anything to tell them, that since his illness and then the operation his life had stopped, and he had nothing new to say. All he could contribute – had he wanted to join in – were remarks about being a patient which they were only too familiar with. But that would change just as soon as he was completely fit and well.

He excused himself from the table straight after pudding at 8.30 on the grounds he was tired – they understood. His mother fussed around him and asked if he needed help undressing, which was embarrassing. Then she produced the plastic pill pot already containing his night-time meds together with a glass of water for him to take up to bed. He called a collective good night to the three of them as he went up the stairs, and guessed they'd probably start talking about him as soon as he'd left the room.

Chapter Nine

'Jacob's very quiet,' Eloise said, her brow furrowing with concern. 'He's hardly said a word to me all evening.'

'Nor to me,' Elizabeth said gently. 'But it is only his first day home. Everything must seem very strange, and he's recovering from a huge operation. It will take time.'

Andrew agreed, and Eloise knew she mustn't take Jacob's attitude personally. She remained at the table talking to Andrew and Elizabeth for nearly an hour and then they transferred to the living room to watch the late evening news on television. At 10.30 Eloise kissed them both good night and made her way upstairs. They were lovely people and made her feel so welcome – more than Jacob had done tonight, she thought, but quickly dismissed this as unkind and selfish. Of course it would take time for him to adjust and recover. She assumed he wouldn't be visiting her room tonight.

Quietly crossing the landing so as not to wake Jacob, she entered the guest room that had become hers. It was comfortable, with a single bed and a faint smell of jasmine from the reed diffuser Elizabeth had placed on the chest of drawers. Over the last few years – since she'd begun staying – this room had gradually become her home from home, and she kept a toothbrush and toiletries in the small en-suite bathroom, and a change of clothes in the wardrobe. She felt relaxed and at ease here, not only in this room but in the whole house.

She washed, changed, and then, yawning, climbed gratefully into bed. The end of the school week was always tiring with the children excitable at the prospect of the weekend, and tonight she'd met heavy traffic on the way over too. But she was here now and there'd be plenty of time to unwind and de-stress over the weekend. She wasn't returning home until after dinner on Sunday as she had often done before Jacob's operation. But this time when Elizabeth had telephoned to check she would be staying the whole weekend she'd been concerned.

'Are you sure it won't be too much trouble with Jacob just home?' she'd asked.

'Don't be silly, of course not,' Elizabeth had chided warmly. 'It will do Jacob good, and you know I always appreciate your company. You already feel like my daughter-in-law.'

This had pleased Eloise immensely. She had always got on well with Elizabeth and had come to feel she had a place in their family, assuming, as Elizabeth did, that one day she really would be her daughter-in-law. Jacob had said as much before his illness – 'As soon as we've saved enough for a deposit on a home of our own I'll propose.' So it was an unannounced engagement where they'd implicitly promised themselves to each other and lived their daily lives in the comfortable knowledge that they were a couple. And while their plans to marry had been put on hold with the onset of Jacob's illness, Eloise had no doubt that once he'd recovered and returned to work, their plans and saving would continue and reach fruition.

With these happy thoughts as bedfellows, Eloise quickly fell into a deep and dreamless sleep. She was fast asleep, lying on her side, when the door to her room silently opened and then closed again. She didn't stir. The room was pitch black; at the rear of the house there were no streetlamps, just meadows where cows grazed. Outside a thick cloud covered a moonless grey sky so even though her curtains were parted no light shone in.

The first she knew that someone was in her room was when a hand covered her mouth and she woke with a start. Then his familiar breath, hot on her cheek as he hissed close to her ear.

'Sssh. Be quiet or they'll hear you.' It was a moment before he removed his hand.

'Jacob, you scared me to death,' she said, turning to him. Her heart was still pounding from the shock. 'Why didn't you tell me you were coming to my room?'

'A surprise,' he said, and climbed into bed beside her.

She moved over to make room for him, propping herself

on her side to look at him. Her pulse began to settle. Jacob eased himself onto his back and she snuggled close, draping one arm over his stomach, well away from the angry scar on his chest. He'd lost that clinical smell which had pervaded his room at the hospital, and now smelt of his deodorant and the fabric conditioner Elizabeth added to the laundry. She breathed it in, homely and comforting.

'What time is it?' she whispered, enjoying the warmth and intimacy of his body. It had been a long time since they'd had the opportunity to lie close.

'Twelve-thirty,' he whispered. 'My parents are in bed and asleep.'

'I thought you were asleep too,' she said with a small laugh.

'I've been waiting for them to come up so I could visit you. Just like old times.' He picked up her hand that was resting on his stomach and placed it on the outside of his shorts.

'Jacob!' she said surprised. 'We can't, can we? Not yet?'

'Why not?' He pressed her hand onto him and felt him stir.

'You're not well enough, are you?'

'Let's put it to the test,' he said roguishly. He eased off his shorts and then curled her fingers around him, growing firmer under her touch.

She assumed he wanted her to masturbate him as she had done when he'd been too ill and weak before the operation to make love properly. He'd touched her too, although she hadn't got much pleasure from it. A large part of making love for her was the warmth and weight of his body on hers as they moved together as one. But she appreciated that men were different in their sexual wants and needs, and it had helped restore some of his confidence – his masculinity, he'd said.

'He may need a bit of encouragement,' Jacob said, moving her hand to work up and down the shaft of his penis, before reaching out and switching on the lamp.

'Jacob!' she said, startled. She blinked into the light.

'That's better. I need to see.'

He threw back the duvet so he could watch properly, see her hand on his dick, but the movement was too delicate.

'Harder. Faster,' he said, and gripping her hand showed her what to do. How he would have liked to have shoved it in her mouth as the bloke on the film he'd watched on his laptop had done, but he didn't think she was ready for that, not yet. Not prim Eloise. Next time, he promised himself.

He was big now, he could see how big he was, and getting bigger by the second. Hard, proud and bold as the blood coursed through his veins. He was standing to attention as he hadn't done for a long while. Watching her hand move up and down was adding to his pleasure. 'Take off your nightdress,' he said, tugging at it.

She didn't and her hand lost some of its firmness. 'I need to see you,' he said again urgently. Why didn't she understand? He tugged harder, yanked at the buttons at the top of her nightdress and they gave way. She gave a small cry, presumably of pleasure. Women liked forceful blokes, didn't they? He roughly pulled the nightdress from her and rubbed his hand over her breasts and then down between her legs, making her cry out again.

'Sit on me,' he demanded, tweaking her nipple. 'It's the only way I can have you.' While this was true, more importantly it was part of the image he'd nurtured all afternoon, having downloaded it from the internet. The very thought of the picture fuelled his pleasure.

'Sit on me,' he said again, pushing her body down the bed and towards his crotch.

She was hesitant to begin with, resisting a little. Playing hard to get. But with another firm push she did as she was told and sat astride him, knees bent. She was clearly reluctant to open her legs really wide and display herself to him as he would be able to see everything, and with her legs as they were, he struggled to get himself in. Taking hold of her knees, he forced her legs wide apart, as wide as they would go, and then with one good hard shove he was in. She cried out again and so did he. It was fucking ecstasy! He looked at his dick fully inserted in her opening and at her breasts with their large reddening nipples. Grabbing her hips, he moved her up and down to show her what to do as he began thrusting, as much as he was able to with the mattress below and his chest muscles complaining. But each thrust was sheer pleasure and as she grew moister it became easier. His pleasure raged and he could feel his new heart beating wildly, faster than it had before. Briefly he wondered if it would stand the strain; they were really pushing it now, testing it to the limit. But he felt his heart was on his side and willing him to succeed and if he didn't, what a way to go!

Up and down, up and down, the usually conservative Eloise glued to his dick like a stuck pig. Was she enjoying it? He couldn't tell and he didn't know or care. If she wasn't she'd just have to put up with it, for she was staying there until he'd finished, for sure. He needed this, his heart did, and as he couldn't lie on her, or she him, she'd have to stay astride him, riding on his dick. He grabbed her nipples and began twisting them, hard. She cried out and tried to push his hands away but he held on tight; he was past the point of no return. He watched her face contort as he pulled and twisted and thrust as hard as he could, harder than he'd ever done before in his life. The gradual build-up to the moment, the absolute height of pleasure, and then stillness as he discharged into her.

'Jesus! Fucking Jesus!' he cried out. And in the room next door his father woke, convinced he'd just heard the devil.

Chapter Ten

'Good to have you back,' Eva said as she and Rosie took their places at the cashier's counter of the high street bank. 'I've missed having you here.'

'Thanks.' Rosie smiled. 'It's good to be here again. I hope I can still remember what to do.'

'You'll be fine. Nothing's changed. Are you free for a quick coffee after work? I've got some news I'm dying to tell you.'

Rosie hesitated and then realized she didn't have to go straight home any longer. 'Yes. I'd like that.'

'Great. We'll chat later. Here we go, ready for the onslaught.'

It was exactly 9 a.m. and the deputy manager was unlocking the main door ready for business. A small queue had already formed outside and as soon as the door opened it quickly dispersed itself at the counter of cashiers. Rosie smiled and said a bright good morning to her first customer. She was pleased to be back at work – another step towards normality. She'd taken two weeks off after Shane's accident. She was due some annual leave and she'd told her boss that she needed it for personal reasons. As well as clearing out his belongings, she needed time to recover and come to terms with what had happened – and hopefully move on. Her mother had suggested she stay with her for a while but Rosie felt she needed to stand alone to prove to herself that she could, that Shane no longer had a hold over her and she wasn't afraid of him any more.

While Shane had been in the hospital, she'd sent him a letter saying that if he ever came near her again she'd call the police. That night, Rosie had called out the local locksmith and had the locks on her flat changed, so that if upon his recovery Shane did try to visit, he'd find himself unable to enter. Once the job had been done she'd felt an overwhelming sense of relief. At last, her flat was safe. Now all that remained of Shane was in her head and she knew it would take time before he left her completely, if he ever did. She was trying hard not to think about him, to shake off the moments of panic that gripped her when she thought about him coming out of hospital, perhaps angrier than before. She'd told her mother a little of what had happened but not all. Some things – the sexual things he'd done to her – she couldn't say. She'd found it a little easier to share this with a group for survivors of domestic violence she'd joined online. The anonymity helped and of course they were on the same page as her, having experienced similar or worse. There were two men in the group, which surprised her; she'd never thought that some women could be as evil as men. But while the group had helped, ultimately she knew her full recovery would be down to her. Clearing out the flat and going back to work was the next step.

Mondays were always busy at the bank and the time flew by. As she dealt with each customer's request or inquiry her confidence grew, and by lunchtime she was starting to relax. Eva was on a different lunch break to her so she went out for a short walk and a breath of fresh air before returning to the staff room to eat her sandwiches and make a cup of tea. Other colleagues who didn't know her as well as Eva were there and they asked her if she'd had a nice holiday and seemed pleased to see her back. Their kindness touched her. It was a pity she hadn't been able to confide in anyone and ask for help when she'd needed it. She still felt responsible for letting Shane into her life and allowing the abuse to continue, although the online survivors group tried to reassure her it wasn't her fault.

At 4.30 the deputy bank manger locked the door, and they cashed up, shut down their terminals and packed away for the night. An hour later, she and Eva called goodbye to their colleagues and left the building. The coffee shop was a short walk up the High Street and they settled with their drinks either side of a corner table where they could talk without being overheard.

'Rosie, I'm pregnant,' Eva announced with a huge smile as soon as they sat down. 'I did two tests at the weekend and they were both positive.'

'Oh Eva, that's fantastic,' Rosie said. 'Congratulations! I'm so pleased for you both.' And she was genuinely pleased. She knew that Eva and her husband, Syed, had been trying for over a year for a baby.

'Promise you won't tell anyone at the bank yet,' Eva said. 'I'm going to wait until I'm three months.'

'I promise,' Rosie said.

Eva shared her plans – to take a year's maternity leave and then return to the bank part time as they needed her income to pay their mortgage. Then her attention turned to Rosie. 'But enough about me. How are you? Do you want to tell me what the personal reasons were that suddenly made you take time off? You know it won't go any further.'

Rosie looked carefully at her friend. How easy it would be to tell her the truth but then she'd have to live with her shock and sympathy and she didn't want that. She was trying to move on.

'The guy I was seeing had an accident – wrote my car off.' She paused. 'We're – we're not together any more, so there's been a lot going on in my life. It was all getting on top of me. I just needed a break.' She shrugged, trying to be casual, and took a sip of her coffee.

'OK. I can understand that. So he's out of your life for good?'

'Yes, completely.'

'A carefree singleton. Well, we'll have to see what we can do about that!' Eva laughed.

'I'm in no rush to start another relationship now,' Rosie said. 'So how are you feeling?' She was anxious to steer the conversation back to safer ground. 'No morning sickness?'

'No, not yet, but I won't mind if I am sick. I mean it's all part of being pregnant and will be worth it in the end.'

'Absolutely,' Rosie agreed, and they continued talking about Eva's pregnancy.

Once they'd finished their coffee, Eva said she'd better go as Syed would be home soon and she wanted to have dinner ready. They left the coffee shop together and then went their separate ways. Rosie was returning to an empty flat but she didn't mind, not at all, for empty was far better than having Shane waiting for her. She'd started to relax again in the flat; she could watch some television, listen to her music, then go to bed without being in constant fear. Every night, she went through a little ritual of checking the doors and windows were locked and that there were no shadowy shapes lurking in the street. But every night, she saw nothing. It looked like Shane was leaving her alone. And once she'd saved up enough she'd buy herself another car.

Chapter Eleven

Elizabeth had telephoned Eloise on Sunday to see how she was, but her call had gone through to voicemail so she'd assumed the poor girl was still ill in bed. She'd left a message saying she hoped Eloise felt better soon. She waited until midday on Thursday before trying again; she knew how irritating it was to keep having to answer the phone if you weren't feeling well. This time Eloise did answer.

'Hello, Elizabeth,' she said quietly.

'Hello, love. How are you? Feeling a bit better?'

There was a pause before she replied. 'Did Jacob tell you I was ill?'

'Yes of course, love. When Andrew and I returned on Saturday and found you'd gone we were obviously concerned. How are you feeling now?'

Another pause. 'Better, thank you.'

'Good. What was it? The flu? Jacob didn't seem to know.'

'I'm not sure. But I'm all right now.' Her voice sounded flat.

Elizabeth hesitated. 'Are you really all right? You sound a little . . . I don't know . . . a little subdued,' she said, for want of a better word.

'Yes. I'm all right.'

'Well, that's good. It was fantastic news about Jacob's test results, wasn't it? He hates those biopsies but it's so reassuring to know there's no sign of rejection.'

'Yes. I'm sorry, Elizabeth, I have to go. I'm on play-ground lunch duty.'

'Oh, OK. I'm pleased you're feeling better. See you at the weekend then. Will you be coming Friday night or Saturday?'

'I'm not sure yet.'

'Don't worry. Come as soon as you can. We're all looking forward to seeing you.'

'Thank you,' Eloise said a little stiffly. 'Goodbye.'

'Goodbye, love.'

Elizabeth slowly set down her phone on the table in front of her, not sure what to make of their conversation. Eloise hadn't sounded herself, she'd seemed distant and restrained, as if she was hiding something. One of the characteristics Elizabeth had always liked about Eloise was her bubbly personality. She had a zest and enthusiasm for life which Jacob had had too before he'd fallen ill. It took a lot to get Eloise down. Perhaps she and Jacob had had an argument. Maybe about her leaving early? He was so insensitive and tetchy at present that if the poor girl had said she wasn't feeling well and wanted to go home, he could easily have thrown a strop. Elizabeth could picture it only too clearly and if that was the case then he needed to apologize. She and Andrew were having to make allowances for him continuously and think carefully before they spoke.

Elizabeth thought hard; another possibility for Eloise's mother was that she'd just found out Eloise was pregnant. But no, she dismissed that straightaway. Jacob had been in hospital for the last month and before that he'd have been too weak. She assumed they were having a physical relationship, as young people did nowadays before marriage, but because of his illness he hadn't been well enough. Yet something was bothering Eloise.

Elizabeth ruminated on it for the next half-hour and when she called Jacob down for lunch she said, 'I'm not prying, love, but is everything all right between you and Eloise?'

'Yes of course,' he said, immediately on the defensive. 'Why do you ask?'

'I phoned her a little while ago to see how she was and she didn't seem like her usual self.'

'I told you, she's ill,' he said, irritated.

'She was back at work. She said she was on lunch duty when I called.'

'So?' he demanded.

'I'm just concerned, that's all. She's a sensitive girl, and all of this can't have been easy for her.'

'And it's easy for me?' he shot back.

'No, love. Of course not.' She knew she wasn't handling this right, but it was so difficult to talk to him at present. Perhaps she shouldn't have said anything at all. 'I'm just concerned for you both.'

'Well, don't be!' he snapped. His face was set as he glared at her. 'What goes on between Eloise and me has nothing to do with you or Dad. You both need to keep the fuck out of my life. Understood?' Grabbing his plate of food from the table, he stormed upstairs.

'Jacob?' she called after him. But his bedroom door slammed shut and then there was silence.

Elizabeth remained where she was, her mouth dry and her pulse beating wildly, shocked to the core by what had just happened and at a loss to know what to do. It wasn't the first time he'd sworn since coming home but she'd never felt threatened by him before. The way his face had contorted with anger. The look in his eyes as he glared at her, the tone in his voice; she had seen and felt pure hatred in her son! The aftercare notes from the hospital had said transplant patients could become frustrated by their long recovery but this was more than frustration. Much more. She and Andrew couldn't do anything right and the way he treated them suggested he loathed and detested them. But why? Then she caught herself. Of course he didn't detest them. He was recovering from a major life-changing operation, and it didn't get more serious than a heart transplant. He was also having to take a vast array of pills which, though necessary, all came with possible side effects. With small relief Elizabeth acknowledged that it was quite likely his medication was responsible for his mood swings and aggression. She'd check the list. If it was the medication then presumably something could be done about it. The surgeon had mentioned that if the side effects of any of his drugs became too unpleasant then they could try him on another brand.

Mitsy ventured out from under the table and Elizabeth stroked her head. 'We're just going to have to be patient,' she told her. 'It's bound to take time.' The dog looked up questioningly. Since Jacob had returned from hospital he'd hardly had anything to do with her; she'd stopped vying for his attention, and now kept out of his way. 'It's bound to take time,' Elizabeth repeated, as much for her own benefit as the dog's.

'No Eloise?' Andrew asked when he returned from visiting a parishioner on Friday evening.

'Apparently not,' Jacob said sarcastically, glancing at her empty chair at the table.

Elizabeth saw her husband take a breath. She knew he was about to reprimand Jacob and quickly stepped in. 'She's coming tomorrow morning,' she said. 'Your dinner's ready.'

Andrew nodded and went upstairs to wash and change before eating, avoiding looking at his son. He'd been later than he expected so Elizabeth and Jacob had started dinner without him. When he returned Elizabeth pinged his plated meal in the microwave. Jacob gobbled down the last of his food and, as his father sat down, left to go to his room.

'What have I done now?' Andrew sighed. 'I've just come in.'

'You haven't done anything,' Elizabeth said, setting his plate in front of him. 'You know how he is at present.'

'I'm not sure I do any longer.'

She joined him at the table but didn't resume eating until he'd said grace. 'How was Mr Tilney?' she asked. Andrew picked up his knife and fork.

'Comfortable. His family are with him.' He paused. 'You're definitely going to ask about adjusting Jacob's medication at his next appointment?'

'Yes. Monday,' Elizabeth confirmed. She smiled encouragingly, although she'd checked the list of possible side effects and the most serious had been the increased risk of infection from the immunosuppressants. Nausea, vomiting and hair loss were mentioned, but nothing about mood swings or sudden anger.

'So how was your day?' Andrew asked.

'Good. The church is ready for tomorrow. It's looking lovely. Let's hope the weather stays fine.'

She and a band of volunteers had spent the afternoon thoroughly polishing and dusting the church, arranging the flowers, and making sure everything was ready for the wedding that was due to take place the following morning.

69

The wedding was causing considerable excitement in the village as the couple getting married were minor celebrities, having appeared in a long-running television soap. They weren't locals but had chosen Maybury church for its charm and olde-worldliness, and Andrew was taking the service. It was rumoured that camera crews might be present, and the press certainly would. Most of the village would be turning out to watch.

'Once Eloise arrives the three of us will walk over,' Elizabeth said brightly. 'It'll be lovely to watch a full white wedding after everything that's been going on. And it might give Jacob and Eloise some ideas.' Andrew nodded and smiled, for they'd both assumed that when their son did marry, it would be in Andrew's church. The image of Jacob completely recovered, in a new suit bought specially for his wedding, and waiting at the altar for his bride, brought a lightness to Elizabeth's thoughts that hadn't been there for a long while.

Jacob remained in his room for the rest of the evening, as he had been doing most evenings since returning from hospital. Aware he needed to take regular rests as part of his recovery, Elizabeth and Andrew didn't disturb him. But at nine o'clock Elizabeth went into the kitchen where she kept his medication and transferred the pills he needed from the Dosette box into the little plastic cup as she did at regular intervals throughout the day. She poured a glass of water and carried that and the pills upstairs. She knocked on Jacob's door and waited for his, 'Come in,' before entering. He was sprawled on his bed, the laptop that he now spent so much time on open on his lap.

'How are you, love?' she asked. Going over to him, she carefully set the glass and pills on his bedside cabinet. He grunted an acknowledgement, his gaze staying on the screen. She turned and as she did she caught sight of what he was watching. 'Jacob!' she said, horrified.

'What, Mum?' he asked, meeting her gaze confrontationally, and making no attempt to hide the screen or lower the lid. 'Is there a problem?'

Hot, flustered, and unsure of what to say, Elizabeth backed away. 'That's not nice,' she said, shocked.

He laughed unkindly. 'Well, you don't have to watch it, do you?'

She hurried from his room to her own, where she sat down shakily on her bed. She'd wait until she was calmer before going down to Andrew. She wouldn't tell him, he didn't need more upset. But what had shaken her more than actually catching Jacob watching porn was his blatant disregard for her. He hadn't been embarrassed or ashamed. It was as though he didn't care or have any respect for her any more, which wasn't like the Jacob she knew, not at all.

Chapter Twelve

Jacob sat in the passenger seat next to his mother as she drove, his gaze fixed rigidly ahead and earbuds in so he didn't have to look at or talk to her. Elizabeth was grateful she didn't have to make conversation or try to smooth over the last confrontation with her son, for her thoughts were full of what she would say to the doctor, diplomatically, so that Jacob didn't become upset and angry again. Their disagreement this morning had been over his wish to drive them and he was clearly still in a bad mood. True, it was only a few days until the six-week post-operation milestone – when he could drive again – but Elizabeth had erred on the side of caution and had wanted to check with the doctor first that it was all right. Jacob had exploded into anger, swearing at her and kicking a chair. Thankfully Andrew had already left the house so hadn't witnessed this last scene.

The bad atmosphere had been building over the weekend, Elizabeth admitted as what had promised to be a pleasant few days had quickly deteriorated into one angry scene after another. When Eloise had arrived on Saturday morning she'd received a frosty, offhand reception from Jacob. Then without giving a reason he'd refused to go to watch the wedding. Andrew was already at the church so she and Eloise had gone together, but Eloise had been very quiet and seemed to take little pleasure in the ceremony, presumably worrying about Jacob. When they'd returned to the rectory, Elizabeth had left them alone in the living room, believing they could do with some time together to repair their differences while she busied herself making lunch. Half an hour later Eloise had come to find her, looking as though she might have been crying, and said she was going now as her mother wasn't well.

'Oh dear, I am sorry. I expect she's got what you had,' Elizabeth sympathized, while suspecting it might be an excuse. But what could she say? She'd asked where Jacob was and Eloise had said he'd gone up to his room for a rest. Eloise couldn't be persuaded to stay for lunch so Elizabeth had seen her off at the door, sending her mother, whom she had yet to meet, her best wishes for a speedy recovery.

Once she'd gone Jacob had appeared and taken his lunch up to his room, which had irritated Andrew who'd just come in and had expected them all to eat together.

Then on Sunday morning Andrew had made the

mistake of saying that now Jacob was quite a bit better it would be nice if he started going to church again. Elizabeth and Jacob usually went together and if Eloise was staying with them for the weekend she came too. Elizabeth had been in the adjacent room when Andrew had broached the subject with Jacob and had heard every word of their heated exchange. It had culminated in Jacob shouting, 'He's your God, not mine! Stuff your religion. I never believed. I hate your fucking church.' Which simply wasn't true. For even if Jacob hadn't had the strength of faith his father had, he'd never minded going to church before. And as the Reverend's son there was a certain expectation − duty, even − for him to go, although Elizabeth would be the first to admit that duty was no longer a word in Jacob's vocabulary.

'It'll be better once he can get out more,' Elizabeth had said placatingly to Andrew after Jacob had stormed off. He was clearly badly shaken.

Andrew had nodded half-heartedly, not wholly convinced. 'Just make sure you talk to the doctor about his medication. Something has to change.'

Jacob had spent the rest of the day in his room, only coming down to eat and take his pills, which Elizabeth no longer took up to him, but set out in the kitchen, calling up to her son when it was time.

She glanced at Jacob now as she parked in the hospital car park. Expressionless and unfazed by the bad atmosphere, he was head down, selecting music on his phone. He stayed in the car while she bought a ticket from the machine and placed it in the windscreen. Then with his earbuds still in and without acknowledging her at all, he got out and fell into step beside her as they walked to the main entrance. It wasn't until they were in the department that he took out his earbuds, but then of course it wasn't to talk to her, but to the nurses, some of whom were young and attractive. She saw him turn on the charm and thought of Eloise. Jacob had never overtly flirted with the nurses before.

The routine was similar and they'd attended so many of these check-ups that they knew what to expect. As usual it took nearly an hour to run all the tests, monitor his heart rate and weigh him, before they were called in to see the doctor.

Dr Shah, one of the implant team who they'd seen before, sat behind his desk going through the latest test results. He glanced up and greeted them as they entered, then continued reading as they took the two chairs opposite. Jacob strummed his fingers on his knee and fiddled with the wire of his earbuds, now looped around his neck. He began tapping his foot impatiently as Elizabeth sat perfectly still, her thoughts racing with what she had to say.

'Well, young man,' Dr Shah said, finally looking up. 'You're doing very well. All your test results are good. Spot on. Let me have a look at you.'

It was the usual routine and Jacob went over to the couch so Dr Shah could examine him. He admired the scar, felt his chest, and then listened to his heart.

'Perfect. A wonderful strong beat. I'm very pleased. It's behaving exactly as it should. Well done.' The examination over, Jacob returned to his seat next to his mother. Dr Shah sat behind his desk again, making a few notes, then looked at Jacob.

'So how are you feeling in yourself? Fit and raring to go?' He smiled.

'Can I start driving now?' Jacob asked.

Dr Shah consulted his notes again. 'You're six weeks post-op next week and everything seems to be healing nicely so I don't see why not. As long as you're careful and don't overdo it. I assume we're talking about driving a car along a road and not racing?' He laughed at his joke and Elizabeth smiled politely.

Jacob nodded.

'You're starting the cardiac rehab programme next week so there's no reason why you shouldn't drive yourself to and from your appointments if that's what you're thinking?'

'Yes,' Jacob agreed amicably.

'Good. And no side effects from the medication? You seem to be tolerating it all well.'

'I'm fine,' Jacob said.

'You may find that your new heart reacts slightly differently to your old one,' Dr Shah said. 'Especially when you start to exercise. That's perfectly normal. During the transplant the nerves to the heart are cut. The medical term is denervation. They don't grow back but that doesn't matter. Your old heart rate was controlled by your nervous system but your new heart is controlled by adrenalin. It will make your new heart beat faster and take a little longer to slow down. Again, all perfectly normal and it won't limit what you are able to do. The physiotherapist will talk to you more about this and show you how to warm up properly before exercise. The denervation also means that you will no longer feel chest pain related to your heart. The nerve connections that conducted pain are gone. Any chest pain you feel during activity is probably caused by the healing of your chest after surgery.'

'I do get breathless if I exert myself,' Jacob admitted. 'And I seem to tire more easily.'

'You will at this stage in your convalescence, but that isn't because there is a problem with your heart, it's just because you've been out of shape for a long time. As you exercise, your strength and stamina will improve. Another couple of months and you'll be a new man.' He smiled again. 'Any more questions?' He looked from Jacob to Elizabeth.

'Yes, I have a question,' Elizabeth said, steeling herself. 'About the possible side effects of the medication.' Jacob looked at her sharply. 'I wonder if you could advise me?'

'Of course,' Dr Shah said.

Elizabeth took a deep breath. 'My husband and I have some concerns that the drugs could be having side effects, not physical ones but more to do with temperament. I know Jacob won't appreciate me saying this, but he can easily become irritated and frustrated, even angry.' She was being as diplomatic as she could. 'He was never like this before and we were wondering if his medication could have anything to do with it, and if so, whether it could be adjusted. I remember you saying there are different brands.'

Dr Shah shifted his gaze from Elizabeth to Jacob. 'Do you feel you're more easily irritated and angry now than you used to be?'

'Yes. Because I'm fed up with not being able to do what I want,' Jacob retorted.

Dr Shah was nodding. 'Exactly my feeling.' He returned his gaze to Elizabeth. 'This is about the emotional effects of a long-term life-threatening illness followed by major surgery and months of convalescing. In some patients the drugs can cause physical symptoms like stomach cramps – but Jacob isn't saying that. Let me assure you that the drugs prescribed are not responsible for any change in Jacob's level of patience. Personally I think he is coping remarkably well. ' He smiled at Elizabeth, condescendingly she thought, before continuing. 'Jacob is a young man, full of zest and with a vitality for life. Of course he's going to feel a bit fed up and irritable. That's natural, and it will improve and go with time, I'm sure.' Then to Jacob he said, 'You're not feeling depressed are you? If so, I can give you something for that.'

Not more pills, Elizabeth thought, but Jacob was shaking his head. 'No, I'm not depressed,' he confirmed.

'Good,' Dr Shah said. 'I think it would help if you start regaining your independence as long as you don't overdo it. So by all means start driving again. Another month or so and you'll be back to your old self – indeed fitter with your new heart. Then we can start talking about you returning to work.'

'Fantastic,' Jacob said.

'And, as your mother has brought up the subject of changes in personality,' Dr Shah continued, 'you can disregard all that stuff and nonsense you read from time to time in the tabloid press about transplant patients taking on some of the likes and dislikes of the donor. It's fanciful nonsense that sells newspapers, nothing more. The heart is an organ like any other. It pumps blood around the body. And although we attribute emotion to the heart – Valentine cards and the like – you can't transplant personality or emotion.' He laughed at the ludicrousness of the suggestion. Elizabeth smiled weakly and felt a complete fool. Jacob smirked. He was enjoying this, she thought, although he didn't say anything until they'd left the consulting room.

'You'll have to do better than that,' he sneered as they walked quickly down the corridor together. 'You and Dad need to get off my case.' He strode away from her and Elizabeth had to run to catch up with him.

'Jacob, we're only concerned for you.'

'Well, don't be! Go and smother someone else. I don't need all your concern, it's suffocating.' A passer-by glanced at them.

She followed him through the revolving door out of

the hospital. He stopped. 'I've got some things to do in town. I'll see you later,' he said, and headed off in the opposite direction to the car.

'Where are you going?' she asked, horrified. She ran a few steps to catch up with him. 'You're not well enough to be out by yourself.'

He stopped dead. 'Yes I am. You heard what the doctor said. I need to regain my independence. And where I'm going is none of your business.' He set off again.

'But how will you get home?' she called after him. 'Shall I wait for you here?'

'No! For Christ's sake, no!' he yelled over his shoulder. 'I'll use the buses like everyone else.' He continued along the pavement towards the main road.

It crossed her mind to run after him but what good would that do? It was likely to make him more angry and she couldn't physically stop him from going. She wished she could pick him up, put him in the car and take him home as if he were a child. Perhaps she *was* being overprotective, although she was sure the doctor hadn't meant this when he'd said he could start regaining his independence by driving a little. Fearing for his safety, she returned to the car to call Andrew for advice. He'd know what to do.

Chapter Thirteen

'He's a silly boy,' Andrew said. 'What's he trying to prove?'

'That he can manage alone and be independent, I suppose,' Elizabeth offered. 'But he gets so angry with me. It's frightening.' She had yet to tell Andrew what Dr Shah had said about the side effects of the medication having nothing to do with Jacob's behaviour.

'I suppose it might do him some good,' Andrew said reflectively. 'Make him realize he's not invincible and he needs us. Try not to worry, I'm sure he'll phone you soon.'

'Do you think so?' Elizabeth asked uncertainly. 'I am worried.'

'Once he needs a lift home, he'll phone. I can't see him using the buses. It will be an uncomfortably long journey.'

'I'll wait around here for a while then,' she said, only partly reassured.

★ ★ ★

The ticket had an hour to run and Elizabeth sat in the car with her side window slightly lowered to let in some fresh air, resisting the urge to phone Jacob. She was also thinking about what Dr Shah had said. Not so much about Jacob needing his independence, nor him telling her that the medication wasn't responsible for Jacob's behaviour, but what he'd said about cutting the nerves to Jacob's heart, and that they'd never grow back. She couldn't remember being told that before the operation but then there'd been so much to take in it might have been mentioned and she'd forgotten. Now his words stuck and resonated with unsettling familiarity, for that was exactly what if felt like to her – the nerves to Jacob's heart had been cut, severing emotion. Denervation, Dr Shah had called it. He'd said that it was nothing to worry about, part of the procedure, and had no negative after-effects. But how could he be sure? Doctors didn't know everything. They didn't get it right all the time. She checked her phone for messages – there were none – and then googled *denervation*.

A surprisingly long list of websites offering information on denervation appeared and opening the first, she quickly learned that radio-frequency denervation was most commonly used to treat chronic back pain. The nerves around the joints in the back were deactivated, thus alleviating the symptoms. But this wasn't the denervation Jacob had had and she googled again, this time typing in *denervation and heart transplants*. There was a lot of technical data that she didn't understand, but then she searched for *side effects of denervation in heart transplants* and found exactly what Dr Shah had said: that it was part of the procedure and the heart took longer to react after denervation as it was now controlled by adrenalin; that the patient could no longer feel chest pain as the nerves never grew back. She opened and closed a number of websites, all of which said similar. Sighing, she sat back in her seat. With this conclusive evidence, she had to admit that denervation wasn't responsible for Jacob's cold, volatile and often hostile behaviour.

There were ten minutes left on the ticket and uncertain what to do for the best, Elizabeth summoned the courage to phone Jacob, acknowledging it did need courage to even speak to him when he was like this. Her call went through to his voicemail and she left a message: 'Hi Jacob, it's Mum, love. I'm still close to town. Do you want a lift?'

Then she gazed out of the window, watching people pass on their way in and out of the hospital. The last few minutes of ticket time elapsed and Jacob didn't return her call or text. She could have bought another ticket but what would have been the point? She couldn't sit there in the hospital car park indefinitely waiting for him. He might be making his own way home now. Just before the ticket expired she texted: *Going home. Call me if you need a lift. Take care. See you later. Love Mum. X*

She waited another minute or so to see if he would contact her and then started in the direction of home. Her phone was on the passenger seat beside her and as she drove she occasionally glanced at it, willing it to buzz with an incoming call or text message when she would immediately pull over to answer it. But it remained fiercely silent. Perhaps Andrew had been right when he'd said Jacob had to do this to realize he needed them.

But she wasn't trying to suffocate him as Jacob had claimed. That was unfair. Yes, she'd mothered him more than one would a healthy young man but that was to be expected, surely? What mother wouldn't have fussed over her son during a chronic illness, heart transplant and long rehabilitation? He'd been so weak and dependent on her for so long it had become second nature to nurse him. Had a new heart not become available when it did, it was doubtful Jacob would have lasted the year. And the old Jacob – the one she'd nursed while waiting for a transplant – hadn't minded being looked after, indeed he'd thanked her many times. It was the new Jacob that found her so irritating and pushed her away. But then of course he was healthier now than he had been for a long while and Elizabeth recognized she'd have to learn to take a step back. Quite a few steps, in fact, and only help when asked.

It was just after two o'clock when she arrived in the village and rather than go straight home to an empty house she decided to visit Mary Hutchins. Mary was 92 and still lived alone in a cottage on the edge of Maybury. Elizabeth usually popped in once a week for a chat and a cup of tea, and to make sure Mary was keeping the house warm and eating regular meals. Other villagers visited her too and took her to her hospital appointments. Between them, their help allowed Mary to retain her independence and stay in her own house rather than go into a care home.

Elizabeth parked in the lane outside Acorn Cottage and checked her phone again before getting out. She opened the small latched gate, went up the garden path, and knocked on the door. The net curtains at the front-room window lifted and Mary looked out, smiled and signalled for her to use the key from under the mat to let herself in.

Chapter Fourteen

Jacob had quickly realized he wasn't up to walking the half-mile from the hospital into the town and was now waiting for a bus, wishing he'd followed his exercise plan. Since leaving the hospital he was supposed to have been walking a little further each day, but walking around the village hadn't appealed. The place was dead, full of old people, chickens and cows; there wasn't even a pub any more or a village shop. So apart from giving Eloise one good fuck and wanking every day to the porn on the internet he hadn't really had much exercise at all, and suddenly he was feeling it. As he waited he checked his phone again. But other than the voicemail and text message from his mother there was nothing new. He was expecting a message from Chez to say exactly what time to meet. Following Chez's instructions he'd texted him to say he was on his way and would be about thirty minutes.

Txt wen ur on ur way man, Chez's message had said. *I can't b hanging rownd wiv stuff on me so don't b l8.*

Jacob had to get some cash from the bank first, but the timing should be OK. He'd be at the bank in about ten minutes, then once he received Chez's text he'd make his way to the disused storage depot a few minutes out of town, where Chez had said there was no CCTV. There Jacob would give Chez the money in exchange for the cannabis he was supplying.

The bus arrived, he got on, sat down and checked his phone again. He hadn't met Chez yet, but did have a description of sorts – black jeans and a hoodie, and there wasn't likely to be anyone else at the disused depot.

He'd been surprised just how easy it had been to arrange to buy cannabis. While messaging in one of the online chat rooms he'd mentioned he'd had a heart transplant which instantly rocketed him to being something of a minor celebrity – a hero – the first dude any of them knew who'd had a transplant. Then someone typed in that their gran had her leg off last year and he'd given her some cannabis, and it made her so high she didn't mind losing her leg and having to hop around. Jacob had typed, semi-jokingly, he could do with some of that stuff now, and five messages later the meeting had been set up. A hundred pounds for a quarter-ounce. It was good quality, strong stuff, Chez had said.

Jacob got off the bus and headed for the bank. It felt good being out by himself, in control, and away from the rectory and his parents. They were doing his head in and it had to stop. Freedom rules, he thought, for now he'd done it once – reclaimed his independence – it would be easy to keep going. He had plans. A car was next. A decent one. He'd had an old banger that had finally given up on him just before he'd become ill. Originally he'd been going to save up for another car but that wasn't going to happen with no salary coming in, and he couldn't wait for ever. He'd been researching new cars online and had found there were some really good deals. Decent cars, fast ones that would give him power and status, that didn't need much of a deposit. Once he'd met up with Chez and got his stuff, his plan was to go to the showrooms in town. He'd already spoken on the phone to a guy called Gary there who'd said that if his credit was OK, he could drive a car away. He felt his heart step up a beat at the thought. A new, flashy fast car was just what he needed.

'Shit!' Jacob said aloud, arriving outside the bank. A sign over the cash machine read: *Out of order. We apologize for any inconvenience.* 'Shit,' he said again. How long was the queue at the counter? He couldn't risk being late for Chez.

Inside the bank he was relieved to see that there wasn't a queue, and one of the cashiers was already free. He went up to the counter and the cashier, blonde and attractive, smiled at him, greeting him with a bright, 'Good afternoon. How can I help you?', like she was genuinely pleased to see him.

'Good afternoon. My day just got a lot better. Unfortunately, I just want your money for today.' He held her gaze and saw her blush. He liked that, shy, not confident and overpowering. Eloise had become far too assertive lately and often reminded him of his mother.

She passed him the PINsentry reader and he inserted his card and entered his PIN. He slowly slid the card reader back across the counter and didn't immediately remove his hand, so that as she took it her fingers brushed his. He saw her flush again.

'How would you like your money?' she asked.

'However you'd like to give it to me,' he said suggestively, holding her gaze.

The cashier sitting next to her heard and in a loud whisper, intended for him to hear, said jokingly, 'You'd better watch that one.'

He laughed. 'Twenties will be fine, thank you. Has anyone told you you've got a lovely smile?' It sounded cheesy but it worked.

'Thank-you,' she said shyly.

He watched as she counted out his money. He could tell his gaze was making her self-conscious, unsure of herself.

'Thank you so much,' he said charmingly, taking the notes she passed him. 'I'll know where to come in future.'

She threw him a small smile and he moved away so she could serve the next customer. He stood to one side and sorted out his money. One hundred pounds in his pocket for Chez and the other fifty he tucked into his wallet.

Before he left the bank he turned and caught the blonde cashier's eye. He grinned at her and she smiled back. His day was getting better by the minute. Next time he came in – and there would certainly be a next time – he'd ask her for her name.

Outside, his phone bleeped with a text message. It was from Chez. *Meet in 10.* Perfect timing, Jacob thought and texted back, *OK. I'll be there.* He began a steady walk up the High Street towards the end of the town. After a couple of minutes he felt his heartbeat quicken as the adrenalin kicked in, just as the doctor had explained it would. Although he probably didn't have this kind of exercise in mind, Jacob thought to himself – most likely he'd been thinking along the lines of using a treadmill in a gym rather than going to buy weed.

He timed his walk so he would arrive in exactly ten minutes, as Chez had said neither of them should be seen hanging around. But when he entered the disused depot and stood by the rusty containers as Chez had stipulated, there was no one to be seen. Then suddenly out of the shadows a short hooded figure appeared and came towards him. He walked right up to Jacob and leant in, head down.

'Hey man, you got the cash?' he asked agitatedly. His hoodie was so far over his head that Jacob couldn't see his face, but he delved into his pocket for the roll of notes. 'You Chez?' 'Yeh of course?' The dealer shifted on his feet and angled closer. 'Come on, man, hurry up. You need to have it ready.'

Jacob pulled out the money and handed it to Chez, who stuffed it into his own pocket. In the same movement he pushed the packet of cannabis into Jacob's hand. 'Put it away, man,' he hissed and was off, quickly disappearing out of the depot. Jacob stood for a moment, clutching the bag of weed. It had been as easy as that.

Chapter Fifteen

'But you told me I could drive a car away!' Jacob fumed, his anger finally exploding. 'What the fuck are you playing at?' He'd spent an hour with Gary on the forecourt choosing a car and then when they'd gone inside to do the paperwork, he'd told him he couldn't have the car after all.

'I'm sorry,' Gary said again, trying to pacify his very irate customer. 'Our offers rely on your credit rating. I did say that on the phone. You have no income at present so the finance company will only loan you three thousand pounds.'

'Which isn't going to buy me a fucking car!' Jacob thundered, and struck the table with his fist. 'Fucking wanker.'

Another guy in a suit came over. 'Hello, I'm Craig, the manager. Is everything all right here?'

'No. It fucking isn't,' Jacob stormed. 'This prick has just wasted half my day.'

Gary slid the forms containing Jacob's details and the response from the finance company across the desk so his manager could see. Craig turned the pages and then, straightening, addressed Jacob.

'I'm afraid what Gary has told you is correct, sir. Without any income no finance company is going to advance you the money you're asking for. You could choose an older, cheaper model, although we don't have any here we can show you. Or come and see us again when you've returned to work. I'm sure we'll be able to help you then.'

'I'm not waiting fucking months for a car!' Jacob fumed. 'Fuck you!' He stood with such force that both men started. 'You can stick your cars up your arse. Fucking wankers!' He stormed out of the garage, kicking the glass door as he went.

Idiots! How dare they treat him like that? Arseholes! What a waste of fucking time! He was hungry and thirsty too, which wasn't helping his temperament. He was supposed to eat and drink regularly throughout the day and he hadn't eaten since breakfast. His heart had speeded up; adrenalin from all the aggro in the car showrooms. Ba-dum ba-dum ba-dum it went. He had to calm down.

Food and drink first, that was the priority, then he'd be able to think more clearly about what he should do. He began to retrace his steps back along the High Street. He was craving carbs and fat, not the lean nutritious muck his mother kept giving him. Fast food, that's what was needed, it would enter his bloodstream quickly and raise his glucose levels. He knew low glucose levels left him agitated and in a bad mood. He'd been feeling the craving for what his mother called junk food for some time.

He stopped outside the kebab shop. A large solid meat doner kebab turned slowly on its rotisserie in the window. Hot, sizzling, dripping and spitting fat. Just what he needed. His mouth salivated as he went in.

'A doner kebab in pitta bread with a large chips and a can of Coke,' he ordered.

'Eat in or take away?' the guy behind the counter asked.

'In,' Jacob said. 'And give me the Coke straightaway.' It was cold, fresh from the fridge. 'Cheers, man.'

'You're welcome. Take a seat and I'll bring it over when it's ready.'

Jacob crossed to one of the tables, popping the ring pull on the can as he went. He sat down and took a large swig. Spot on. The sugar and caffeine hit the back of his throat and then his stomach. Jesus. It felt good. He hadn't had a cola drink in months and wasn't supposed to; it was bad for him. But hey, life was for living and he intended to live his new life to the full. As he sipped the Coke he checked his phone to find two new texts, one from Chez: *Enjoy man. See u soon and remember it didn't come from me.* The other from his mother: *Please text or phone to let me know you're OK. Your father and I are worried about you.*

He set the phone on the table and swigged some more. He was now in a better frame of mind to start phoning other garages. He took one of the copies of the local newspaper from the rack, nodding to a bloke at another table. The adverts placed by car dealerships started on the front page and continued inside. Dozens of them. No deposit. Low interest rate. Easy terms, but that's what wanker Gary had said. Jacob keyed in the number of the garage with the largest advert and explained his situation to the salesperson: that he needed a decent car but was off work sick at present.

'It's difficult, mate, to get finance without any income,' the guy said.

'How difficult?' Jacob asked.

'Impossible.'

'Wanker,' he said and cut the call. He tried another garage and got the same reply. His food arrived and he asked the guy if he could borrow his Biro. Jacob crossed off the two garages he'd phoned as he ate.

Swallowing a few more mouthfuls and enjoying every bite he then phoned another garage and got the same response. Then the next and the next, and so he continued, eating, swigging, phoning, cursing and striking an angry line through the adverts. By the time he'd finished his food he'd phoned virtually every garage in the paper and was seriously pissed off.

'Fucking wankers,' he said out loud.

The bloke at the other table looked over and nodded.

While the guy serving, who'd heard enough to know what was going on, said, 'Why don't you ask a relative to lend you the money? That's what I did. Borrowed it off my brother. I pay him each month plus a bit of interest, but nothing like those sharks.'

Jacob was about to dismiss the idea on the grounds he didn't have a brother but then thought of his parents. They were tripping over themselves trying to please and pacify him in order to aid his recovery. A new car would certainly help their cause. His mother had been there when the doctor had said he needed his independence. Impossible without a car.

'Thanks, man,' he said as he stood to leave. He tossed the Biro over the counter and the guy caught it.

'You're welcome, man. Good luck.'

Outside, Jacob was feeling much better now. The food and drink had raised his glucose levels; he had weed in his pocket for later, and he also had the solution to his car problem. It didn't get much better than that! Once he had his new car he'd drive to the showrooms and show wanker Gary and his manager. Rub their noses in the custom they'd missed.

As he walked he texted to his mother: *Sorry, Mum. I've been looking at cars. I'm ready to come home now. Would appreciate a lift. J x*

His phone rang immediately as he knew it would. 'Oh darling, I'm so glad you're all right. I know I mustn't fuss so much. I'm sorry. I'm home now so rather than hang around and wait for me to drive all the way there why don't you take a taxi? There's a stand in the High Street.'

'Won't it be expensive?' he asked.

'Don't worry, love, I'll pay for it. You just come home.' Which was exactly what he'd thought she'd say. Predictable or what!

At the rectory Elizabeth had been so relieved to hear from her son that her eyes had filled. She texted Andrew to say she'd spoken to Jacob and he was on his way home. Then she checked she had plenty of cash, and left her purse out ready. Jacob had sounded so much better on the phone, more like his old self. He'd thanked her and had called her Mum. His text message had been polite too, and he'd signed off *J x* just as he used to. Yes, the time he'd spent alone had obviously done him good. That little independence. Thank goodness. 'Thank you,' she said out loud, glancing up to the heavens. We're slowly getting back to normal, she thought, and not a moment too soon. I don't think I could have taken much more.

Fifty minutes later the cab pulled up outside the rectory and Elizabeth grabbed her purse and rushed out. Jacob was just getting out of the cab and smiled at her. 'Hello, Mum.' He looked as though he was pleased to see her.

The driver lowered his window and she paid him, adding a generous tip. 'Thank you, ma'am,' he said.

'Thank *you*,' she replied.

As she and Jacob walked up the garden path he kissed her cheek. 'Sorry about this morning, Mum. I didn't mean to upset you.'

'That's all right, love.' She smiled happily. 'I understand. Forget it. You said you'd been looking at cars. Did you find anything suitable?'

'Yes, although I want to discuss it with you first. When you have a moment,' he said, which pleased her immensely.

He let her fuss around him for a while as it kept her happy. She wanted to take his temperature and blood pressure as she thought he looked a bit flushed. He was supposed to take them each day or if he felt at all unwell but he felt fine. He thought his colour was probably due to the promise of a new car and the Coke and greasy food, but if allowing her to play nurse helped butter her up so much the better. The readings were slightly high but within normal. She packed away the blood pressure monitor and joined him on the sofa. 'Tell me about the car you've seen,' she said. 'I can't wait to hear.'

'It's a black Peugeot, 1600cc. There's a special deal on at the moment. It comes with free insurance, a three-year warranty and breakdown cover. It's a really safe and comfortable car, Mum. You'd love it. It's on special offer at fourteen thousand pounds. I was hoping you and Dad could lend me the money.'

'That's a lot,' she said, unable to hide her shock. 'Surely there are cheaper cars, second-hand.'

'There are, Mum, but they're crap.' He quickly corrected himself. 'They're rubbish. You remember the trouble I had with my old car? How it kept breaking down on the motorway? It was so unsafe, and I ended up throwing good money after bad to have it repaired. It makes sense to get something decent that will last, and is safe to drive.' He thought the safety angle was a good one.

She hesitated. 'Even so, love, it's an awful lot to spend on a car. I'm not even sure we have that sort of money.'

'I'll pay you back each month as soon as I return to work. It shouldn't take more than a year. I could pay you some interest as well if you like.'

'No, love, we wouldn't charge you interest!' she said with a smile. 'Of course not.' She paused again and looked at him thoughtfully. 'And you're set on this model?'

'Yes, Mum, it would make me so happy.'

She could see how happy he was now. What a difference the thought of a new car had made already. 'Let me have a chat with your father. I think it's better if I talk to him and explain.'

'Thanks, Mum. You're a star.' He kissed her cheek again. 'You really are the best.'

That evening after dinner Jacob lay propped on his bed, laptop balanced on his stomach, typing as he listened to the raised voices of his parents coming from the living room below. He'd eaten with them, which had pleased his father, and then he'd left them on the pretence of needing to rest, but really so his mother could speak to his father about the car loan. He'd thrown her a conspiring look as he'd walked from the room and she'd winked back. His father had seemed in a good mood, pleased Jacob was at the table, and even more pleased when he'd asked him about his day and mentioned he was thinking of playing the organ again in church. But now he was being an absolute prick. Jacob could hear most of what he was saying and it wasn't good. Half an hour later when his mother came up with his tablets he knew what the answer was.

'I'm so sorry, love,' she said, red-eyed. 'Your father says he'll help you buy another car when you're back at work, but not such an expensive one. You see, love, morally, he doesn't think it's right to spend so much on a car when there are people starving in the world. You do understand, don't you?'

Her feebleness irritated him. 'And you can't lend me the money?'

'I haven't got it. I would if I could but I don't have an income. All the work I do is voluntary.' Which he knew. 'I'm so sorry. I know how much it means to you.' He ignored her and resumed typing.

She hesitated, and then leaving his pot of pills and glass of water on his beside cabinet quietly left the room.

Shit. Fucking shit! He didn't have a plan B but he wasn't going to give up that easily. He needed a car and had his hopes pinned on a decent one that would make him proud. His old car had been small, unreliable and lacking in distinction. To feel really good about himself, big and powerful, he needed a car that reflected the new him.

He typed his dilemma into the chat room: *Need wheels but no fuckin money.* Various solutions were immediately offered by others, including stealing a car. Apparently *Hellboy* could show him how. Holding up a corner shop – *Snake* knew someone who could get him a gun – *easy man.* Then Chez popped up: *have a smoke, man, and it will all become fuckin clear.* This suggestion appealed. He signed out of the chat room and took the packet of weed from his jacket pocket together with the papers and lighter he'd bought while in town, and then sat in the chair by his desk. With a book beneath to catch any bits that might fall – this stuff was too expensive to waste – he began rolling the joint. He'd never smoked before, let alone rolled a joint even at uni, but he'd watched an online video so he knew what to do. Even so, it took a fair bit of concentration and a few goes before it was good enough to light.

Crossing to the bedroom window, he opened it as far as it would go and lit up. He inhaled deeply and to begin with felt nothing apart from hot smoke and a vague sense of déjà vu, as though he might have done this before. Then the weed hit his brain and he started to drift, the world slowed and the sounds around him became far-off and unreal. The tree outside his window seemed friendly and was waving its branches at him. He smiled and waved back happily. Thoughts came and went, some familiar – he could trace them back and tie them down, but others so bizarre it was almost as if they'd come from someone else. An alien maybe? He laughed. He saw a small pile of dried bird shit on the windowsill and thought the bird should have been more careful. He tried to pick it off, but his finger was too big and clumsy and he laughed at his attempts. He took another drag and another, and the feelings intensified. A buzzing sound filled his head and time vanished. Desperately thirsty, he drank the water his mother had left. He looked at the alarm clock. Over an hour had passed; it didn't seem possible. He returned to the window as light as a feather, flying with his thoughts. Then suddenly, miraculously, he had the answer to his problem just as Chez had said would happen. 'Hey man, that's cool,' he said out loud. 'Why didn't I think of that?' And he laughed because of course he had.

Chapter Sixteen

'You can go first,' Jacob said to the guy standing behind him in the queue. 'I'm waiting to see a particular cashier.' He stepped aside to allow him to pass.

'Thanks, mate.'

'You're welcome.' He was in a good mood.

Rosie must know he was waiting to see her. He never saw any other cashier now. He waited at the front of the queue, letting others go first until she was free. He'd seen her flush and grow self-conscious as soon as he'd walked in. She always did. God, she was attractive, it gave him a boner just looking at her and thinking what he'd like to do to her. The old woman Rosie was serving was taking ages, fluffing around in her handbag, trying to find a form, and then her purse, and finally paying the bill. As soon as she moved away Jacob went to the counter.

'Hello, gorgeous, how are you?'

Rosie smiled, beautiful and demure. 'Hello, what can I do for you today?' It was his fifth visit and each time they'd become a little more familiar with each other.

'I'd like cash please. Two hundred pounds. I know the ATM is working but I'd rather you gave it to me.' She laughed; it had become their little joke.

He held her gaze seductively as she passed him the card reader.

'I was wondering if you were free for a coffee today? It's your lunchtime soon isn't it?'

'How did you know?' she asked, surprised.

'Ah. I've been watching you,' he said roguishly, and entered his PIN. 'You have your very own stalker.'

She laughed again and retrieved the card reader, then entered the transaction into her computer.

'You haven't answered my question,' he said.

'I don't have long at lunch.'

'I know, and you like to go for a little walk first before you return to the bank to eat.' He'd seen her doing so.

'You really have been stalking me,' she joked.

'Go on, Rosie,' her colleague said. 'You know you want to.'

Rosie met his gaze as she passed him the money and the receipt. 'I'll be free in ten minutes.' Which he knew.

'Great. I'll wait for you outside.' He grinned and then left the counter so she could serve the next customer.

Outside, he stood on the pavement examining the receipt for the money he'd withdrawn. There wasn't much left; his balance was exactly £31.04. The stuff he was now buying regularly from Chez had drained his bank account dry, and Chez wouldn't be moved on price. Jacob had already tried to bring him down. He was seeing him later today and would ask him again if he could give him a better deal now he was a regular, and if he still refused he'd set about trying to find a cheaper supplier. But Jacob knew you had to be careful online as you didn't know who you were talking to in chat rooms. One of the guys said he'd been busted after chatting to an undercover cop.

Five minutes later Rosie came lightly down the steps of the bank, her long hair flowing freely around her shoulders. She smiled at him.

'Hey, my lovely,' he said, and kissed her cheek. 'I've been wanting to do that for ages.'

She laughed, but he could see she'd liked it. Women liked assertive, dominant guys who took the lead.

'I thought we'd go to The Coffee Shop,' he said.

'Yes. I like it there.' She fell into step beside him.

'I'd offer to buy you lunch but as you saw from my account I'm a bit short of funds right now.' Good move, he thought, introducing the subject of money straightaway.

'A coffee is fine with me,' she said. 'I'll have my sandwiches at the bank later.' They continued down the street, close but not quite touching, making light conversation.

Being the gentleman, Jacob held open the door to the café so she could go in first. It was busy at lunchtime but as they waited at the counter a table became free.

'You grab that,' he said, pointing. 'I'll bring the drinks over.'

She did as he directed and a couple of minutes later he joined her.

'Thank you,' she said, taking a sip. 'The coffee here is nice. I come here sometimes after work.' He didn't let on that he knew – that he'd seen her come in here with her colleague.

'That's something else we have in common then,' he said, smiling charmingly. He could be such a smooth talker when he wanted to be. 'So tell me a bit about yourself. Have you always worked in the bank? And more importantly, do you like it?' He took a gulp of his coffee, which wasn't bad but was nothing to get excited about.

'I started at the bank straight from school,' she said. 'They trained me. Some days I think I'm in a bit of a rut, but most of the time it's all right. My colleagues are nice, and the salary isn't bad so I can't complain.' He nodded, interested. 'What do you do?' she asked.

'At present I spend a lot of my time being prodded and poked by a team of doctors and nurses who take my blood, and a physiotherapist who tortures me on a treadmill.' She looked at him questioningly. She was supposed to. Women liked a bit of intrigue and humour. 'I'm recovering from a major operation,' he said, then explained about his heart transplant. He knew she'd be impressed; everyone he told was.

'That's amazing,' she said. 'I've never known anyone have a transplant before.'

'No. We're an elite breed,' he said smoothly.

'You seem very well. Are you fully recovered now?' she asked, sounding concerned.

'Everything is working as it should be,' he said suggestively and held her gaze again. She looked away, embarrassed, and he knew he needed to ease back a bit. Be more subtle. She seemed the type that would appreciate a bit of tact. 'So what do you like to do in your free time, when you're not at the bank?' he asked.

'Oh the usual things, read, listen to music, go to the cinema, or to a friend's.'

They continued talking and very soon he learnt that she lived alone in a rented flat and her last relationship had ended three months ago. She didn't own a car but was saving up for one.

'That's a coincidence,' he said. 'So am I. Well, actually I'm hoping to get a loan to buy one. Living out in the sticks a car is essential. The buses take forever and taxis are expensive.'

She nodded. 'Where I live is only a ten-minute bus ride away.'

'Lucky you. Would you be able to arrange a loan for me at the bank?'

She laughed. 'I wish!' And just for a second he felt a niggle of irritation; he didn't like being laughed at. But already he was realizing his plan was crap and wasn't going to work. He'd found before that ideas and decisions made while stoned fell apart in the cold light of day.

'Perhaps you could put in a good word for me?' he tried.

'I'm afraid I don't have any say in those matters. You'd have to speak to the financial adviser. I could make an appointment for you to see her.' She was trying her best.

'I might take you up on that,' he said amicably, although he had no intention of doing so. Unless she could pull a few strings for him, which it appeared she couldn't, it would be a complete waste of his time. If a finance company wasn't going to loan him the money then a reputable bank certainly wouldn't. The conversation had fallen a little flat so he changed the subject and told her her hair looked lovely, which she appreciated.

They continued talking for twenty minutes, then as they finished their coffees he looked at the clock on the wall. 'It's time for you to go back to work,' he said thoughtfully. 'You need to have your lunch.'

'I could stay a bit longer,' she offered. But Jacob knew that Chez would be texting soon to say he was in town.

'You must eat,' he said, pushing back his chair. 'I'll walk you to the bank.' He was impressed with himself; he could be such a fucking gentleman when he wished.

'Thank you,' she said, and he opened the door for her as they left.

When they arrived outside the bank he told her he'd like to see her again, and then, kissing her cheek, said goodbye. She smiled, but looked disappointed. He knew she'd been expecting him to ask for her number, but that would wait until next time. Treat them mean and keep them keen was his new maxim for women.

Jacob waited until she'd gone back into the bank before he checked his phone. He had it set on silent and had felt it vibrate in his pocket as they'd walked. As he expected the text was from Chez, telling him he'd meet him at the usual place in ten minutes. He headed off along the High Street towards the disused depot. Once he'd got the stuff from Chez he'd catch the bus to the hospital and then after his check-up it was a taxi home paid for by his mother. He'd stopped her coming to all his appointments now.

He wasn't looking forward to going home, not one bit, not after all the arguments. They were getting worse, creating a bad atmosphere. Why they didn't just leave him alone he'd no idea. The Rev, as he now referred to his father, and his wife were really cramping his style and getting right up his arse. He'd been so angry with the Rev this morning that he could have hit him, and his mother had irritated him beyond belief as she'd pathetically tried to smooth things over and get them to apologize. As if!

'Up yours!' he'd yelled, giving them the middle finger as he went. It was time he moved out, he thought. Moving in with Rosie would be nice. She'd admitted she liked her flat but got lonely sometimes. Well, he could fix that for sure.

Chez was already waiting and appeared from behind a skip as soon as he walked in. 'Hey man, I told ya ten minutes. Where you been?'

'None of your fucking business,' Jacob said. He took

the money from his pocket and Chez took out the packet of weed. 'I want a better deal, man,' he said, holding the money and pulling himself to his full height. 'I'm paying through the nose for this stuff.'

'No, you're not, man. You get the same deal as everyone,' Chez said, but he was twitching nervously.

He looked really shocked as Jacob grabbed him by his throat. His eyes widened in alarm. 'Don't do that, man, you're hurting me.'

'I intend to,' Jacob sneered. He was a skinny little runt, a foot shorter than him and wasted. It was easy to lift him by his throat so he had to balance on his toes to breathe.

'OK, man. Give me ninety,' he said, real fear in his eyes.

'Eighty,' Jacob said, squeezing his throat.

'I can't. The boss will kill me.'

'Not my problem.' He squeezed harder.

'OK, man. Eighty,' Chez squeaked.

'Excellent,' Jacob said, and released him.

Chez gasped and rubbed his throat and gave Jacob the packet of weed.

'It better be the full weight you little skunk,' he said, tucking the packet into his jacket. He'd learnt a lot since he'd started buying the stuff, more than Chez realized.

'Of course it is. I wouldn't fleece you, man,' he said, his voice unsteady.

'Good, or else.' He counted out the notes and stuffed them down the front of Chez's hoodie, then walked away.

'Arsehole,' Chez yelled as he went. 'You'd better watch

your back, man. I wouldn't like to be in your shoes when I tell the boss.'

Giving him the V sign, Jacob continued to walk in the direction of the town. 'Go fuck yourself,' he shouted as he left. He didn't look back.

Chapter Seventeen

As the cab pulled up outside the rectory, Jacob took out the money his mother had given him for the fare and paid the driver, keeping back the tip she'd added. Money was tight. He needed every bit. He got out and made his way up the path, loathing the prospect of having to go inside. The sooner he persuaded Rosie to let him move in the better. All these arguments weren't doing him any good and he blamed them. His blood pressure had been up when he'd had the check-up at the hospital and the oxygen level in his blood down. Dr Shah had said it was of a similar level to that seen in smokers. 'You're not smoking are you?' he'd asked.

'Of course not. I never have,' Jacob replied indignantly. Which was true – he hadn't ever smoked the cigarettes he assumed the doctor was talking about.

Jacob had then asked if stress could be causing the

problem and reluctantly divulged that his parents had been arguing a lot, which had surprised Dr Shah. The doctor knew Jacob's father was a reverend, and he didn't really expect ministers to argue with their wives, instead imagining them to discuss matters rationally. However, he readily agreed that stress could be responsible.

'Perhaps your parents would find it helpful to come in and talk to someone here?' he suggested, aware that transplants could put the whole family under a lot of stress. 'We offer a counselling service.'

'Thank you. I'll ask them,' Jacob said politely, with no intention of doing so.

Dr Shah then told him to book an extra appointment so the levels in his blood could be checked again, and if he felt unwell to contact them immediately.

No doubt there'd be more aggro tonight, Jacob thought now, as he turned his key in the front door of his parents' house. Once the Rev got going there was no stopping him. This morning he'd been lecturing him again about the evils of smoking illegal substances. Jacob had tried to be reasonable to begin with and said the weed was for medicinal purposes, and had even bothered to show him a web page on his phone supporting this. But the Rev had droned on and on that he'd seen what drugs did to people when he'd been working in the city: tearing families apart and making the kids aggressive and paranoid, which by implication was clearly what he thought was happening to Jacob. Meanwhile his mother had unwisely brought up the matter of him drinking beer – saying it was bad for his health. That's when he'd exploded. For fuck's sake, it was only a few beers in his room! And from there on it had escalated until his taxi had arrived to take him into town.

Having been expecting the worst, sad faces and more lectures, Jacob was now surprised to see his mother coming towards him smiling convivially. 'Hello, love, how did you get on at the hospital?'

'Fine.' He shrugged. 'Is the Rev out?'

She was about to correct him and say 'father' but thought better of it, and nodded instead. 'Sit down, dear, I need to talk to you.'

He hated her calling him dear or love, but then he hated most things about her now. 'I'll stand,' he said. 'It won't take long.' He was craving a joint. He had at least three a day now, often more.

She touched her face nervously, uncertain of how to begin. 'Eloise telephoned while you were out.' He made a move to go. 'No, hear me out, please,' she said quickly. 'I know you said it's all over between you, but she's been trying to contact you. She thinks you should talk and so do I. I asked her here for the weekend but she can't make it. Her parents are away and she's house-sitting – looking after the cats. She suggested you went there on Saturday. I really think you should. It would give you both some space to talk things through. You've known her a long time. Will you go, dear?' She stopped, breathless, and looked at him hopefully.

He was about to dismiss it out of hand and tell her to

keep her nose out of his fucking business when it occurred to him that it might be preferable to spend the weekend with Eloise, who had clearly forgiven him, than with his parents. Interesting, he thought, that despite all Eloise's tears and protests, and running away at the first opportunity, she'd actually enjoyed the way he'd fucked her, and now wanted more. Well, there was a lot more where that came from. He was stronger now and more virile.

'OK,' he said easily. 'But haven't you forgotten something?'

'What?' Elizabeth looked at him, concerned.

'I haven't got a car. Have I?'

'You can borrow mine,' she said without hesitation. 'I can manage without it this weekend. I'll be spending most of my time with Mary Hutchins, she's ill in bed. I am pleased you've decided to see Eloise, love. I hope you can sort something out. Shall I phone her or will you?'

'I will.'

'And Jacob?'

'What?'

'Mary Hutchins was asking after you. It would be lovely if you could pop in and see her like you used to. She's very poorly.'

He shrugged and continued up to his room where he locked the door. Having switched on his music he sat in the chair by the window and began rolling a joint. He could roll joints efficiently now, without dropping any; he'd had a lot of practice. He opened the window, lit the tip of the joint, inhaled, and then sat back and waited for it to hit. He was soon in the best place ever. Time contracted or telescoped depending on what he was thinking, and his senses sharpened. He gazed at the passing clouds shaped like objects and people's faces. He heard the birds' chatter, the sound so intense that he felt he was part of their conversation. Human voices sounded in the distance, he heard the hum of a car pulling into the village. Images of Eloise and Rosie came and went and his thoughts drifted to the two of them together. Very nice. Rosie was sucking his cock, he could feel her mouth wet and warm sliding up and down, and the tip of her tongue teasing his foreskin. He put his hand on her head and forced her mouth further down so his prick hit the back of her throat, while Eloise sat astride his face. He could taste and smell pussy. No more playing hard to get for Eloise. He knew what she liked – the same as all women – a bloody good fuck. And if she or Rosie started playing hard to get he'd teach them a lesson they wouldn't forget.

The landline rang in the distance and then stopped. He assumed his mother had answered it downstairs. Eloise again? God, she was keen. He'd text her later and say he'd be there around midday on Saturday. The house to them-selves sounded good. He took another drag, closed his eyes, rested his head back, and imagined everything he was going to do to her over the weekend.

Downstairs Elizabeth's face had turned ashen as she listened to Dr Shah tell her that Jacob's test results today were causing concern and he needed to get in touch. 'Please persuade him to make an appointment,' he said. 'I appreciate the biopsy is an uncomfortable procedure but at present it is the most accurate method we have for looking for signs of rejection.'

'Do you think his new heart is being rejected?' Elizabeth asked, sick with fear.

'No. But I need to check to be sure.'

'I'll speak to him,' she said. 'I'd no idea. Jacob didn't say anything when he came home.'

Dr Shah paused. He knew tact wasn't his strong point – his colleagues had told him – but he tried his best. 'I appreciate you can't come to Jacob's appointments any more because you're very busy, but recovery is a long journey and a difficult one to do alone.'

'He's not alone. My husband and I are here with him,' she said, shocked. 'And I'm not so busy I can't attend his appointments, but Jacob doesn't want me to. He wanted his independence and you said it was good for him.'

Dr Shah drew a breath and reminded himself to be patient. 'I don't wish to pry but Jacob is my responsibility and I need to make sure everything possible is being done to aid his recovery. As with any chronic illness or operation, recovery can be hindered by worry and stress. Jacob appears to be under quite a lot of stress at home at present. I've suggested it might be useful for you and your husband to come and have a chat with one of the counsellors here.'

For a moment Elizabeth thought Dr Shah was finally acknowledging that there had been a dreadful change in Jacob's behaviour since the transplant and was now offering help, until he added, 'I'm sorry that you and your husband are having marital difficulties, but please try not to let it impact on Jacob. It's possible to keep separation amicable. My wife and I did.'

The awful truth dawned. 'Did Jacob tell you that?' she gasped in disbelief.

'Yes, while we were discussing the effect stress can have on recovery.'

'But it's not true,' Elizabeth cried. 'The only problems my husband and I are having are with Jacob!'

Dr Shah paused and drew a deep breath. 'Please try not to hold your son responsible for your marriage breakdown,' he said, as diplomatically as he could. 'And persuade Jacob to book that appointment for the biopsy. Concentrate on him. You know where I am if you need me.' And with that he closed the conversation.

Elizabeth stood, unable to believe what she'd just heard. How could Jacob have told the doctor those dreadful lies? And why? To make them appear as bad as he seemed to believe them to be? It was wicked and it didn't make sense. Her hand trembled as she returned the phone to its cradle. She'd always offered to go with Jacob to all the appointments, but he'd consistently refused, often being rude and hurtful in the process – *I don't need you any more*.

So she and Andrew had given him his independence, which was supposed to aid his recovery. She'd paid for all the taxis and had given him extra money when he wanted it, which was often. She always asked how he'd got on at the hospital but he never shared anything with her now, sometimes telling her to mind her own f–ing business. He'd told Dr Shah she and Andrew were divorcing! For what purpose? To gain sympathy? What other lies had he told him? This was her son and although she hated herself for admitting it he'd become a deceitful, sly, manipulative liar, and to some extent she blamed herself. She'd let him get away with it, pandering to his needs and making excuses for his appalling behaviour, but with good reason. Volatile and unpredictable, Jacob exploded into anger at any opportunity and it was frightening. I doubt he's told Dr Shah that, Elizabeth thought bitterly.

Summoning all her courage she went upstairs to confront him before she lost her nerve. She knocked on the door and tried to open it but it was locked. 'Jacob. We need to talk. Open this door please.'

She could hear his music and could smell the stuff he smoked coming from under the door. 'Jacob. Let me in now. Dr Shah just phoned and I'm not pleased.'

Suddenly the door opened with such force that she instinctively stepped back. Jacob towered over her, eyes wide and staring. 'Fuck off will you!' he shouted in her face, and slammed the door shut.

Chapter Eighteen

'Read it please,' Elizabeth said to Andrew.

He pulled his chair over so he could see the computer screen. They'd been working separately in the study, he on parish business at the large oak desk, and Elizabeth at the computer on the smaller one. She'd been searching for articles online. It wasn't the first time she'd made these searches but it was the first time she'd shared any of them with Andrew.

As he read and scrolled down the web page he absently stroked Mitsy's head. Even the dog seemed to appreciate the change in atmosphere now Jacob was out of the house. It was Saturday afternoon and he'd left to spend the weekend with Eloise. Elizabeth thought it was like a breath of fresh air, a reprieve, a chance to move and speak freely again. Andrew neared the end of the article and sat back in his chair.

'Liz, it's a tabloid newspaper. Don't you think it's been exaggerated for effect? Even the journalist says there is no medical evidence to support what the woman is claiming.'

'I know, but I've found other similar stories.'

'I don't doubt it. As Dr Shah said, this sort of thing sells newspapers. But logic tells me it's not possible. A person's likes and dislikes are part of their personality, who they are, their soul. And you can't transplant that.' He took her hands in his. 'I know you're desperate to find a reason for Jacob's behaviour, I am too, but I really don't believe this is it. I think we need to look closer to home, accept responsibility, and work through it as a family.'

'But how can it be us?' Elizabeth asked, anxiously. 'What are we supposed to have done wrong? Do you know?'

He gently stroked her hand. 'Liz, I'm not suggesting we have intentionally caused Jacob his problems, but perhaps we've inadvertently made them worse by not responding to him as we should have done. Clearly something is upsetting him or he wouldn't be behaving as he is doing, or have told Dr Shah all those lies. I think we should take up the doctor's offer of counselling – the three of us, Jacob included. It will give us all a chance to speak our minds openly in a controlled environment. The counsellor won't let it get out of hand and we can explain to Jacob how damaging and hurtful his behaviour is and he can tell us how he's feeling.'

She held his gaze. 'You know I'll try anything if it gets

us back the old Jacob. But I doubt he'll agree to go. He can't bear being in the same room with us at present.'

'I'll speak to him when he comes home. I need to do more, especially now you say you feel threatened by his behaviour. I know it's difficult but perhaps counselling is the way forward.'

'Perhaps,' she said desultorily, not convinced. Andrew hadn't seen as much of Jacob as she had.

'Now come on, love, cheer up. I've got a surprise for you. You've been wanting to eat at The Old Manor House restaurant for some time so I've booked a table for tonight. A romantic dinner for two.'

She smiled and her spirits lifted a little. 'Thank you. That is kind. You are thoughtful. I love you so much.'

'I love you too,' he said, kissing her cheek. 'Now, no more surfing the internet. It won't help. You can prove anything online.'

'All right.' She smiled again and closed the web page, feeling slightly chided for having embraced and believed what she'd read there. Andrew returned to his desk. 'I'm going to pop over to see Mary shortly. I'll take her some dinner too.'

'How is she?' he asked.

'Improving.'

'Good. Give her my regards. I'll try and visit her next week.'

It was after midnight by the time they returned home from The Old Manor House and the evening had lived up to expectations. The food had been excellent and the olde-worlde ambience relaxing. Tired but emotionally rejuvenated, Elizabeth said goodnight and went up to bed while Andrew, always a night owl, stayed downstairs to run through his sermon for the following morning. It was aptly chosen and entitled 'When God Tests Our Faith'. He was planning on including an example from his family and how they had felt they were being tested when they'd been told Jacob had an incurable heart disease. He'd given enough sermons in his career as a minister to know that the congregation appreciated an example or two from his personal life. It made the teaching more relevant to their lives, and if the minister had admitted to erring then so could they. It was so important to make sure he could relate to the congregation and they to him.

He made a few notes in the margin and underlined a couple of salient points he wanted to emphasize. Coming to the end and satisfied with his efforts he tucked the sheets of paper into his briefcase and then saw Mitsy into her bed. He checked the doors were locked, switched off the downstairs lights and went quietly upstairs to their bedroom. To avoid waking Elizabeth he took his pyjamas into the bathroom to change. It had been a lovely evening; he was so pleased he'd thought of the idea, they'd both been relaxed and Elizabeth had laughed freely as she hadn't done in a long while. He appreciated he needed to take more responsibility for Jacob while he was like this. If he was honest he'd been avoiding him and leaving the house when he was angry. He hated confrontation and shied away from it – strength or weakness he couldn't say, it was just who he was. But that had to change now Elizabeth had admitted she couldn't take much more and was sometimes scared of their own son.

As Andrew finished washing he heard Elizabeth's car draw up outside and his heart sank. Jacob wasn't due home until tomorrow, which didn't bode well for him having patched up his differences with Eloise. Was he upset? Angry, or taking it in his stride? He must be disappointed. Was this a good time to talk to him? Andrew briefly considered going down to see him now, but then decided it would be wiser to wait until the morning. What he would say he didn't yet know, but he was hoping for one of those father and son chats similar to the ones they'd had in the long months of Jacob's illness while he waited for a transplant. Most evenings when he'd returned home from his parish work he'd sit and talk with Jacob. He'd confided in him about his fears of dying and Andrew had reassured him as best he could. They needed to become intimate again, once he'd opened up the pathway of communication.

Leaving the landing light on for Jacob, Andrew crept silently into his bedroom and closed the door. He eased back the duvet and climbed into bed without disturbing Elizabeth. She was fast asleep on her side and facing away from him. He moved closer and slipped his arm around her waist, enjoying the comfort and warmth of her familiar body. As he did every night before he went to sleep he said a silent prayer of thanks, asking for forgiveness for his sins and the strength to face the challenges of the next day. But tonight quite suddenly and to his surprise another prayer came into his mind, one he hadn't even realized he'd remembered. It was called 'Now the Light Has Gone Away'; his mother had taught it to him as a child – long before he'd entertained any ideas about following a career in the church. Now with a stab of emotion he remembered teaching this prayer to Jacob as a child. Perhaps he'd remind him of it when they talked. It was memories like this that bonded a family – a treasure trove of shared experiences – that saw them through the bad times and reunited them. And with a feeling of inner peace and tranquillity he thanked the Lord and closed his eyes ready for sleep.

Chapter Nineteen

Mary Hutchins had lived in Acorn Cottage most of her life. Her father had brought his wife and young family to live in the village when Mary had been a toddler, the youngest of three children. Mary's older brother and sister had died some years before, and with no family of her own she appreciated her many good friends in the village. She loved the cottage and had only lived elsewhere when she'd married, returning to the house a year later as a war widow. Mary's biggest regret was that she'd never had children, but she knew she had a lot to be grateful for. It was at times like this when she wasn't feeling well that she knew how lucky she was to have so many kind people in the village looking after her.

Turning her head slightly, she looked again at the clock on the bedside table. It was nearly 1.30 a.m. How long the night seemed when she couldn't sleep. It stretched on forever. Lack of exercise was to blame, she decided. She didn't usually have this problem sleeping; she'd spent too long in bed with just short walks to the bathroom. Tomorrow she needed to make a big effort and get dressed and properly on the move. She was over the worst of the flu now and all this lying around wasn't doing her any good. The doctor had ordered bed rest, plenty of fluids, and paracetamol for her temperature and headache. Her friends in the village had been very conscientious in seeing his instructions were followed, but now she needed to get her old bones going again. Once she was up and about she was sure she would start to sleep better.

She turned her head the other way so she could see out of the window. She never closed the curtains at night. There was no need. Hers was the only cottage this far up the lane and flanked by the meadowland and wheat fields of Maybury there was no one to see her. She loved looking at the night sky, the stars twinkling far away and the moon waxing and waning on its journey across the heavens. When it was a full moon in a cloudless sky it lit up her bedroom with a brilliant translucent glow that reminded her of the night Peter Pan flew into the Darling children's bedroom in the story she'd read so many times as a child. She still had that book somewhere. But now the moon was just a thin crescent which gave hardly any light at all. She propped herself on one arm and took a sip from the glass of water on her bedside table before lying down again.

She was still far from tired, so tomorrow she would get

going, perhaps even go to church. She knew the Reverend or his dear wife, Elizabeth, would take her in their car if she asked, but she'd wait to see how she felt. She liked to retain her independence and usually walked to church and back again twice on Sundays. She was one of the Reverend's best church-goers and hardly ever missed morning Communion and Evensong on Sundays.

She shuffled her body into a more comfortable position and then closed her eyes, willing herself to sleep. A moment later her eyes shot open again. She thought she'd heard a noise. She listened intently but the sound wasn't repeated. Hopefully the squirrels hadn't got into the loft again, they'd done a lot of damage up there before. Apart from the wind outside there was nothing to be heard. Her hearing was very good; it was her eyesight that was letting her down now. Speaking of which, where were her glasses? She'd been looking for them earlier and usually kept them under her pillow at night, but things kept being moved with so many people in and out of her cottage.

She pulled herself up the pillow and switched on the bedside light. They weren't on the bedside table or the bed. She checked under her pillows, but they definitely weren't there. Her glasses were essential and she wished people would stop moving her things. She was grateful for their help – their concern and the hot food and drinks they brought – but if only they would stop tidying up and putting things in the wrong place. Before long she wouldn't know where anything was. Yesterday someone had moved her front-door key from under the mat where she always kept it to a nearby plant pot, so that her next visitor had spent ages hunting around for it by which time her soup had been cold. She thought everyone in the village knew that her key had to stay under the mat so it could be used when necessary. It also doubled as her spare key if she locked herself out. Anyway, she mustn't grumble. They all meant well and she couldn't have managed without them when she'd been really poorly. But where were her glasses?

She heaved herself into a sitting position and then slowly lowered her legs to the floor and pushed her feet into her slippers. At least they were in their right place – beside her bed and beneath the walking frame. She could see her dressing gown too, draped over the end of her bed where she liked it. It was just her damn glasses. Gripping the handlebars of her walking frame she drew herself into a standing position, then once she had her balance she began a slow shuffle around the room. She crossed to the dressing table with its little crocheted mats and bowl of fragrant potpourri. Her library books were there but not her glasses. They didn't appear to be in the bedroom and she couldn't remember the last time she'd had them. Perhaps someone had put them in the living room, although she couldn't imagine why. If she was going in there she'd better put on her dressing gown; she didn't want to go catching another cold – that could lead to pneumonia.

Guiding the frame to the foot of the bed she slipped on her dressing gown and then went slowly into the hall.

The night light gave a welcome glow; thankfully her last visitor had remembered to switch it on so she could easily find her way to the bathroom in the night. The door to the living room had been shut tight, despite her asking everyone to make sure none of the doors was fully closed as they were difficult to open with her arthritic hands. She reminded herself again she mustn't moan. They'd all been so kind. She inched the walking frame to just in front of the door and then gripped the door knob with both hands, pushing the door open as far as it would go so she could get the frame through. Halfway in she reached up for the light switch on the wall. As she did she heard a startled cry, then there was an excruciating pain in her head and nothing. A sense of falling and blackness engulfed her.

Chapter Twenty

At 8.30 the following morning Suzy Richards, the grand-daughter of one of Mary's dearest and oldest friends, arrived outside Acorn Cottage. She was home from university for the weekend and had offered to bring Mary her breakfast before she returned to uni. She always tried to see Mary when she was home and looked upon her as another grandmother. She was concerned to hear she'd been poorly. She set down the Thermos bag containing the porridge and freshly brewed tea and removed the key from under the doormat. You couldn't have kept your front-door key under a mat where she lived in the digs. You'd have been robbed for sure, but here in the village it was different. It was like a time warp, she thought, quaint but sometimes boring. Nothing ever happened here which was why she'd picked a city university.

Having opened the door, she returned the key to under

the mat, then went into the small lobby, closing the outer door behind her. Mary kept her umbrella, walking shoes and boots in here. It hadn't changed in all the years Suzy had known her. The inner door was never locked and she entered the living room, with its solid 1950s furniture that was now in fashion again. Daylight crept in through the small latticed casement windows.

'Mary, it's Suzy,' she called, not wanting to startle her by suddenly appearing. 'Are you in bed?'

She started across the living room and then stopped dead. 'Oh Mary! What's happened?' Dropping the Thermos bag, she rushed to her side. 'Mary? Can you hear me?'

Mary was on her back, half in and half out of the living room. Her eyes were closed, her legs and arms splayed out awkwardly, and she was bleeding from a head wound. 'Mary, can you hear me?' Elizabeth said again, taking her hand. It was freezing cold.

Delving into her pocket, she grabbed her phone and dialled for the emergency services. The operator asked if she required police, fire or ambulance.

'Ambulance,' she cried.

'I'm connecting you now.'

'She's ninety-two and I've just found her,' Suzy babbled as soon as she was put through. 'She might have been here all night. I don't know. Please come quickly.'

The call handler talked calmly, asking for her details and the address of the property. 'An ambulance is on its way,' she reassured her. 'Is the lady breathing?'

'I think so.' She put her face close to Mary's and felt

the faintest draft of a warm breath on her cheek. 'Yes, she's breathing,' she said, relieved.

'Good. Is the wound still bleeding?'

'No. It's congealed, dark red. But she's so cold. She's in her nightwear.' She was fighting back her tears now, trying to stay calm so she could understand what the call handler was asking her.

'Is there something in the house you can cover her with, a duvet or blanket?'

'Yes, of course.' She should have thought of that.

'I'll stay on the line while you find something.'

She rushed into Mary's bedroom and dragged the eiderdown from her bed and into the living room, laying it over her. 'I've covered her. Shall I get a pillow for her head? She's on the hard wooden floor.'

'No. Don't move her in case she has a neck or back injury. The ambulance is on its way. It will be with you soon. Are you a relative?'

'No, she hasn't got any relatives. She's my gran's friend.'

'So she lives alone?'

'Yes. I came in to bring her breakfast and found her like this. She hasn't been well. She must have got up in the night and fallen.'

'All right love, stay calm. The paramedics will be with you soon. Can you stay with her until they arrive?'

'Yes, of course.'

'Good girl. I'm going to take another call now but I'll leave the line open and I'll check with you again in a minute. OK?'

'Yes. Thank you.'

Suzy continued to kneel beside the old lady, gently holding her hand. She wasn't allowed to move her but she looked so frail and uncomfortable lying there on the floor. Her face was pale, bloodless, like porcelain. Suzy had thought she was dead when she'd first walked in.

'Mary?' she tried again. 'It's Suzy.' But there was no response.

She should phone her parents but the call handler had kept the line open on her mobile. She'd use Mary's phone. Gently tucking her hand under the eiderdown Rosie then crossed to the coffee table where Mary's phone sat next to the fruit bowl. Her father answered, and her voice shook as she told him what had happened.

'We'll be straight over,' he said.

She returned to sit beside Mary and presently she heard the ambulance siren in the distance as it entered the village. At the same time the call handler came back on the line and confirmed the ambulance would be with her in two minutes.

'Thank you.'

She briefly left Mary to open the front door, wanting to be ready for her father and the ambulance crew. As she returned she thought she heard Mary murmur something, but it was so quiet she couldn't be sure.

'Mary?' she asked, but there was nothing.

Both her parents came in at the same time as the paramedics, who introduced themselves as Nick and Dave. Suzy went over and stood beside her father and he put a comforting arm around her. They watched as the paramedics began their work.

'Who found her?' Nick asked as Dave checked Mary's vital signs.

'I did,' Suzy said.

'Mary had the flu but was starting to feel better,' her mother explained. 'She'd been getting up for short periods. I suppose she got up in the night and fell.'

He nodded. 'As soon as we've finished checking her over and are happy she can be moved we'll take her to the hospital. She lives alone?'

'Yes,' Suzy's mother said. 'She has many friends in the village and we all help look after her.'

'That's good of you,' Nick told her as Dave examined the wound on Mary's head.

'I wonder if something could have fallen on her,' Dave said after a moment, giving the room a cursory glance.

'What makes you say that?' Suzy's father asked.

'She's unlikely to have sustained this injury in a fall. The wound is on the very top of her head.' He placed the large sterile pad Nick passed him over the wound. 'Something heavy, possibly a brass ornament falling from a shelf could have done it. Or one of those old-fashioned ceiling dryers.'

'I don't know,' Suzy said anxiously. 'I didn't see anything. I just came in and found her there, then brought in the cover.'

He nodded. 'Don't worry, you did right.' He threw her a reassuring smile.

Nick fetched a stretcher from the ambulance and they put a neck brace on Mary. 'A precautionary measure,' Dave explained. Then they carefully lifted her onto the stretcher and carried her to the ambulance. Suzy's mother went with Mary in the ambulance while Suzy, still shaken, returned home with her father. They'd visit her in hospital later.

News always travelled fast in the village and by the time the congregation was filing into church at 10.45 a.m. most of them knew that Mary had taken a nasty fall and was in hospital. Those who hadn't known soon did, and one of the congregation let the Reverend know before the service began so he could include Mary in their prayers and blessings.

At the end of the service the congregation filed out past the Reverend, who shook everyone's hand and thanked them for coming. They never went straight home but stood in small groups chatting even when it was raining – as it was now. Church was the focal point of the village and they huddled together under umbrellas and exchanged their news. Today, understandably, much of the talk was about Mary. While they stood talking, one of the parishioners, Joan Roberts, received a text from Suzy's mother, which she read out: *Mary has regained consciousness although still a bit groggy*. It was welcome news.

Five minutes later Sid Jenkins, chairman of the parish council and self-appointed leader of most issues connected with Maybury village, took a phone call from his son-in-law, alerting him to the fact that a police car had just parked outside Acorn Cottage. He shared the news and then left to see what they wanted. It was very rare indeed that a police car came into their village unless they were just passing through.

Excitement and speculation darted through the village like a bird on the wing, so that by the time most of the villagers were sitting down to Sunday lunch conjecture was running high. The police had been at the cottage for over two hours so they clearly suspected something. Acorn Cottage wasn't on the main thoroughfare, which seemed to rule out a passing opportunist thief, as anyone who didn't know the village wouldn't have even been aware of the cottage's existence. Besides, there were much richer pickings from the larger houses that were visible from the road. And why burgle Mary? As far as anyone knew she only had her pension, no valuables, and just enough savings to keep her cottage warm in winter. The buzz continued all afternoon until the news began to circulate that the police had found no evidence of a break-in, so had concluded that Mary had fallen, which was reassuring but a bit of an anticlimax.

The atmosphere in the rectory on Sunday was pretty good too. On returning from church Andrew had initiated the heart-to-heart with his son that he'd promised Elizabeth. Jacob had been reasonable and receptive, which seemed to confirm that Andrew had handled it just right. He'd waited until Jacob had showered and eaten before asking him to sit down for a chat. Jacob hadn't protested and

Andrew had begun his well-rehearsed speech by admitting that he might not have been as understanding as he could have been, and apologizing. This set the scene and started them off on the right footing, so that when Andrew brought up the subject of Jacob smoking and drinking – in a non-confrontational manner – explaining how worried he and his mother were, Jacob agreed to stop. Just like that. He also agreed to attend the hospital for the appointment he'd missed and to try to be more patient with his parents. Andrew asked how Eloise was and Jacob admitted they wouldn't be getting back together again. Andrew said he was sorry but hoped he would now be able to move on, to which Jacob replied that he was working on it.

So all in all Andrew felt it had been a very productive chat, and when he told Elizabeth she agreed. Jacob had had dinner with them and asked after Mary's welfare, which seemed to confirm that he'd finally turned a corner, and the old Jacob was returning. That night Andrew thanked the Lord for the direction he'd given him, and prayed that Jacob's moods would not change again.

Chapter Twenty-One

On Monday morning the feeling of optimism continued in the rectory as Andrew kissed Elizabeth goodbye and left on parish business, and Jacob left in a cab to attend his hospital appointment. Elizabeth, aware that a number of villagers were going to visit Mary that afternoon and evening, was planning on going the following day. However, she thought she would pop into Acorn Cottage later to check everything was all right and nothing was going off in the fridge or pantry. She'd also bring back any laundry that needed doing, and Mary's mail, which she would take with her to the hospital when she visited.

The landline rang and she assumed it would be parish business as it usually was at this time of day. She answered the phone in the living room with a notepad and pen to hand ready to take any message for Andrew.

'It's Eloise's mother,' the woman said flatly.

'Oh, hello. How are you?' Elizabeth asked brightly, slightly surprised. They'd only ever spoken on the phone twice before. Yet already there was something in her tone which suggested this wasn't just a social call.

'If your son ever comes near my daughter again I'll call the police,' the woman said. 'We would have called them straightaway, but Eloise asked us not to. You and your husband want to be ashamed of yourselves. That boy's a monster.'

Elizabeth felt her stomach contract with fear. She went cold. 'Why? What's happened? I don't know what you're talking about. Jacob hasn't said anything to me.'

'I bet he hasn't!' she scorned. 'He's an animal and wants locking up.'

'But what's he supposed to have done?' Elizabeth cried, rising to his defence. 'You can't just accuse him. I'm sure there's been a misunderstanding.' But a small voice told her that, quite possibly, there hadn't been.

'That animal attacked my daughter. Her face is bruised and her lip cut from where he hit her as he raped her.' Elizabeth gasped, her hand shooting to her mouth as she stifled a cry. 'He forced her to do things, horrible things that she's too upset and embarrassed to say. She can't even tell us.'

'But that's not our Jacob,' Elizabeth said, on a rising tide of panic.

'Do you want to come and see her face for yourself?' Eloise's mother demanded bitterly. 'Or shall I take a photo and send it to you?'

'No, of course not,' Elizabeth cried.

140

'If my husband had his way he'd be over there now sorting out your son and I wouldn't stop him. You tell him that. We're not taking this to the police for Eloise's sake. She can't bear the thought of making a statement. But if I see him here again I will go to the police.'

'I understand,' Elizabeth said feebly. 'But when was all this supposed to have happened?'

'Saturday evening. My husband and I were away for the weekend and Eloise stayed at home to look after our cats. She invited Jacob here so they could talk and hopefully sort a few things out. He attacked her in her bedroom and kept her prisoner for three hours. He did unspeakable things to her. Sexual things, perverted things she can't bear to talk about. Eventually she escaped and locked herself in the bathroom. She told him she'd phone the police if he didn't leave. He didn't know her phone wasn't with her, and he cleared off.'

Fear gripped Elizabeth and she swallowed the bile rising in her throat. Jacob had returned home in the early hours of Sunday morning after, he'd said, failing to patch up his differences with Eloise. Was it possible he'd done these unspeakable things to her? Surely not, but then Eloise wouldn't make it up, would she? 'I don't know what to say,' Elizabeth said lamely, her voice faltering. 'I'm so sorry.'

'It'll be those drugs he's hooked on. But that's your problem. If he comes anywhere near my daughter again he won't know what's hit him. We thought you were good people with your husband being a reverend. Just goes to show.' And the line went dead.

Chapter Twenty-Two

In the outpatients department of the transplant centre, Jacob was waiting for his biopsy. The other tests had already been completed and he'd agreed to wait until the surgeon was free. Some of the last test results were giving cause for concern so it was important the biopsy was done as soon as possible to check for signs of rejection, the doctor had stressed. Rosie sat beside him, holding his hand and offering words of comfort and encouragement. When he'd told her how much he hated having the biopsies and had missed one she'd immediately offered to take time off work to be with him. As a thank-you he said he'd take her out for dinner afterwards now he had some money in his bank account.

'The only time I've been in hospital,' Rosie said, making conversation as they waited, 'was when I had a very high temperature as a toddler. But I don't remember it.'

'Lucky you,' Jacob said. 'I'm pissed off with hospitals – when I was ill and then the transplant.'

'But it'll all be worth it in the end,' she reassured him. 'Do you know who the donor was?'

'No.' He checked his phone again, turning it slightly away from her so she couldn't see the screen. He was hoping for a text from a new dealer, but it hadn't been as easy to find one as he'd thought. They all seemed to be working for and controlled by Chez's boss; apparently it was his patch. However, this text wasn't from a new supplier but from his mother. 'Fuck,' he said out loud.

Rosie looked at him, slightly startled. 'Is everything all right?' she asked gently, touching his arm.

'Just a bit of bother from my ex.'

She removed her hand, a little hurt, then chided herself for feeling jealous. Of course he was going to have an ex, probably lots of them. He was an attractive guy, and she reminded herself that she too had a past, and not one she was proud of. She now felt a complete fool for allowing Shane into her life and letting him treat her as he had, but he'd had a rugged charm at the start. A bit like Jacob, she thought, but no, she mustn't think like that, she mustn't let the past ruin her future. As her mother had said, she had to put all that behind her, learn a lesson, move on and find a decent chap. There had been no sign of Shane since the accident, and Rosie was beginning to feel less and less worried about the thought of him resurfacing. She might tell Jacob about Shane one day, if they started seeing each other regularly, but not yet. Guys didn't like lots of heart-rending revelations – too much too soon.

Her phone bleeped with an incoming text and she had no problem in showing Jacob. *Look after him. He's really cute. Eva xx.* She laughed as she showed him the screen.

'Cute!' Jacob replied indignantly. 'Cute is for rabbits.'

'Oh, you know what she means.' Smiling, she texted back: *Don't worry. I am xx.*

Rosie had to remain in the waiting area while Jacob went in for his biopsy. She passed the time by flicking through the old magazines scattered on the table, and texting Eva, who was on a late lunch break. She sent her a photo of where she was for Eva had never been in a hospital transplant centre and was as impressed as Rosie. Once Jacob had had the biopsy a nurse came out and said the procedure had gone well and she could go and sit with Jacob in the recovery room if she wished. She showed Rosie the way. Jacob had been given a mild sedative and instructed to rest for an hour, and have the wound checked by a nurse before he could go. Rosie sat beside him on the couch and held his hand as Jacob yawned and grumbled. He found the whole process irritating and boring, he said, but Rosie thought it was exciting, a bit like the hospital programmes she watched on television. She sent Eva a selfie.

When the hour was up, the nurse came in and said that really the doctor had wanted to see Jacob to discuss the results of the blood and oxygen level tests – the results of the biopsy wouldn't be back from the lab for a few days – but he'd been called away to an emergency.

'So you go and enjoy your day,' the nurse said. 'We'll phone you if there is anything untoward. Otherwise assume the test results are normal.'

As Jacob and Rosie strolled away she linked her arm through his and the nurse remarked quietly to her colleague, 'That's not the same girl who used to visit him in hospital, is it?'

'No. Just shows what a new heart can do!' They laughed.

Outside, Jacob called a cab rather than use the bus to take them into town to the restaurant he had in mind for wining and dining Rosie. He liked to arrive in style and wanted to impress her.

Meanwhile, Elizabeth sat at the kitchen table in the rectory, head in her hands and a glass of water at her side, willing herself not to be sick again. She'd vomited straight after the call from Eloise's mother and then every time she thought about what the woman had said the bile rose to her throat. There was nothing left in her stomach but she dry-retched over the sink. Animal, she'd called him. He'd beaten and raped her daughter, darling Eloise. It was almost impossible to believe such things about her own son. In the past she'd wondered how the parents of murderers and rapists felt, and now she knew. Assuming of course it was true and Eloise hadn't made it all up. But why would she? She couldn't imagine a reason for Eloise to invent something like that, and to some extent Elizabeth blamed

145

herself. She'd persuaded Jacob to go to see Eloise. She'd even lent him her car.

She hadn't telephoned Andrew yet, although she desperately needed to share this, but she wanted to hear what Jacob had to say first. Perhaps there was a different version that would make Jacob less culpable. But what could possibly mitigate and explain what Eloise's mother had said? If Eloise had changed her mind at the last moment about having sex, or Jacob hadn't stopped when she'd asked him to, it still wouldn't account for the bruises on her face or cut lip, or her being kept prisoner for three hours. She'd tried phoning Jacob but he hadn't picked up so she'd texted asking him to phone her, saying only that Eloise's mother had rung her, upset and angry. He hadn't replied; she didn't think he would, and while she hated to admit it, this seemed to confirm his guilt. 'It's the drugs,' Eloise's mother had said. But Elizabeth knew that Jacob's behaviour had started to change even before he'd begun smoking cannabis.

Picking up her glass of water, she slowly stood and went into the study where she switched on the computer. While she waited for it to load she sipped the water and thought of Andrew, who'd dismissed the article she'd found and agreed with Dr Shah that it was press sensationalism. But if she could find more concrete evidence perhaps he'd start to understand and believe her. Then of course if wouldn't be entirely Jacob's fault, and telling Andrew what he'd done to Eloise might possibly make it that little bit easier. If there was another reason.

The Windows screen appeared and Elizabeth pulled her chair closer and googled: *personality change after a transplant.* Sometimes new searches revealed fresh information and she began scrolling down, opening the various web pages. There were lots of 'true' and 'real-life' stories that had been reported in newspapers and magazines relating how kidney, cornea, liver and heart transplants had transformed the recipients' lives so that they were able to see for the first time in years, climb a mountain, canoe, or run a marathon. But these weren't the type of changes Elizabeth was interested in. She was looking for changes in personality, not quality of life and accomplishments.

She continued down the page, found the article she'd shown Andrew, reread it and moved on. She found another web address that looked hopeful, opened the page and read a similar story. This woman claimed to have experienced changes in her likes and dislikes after receiving a new heart. It cited another article and she clicked on the link to it. This article was five years old and gave an account of a woman who believed she'd taken on some of the characteristics of the donor after a kidney transplant when her taste in the arts had become more highbrow. She'd begun reading Dickens and Shakespeare and listening to Beethoven and Bach, much to the amazement of her family, when previously she'd been a fan of Mills & Boon and pop music. But a doctor quoted said many people develop more sophisticated tastes in middle age so the fact it happened straight after the transplant was likely to be a coincidence.

She found another article that examined other similar claims and read the account of a young woman who said she'd felt more masculine, assertive, and tougher after receiving a heart from a man. But of course Elizabeth realized that this could easily have been suggestion – she knew the donor was a male in his twenties and subconsciously had started behaving as she perceived him to be. Then she found a harrowing account of a man in Germany who'd committed suicide five years after receiving an organ transplanted from a man who'd also committed suicide. They'd both hanged themselves. Could that too be a macabre coincidence? Apparently it could. The journalist pointed out that the most common method of committing suicide in men is by hanging. It seemed there was a plausible explanation for all of these accounts.

Elizabeth continued reading. There were a surprising number of such stories online, but she had to admit some were fanciful even to her, and she was desperate to discover proof that Jacob wasn't to blame for his behaviour. According to the parents of a child who'd received transplanted lungs, their son had begun talking to the dead boy, calling him by his name. Another family in India believed their daughter had taken on the personality of the donor so much so that she'd been reincarnated. A woman in America claimed that the identity of her donor came to her in a dream with such clarity and detail she was able to trace the donor's family, who confirmed all she knew about their dead son.

Then suddenly, to Elizabeth's small delight, she found

an article that quoted research rather than narrative recollections. The first was a small sample of fifty-five adults in America who'd received transplanted organs. She read that 95 per cent of them hadn't experienced any personality change after the transplant, but 5 per cent had, which was significant. Elizabeth sat upright in her chair.

These post-transplant changes included changes in food preferences, music, sexual orientation, art, hobbies, and general disposition – the recipient becoming happier, more thoughtful, more confident and so on. Some of the subjects had also reported that some situations and places they'd never known had unaccountably become familiar to them – like déjà vu. But the researchers were quick to point out that these were anecdotal verbatim accounts and couldn't be independently corroborated. Even so, it gave her hope. It had been an objective piece of research and the article referred to another study in Asia. Elizabeth clicked on the link. Unfortunately, this sample was even smaller, only ten people, yet two had reported some change in personality. Again, there was the usual rider that the accounts couldn't be independently substantiated. It seemed no respectable researcher wanted to stick their neck out and risk being laughed at. Further down the page she found a quote by a spokesperson for UK Transplant who said that while they were aware of the reports of changes in personality of some transplant patients, there was no evidence to support it.

But on the third page of web addresses, Elizabeth found a thesis by a PhD student entitled: *Changes In Personality*

After Transplant: The Cellular Memory Phenomenon. Her heart skipped a beat. So it had a name: cellular memory. She took a sip of water while keeping her eyes on the screen. 'The cellular memory phenomenon (CMP), while still not fully scientifically validated, is supported by several scientists and physicians,' the article began, which was news to her. So some scientists did recognize its existence! She wished she'd known that and had been better informed when she'd spoken to Dr Shah.

The thesis continued: 'CMP hypothesizes that behaviours and emotions can be passed from a transplant donor to the recipient through memories stored in the neurons of the organ.' Then there were pages and pages of research data which she pored over at length, trying to make sense of it. While much of the scientific terminology was beyond her the message was clear. Cellular memory had been observed in laboratories using various organisms – bacteria, yeast cells, amoebas, plants, and worms. It had therefore been proven that it was possible to pass on cellular memory in lower life forms. It just hadn't been proven in humans yet.

Flushed with hope, Elizabeth read on and tried to understand the explanation of the chemical and biological processes that had made this possible, but it was very difficult without scientific knowledge. It seemed that multicellular organisms could change their genetic programme in response to stimuli, and remember their origin in the recipient or host, even many cell divisions later. It was to do with DNA proteins – the building blocks of life which she'd heard of – the blueprint of who we were, so that each cell, each strand of DNA, molecule of protein, contained not only our physical being but our personality. It was incredible but it made sense. Why shouldn't molecules contain the blueprint of who we were as a person as well as the colour of our hair and eyes?

The second part of the thesis reported the student's carefully researched case studies – a cohort of 102. He'd traced the recipients and had interviewed them in person if they'd reported any personality change after their transplant. He'd then interviewed the donor's family or friends to validate the claims made, and all of them could be substantiated to some extent. And it wasn't only organ transplants that produced these results, but transplants of corneas, blood, and bone marrow. Heart transplant patients reported the biggest changes and seemed to be most susceptible to cellular memory, possibly because of the 'huge mass of combinatorial coded nerve cells'. His thesis concluded by saying that the whole ethical debate on transplants needed to be reopened as the existence of CMP meant that elements of a person's character – even their soul – could be transplanted along with the organ.

Chapter Twenty-Three

Jacob felt his date with Rosie had gone OK. His only slip-up had been when she'd asked him where he'd got his money from and he'd been about to say, 'None of your fucking business.'

He'd stopped himself in time but not before Rosie had seen his expression change, harden into a flash of anger. She'd looked scared and had made a flustered apology. 'I'm so sorry. It's none of my business. That's what comes with working in a bank and dealing with people's finances all day.'

'No problem,' he said, resuming his composure. 'You weren't to know it's a bit of a touchy subject for me. You see my gran died recently and left me the money in her will. I'm pleased she did but at the same time I feel guilty for accepting it. Can you understand that?' He was impressed by the ease with which the lie had tripped off his tongue.

'Yes, of course,' she said, immediately relieved and smiling. 'But you mustn't feel guilty.' She reached for his hand across the table. 'Your gran wanted you to have that money, so she'll be happy knowing you're enjoying it. Will you be able to buy a new car now?'

'I'm thinking of it. Perhaps you'd like to come with me some time and help me look?' Full marks, Jacob. Well done mate. It was the right thing to say. He could see how chuffed she was to be included in his plans. It didn't take much to keep a woman happy.

'Yes, I'd like that,' she said, gazing into his eyes. 'Let me know when you want to go and I'll book a day off work.'

The only other glitch, well, disappointment really, was that she hadn't invited him back to her flat after the meal. He'd thought that half a bottle of wine and as much sweet-talking as he could muster would have done the business. But when he'd said he'd see her home she'd looked embarrassed and said she hoped he understood but she needed to take things slowly after a previous bad relationship. Not too slowly, he thought, while nodding sympathetically. He hadn't invested all this time (and money) to wait months to get his leg over. He needed a place to stay and Rosie's flat ticked the boxes: central, no bills, and with the bonus she'd be out most days working. But he'd hidden his anger this time and had flashed her a little-boy pout of disappointment. Then he'd done the gentlemanly thing and had walked her to the bus stop, where he waited until the bus arrived before catching a cab home.

★ ★ ★

At 5 p.m. Elizabeth would normally have been taking Mitsy for a walk before starting the evening meal, but now she sat in the living room at the rectory, on edge, phone in her lap, waiting for a reply to her email. With the student's full name and university on his thesis she'd found him relatively easily on Facebook. She had then messaged him to say she had to speak to him urgently about his PhD research and could he send his number, or if he didn't want to give it out could he contact her? She'd included her mobile number. She hoped David Burns would take her message seriously and not think she was a nutcase stalking him on the internet. She'd message again if he didn't reply. She had to speak to him. It was crucial.

As she waited the front door burst open and Jacob stormed in. Elizabeth knew immediately he was very angry.

'Don't believe a word that cow said!' he thundered, eyes blazing. 'She's out to make trouble, and by the sound of it you've fallen for it.'

'No,' Elizabeth protested, rising from her chair. 'I wanted to speak to you first, that's why I tried to call you.' She looked at him, nostrils flared in anger; he was barely recognizable from the son she'd known. 'Tell me what happened please, Jacob. It sounds dreadful. I'm so upset.'

'Will it make any difference?' he demanded. 'Or have I been tried and found guilty in my absence? What did the bitch say?'

'Jacob!'

'Sorry, but you can see I'm angry. What did she say?'

Elizabeth knew that if she told him exactly what Eloise's mother had said it would make him angrier still. 'She said there'd been a problem at the weekend between you and Eloise.'

He met her gaze. 'And she didn't tell you what?'

'Not exactly. No.'

He knew she was lying. The state he'd left Eloise in – screaming and crying and threatening to call the police – she was bound to have told someone, and most likely her mother.

'I'll tell you then,' he said, flopping into an armchair. Elizabeth sat down again, tucking her phone beside her, hoping David wouldn't choose this moment to call. She could feel her stomach cramp with anxiety as it always did now when Jacob was in the same room as her.

'Eloise wants us to get back together,' he said with a sigh of exasperation. 'That's why she wanted me to go there at the weekend. She had it all planned. The house to ourselves. A romantic dinner for two, then bed, and everything would be back to how it was. But I can't do that, Mum,' he implored. 'I don't love her. I thought it was only fair to tell the truth – to be honest and not lead her on.' He paused and looked at her. Was she believing him? He thought she might be. God, she was gullible.

'I told her as gently as I could, Mum, believe me, but she went ballistic. Shouting, screaming and crying. She threatened to kill herself if I didn't take her back. Then she ran into the kitchen and grabbed a knife. I thought she was going to kill herself or me so I wrestled it out of her hand. She was hysterical and I slapped her face to bring her out of it.'

'So that's how she got the bruises, and cut to her lip?' Elizabeth asked sombrely.

He nodded. Clearly she knew more than she was letting on, as he'd guessed. 'I had to slap her quite hard, but it didn't help. She continued to throw herself at me, trying to kiss me and hold on to me. She said she'd do anything to get me back. It was embarrassing. Then when she saw that it wasn't getting her anywhere she said if she couldn't have me no one else would. She said she'd tell everyone I raped her and ruin my life.'

'But why would she do that?' Elizabeth asked, looking at him carefully. 'It doesn't make sense.'

'Jealousy, Mum, the green-eyed monster! I told her there was someone else. I realize now I shouldn't have done. But at the time I thought it might help her come to terms with our relationship ending. You know, make her see it was over, and that there was no going back. But it didn't help. She kept crying and shouting that she was going to say I raped her. In the end I left. Staying was making it worse. God knows what she told her mother but whatever it was it wasn't true. You do believe me, don't you, Mum?'

Elizabeth nodded thoughtfully. 'I assumed there would be another explanation. Perhaps I should phone Eloise's mother and tell her?'

'No. Don't do that. Just leave it. She'll get over it in time.'

'If that's what you want.' She paused. 'So is there someone else? Or did you just make that up to try and help Eloise?'

He allowed himself to smile. 'There is someone, Mum. It's early days yet, but already I like her a lot. She's a nice girl with a good job in the bank. I'll bring her home to meet you and Dad when we've known each other a bit longer.'

'I'll look forward to it,' Elizabeth said.

'Great. Well, I've had rather a busy day so I think I'd better have a lie-down for a while.' He came over and kissed the top of her head. 'Oh, yes, I nearly forgot, the biopsy and all the other test results were fine.'

'Well, that's a relief. Thank you for telling me. I'll tell your father.' She smiled at him and watched him leave the room.

Plausible, yes, quite believable, Elizabeth thought. Eloise wouldn't be the first girl to react badly at being dumped. *Hell hath no fury like a woman scorned*. Convincing and feasible if you didn't know Eloise as well as she did. A kinder, more generous, dependable, rational, level-headed girl you wouldn't find. Not in a million years would she have reacted as Jacob had described. So as much as Elizabeth would have liked to believe Jacob she was almost certain he was lying; although she wouldn't be telling Andrew any of this, not yet anyway.

Chapter Twenty-Four

By the end of Monday evening Elizabeth still hadn't received a message from David, the PhD student whose research she'd read online, so just before she went to bed she sent another message through Facebook. It reiterated the contents of the first but added that she needed to speak to him urgently in connection with the heart transplant her son had received. The following morning she was disappointed to find there was no reply. Then at 8.30 a.m. while she was in the kitchen washing up the breakfast things and wondering how she could contact him, her mobile rang from a number she didn't recognize.

'Hello?' she answered tentatively.

'Is that Elizabeth?'

'Yes.'

'It's David Burns. You messaged me.'

'Oh, thank you so much for phoning. Have you got time to talk now or shall I call you back later?'

'I've got thirty minutes now if you're free. I'm on the train going to work.'

'Thank you so much,' she said again, and closed the kitchen door just in case Jacob woke. She didn't want him overhearing this and Andrew had already left. 'I thought you might think I was a nutcase and not phone.'

He laughed. 'Well, I guessed the wife of a reverend was going to be OK.'

'How did you know that?' she asked, surprised.

'You can find out most things on the internet as you've discovered. I was surprised you'd come across my thesis. I'd forgotten it was still online. It's quite old.'

'Yes, but it's still the most detailed study I could find on cellular memory and transplants.'

'That's probably because it's a topic no one wants to address. From what you said in your emails about your son I'm assuming you have fresh evidence. But I should tell you that I stopped researching cellular memory once I'd completed my PhD. I now work in a completely different field, researching anaesthetics for a large pharmaceutical company. So I'm afraid I wouldn't be interested in interviewing you, although I'm sure what you have to say is very interesting.'

'No, that's not my reason for contacting you,' Elizabeth said quickly. 'I wanted to ask you how likely you thought it was to have a complete personality change after a heart transplant. I don't just mean changes in lifestyle or food preferences, but a change of personality as though it was a different person.'

There was a short silence before David replied. 'It's possible in theory, if you accept CMP. We have proof that cells thrive and reproduce after transplant so it's a matter of degree – what are the limits? How far can they go? I've no idea if it's possible for the DNA of the donor to completely take over the recipient to the extent of them becoming that person.' He paused for a moment. 'Although there's a very interesting case which you might not have come across. It's not well documented. A teenage girl whose blood group gradually changed to that of the donor after a liver transplant. Now that *is* significant. For that to have happened it means that every blood cell in every part of her body was replaced by those of the donor. She therefore had his DNA, which is jaw-dropping.' Elizabeth could hear the excitement in his voice and her hopes rose.

'So physiologically at least that girl was more like the donor than her old self – pre-transplant,' he continued. I don't know if she experienced personality changes, but my guess is she did. She lived in Brazil and her family were very protective of her and didn't want her used as a guinea pig, or I would have flown out to interview them. But what was even more mind-blowing was that she was able to stop taking the immunosuppressant drugs.'

'Really!' Elizabeth gasped, appreciating the significance.

'Exactly. As far as I'm aware it's the only case, but it means that her body had become so like the donor's that it accepted the liver as its own. She was that person. More research needs to be done but she is the living proof that not only does cellular memory exist in humans but it can have a profound and far-reaching effect after transplant surgery.'

'So why has so little research been done on it?' Elizabeth asked.

'Lack of funding and credibility. It's not easy to persuade an institute that's already short of funds to back something that affects only a fraction of the population, and which most of the medical world dismisses as hocus-pocus. When I first showed the outline of my thesis to my professor he split his sides laughing. It was only when I showed him the research I'd already done that he allowed me to go ahead. You see, I had a personal interest in exploring cellular memory as well as a profes-sional one.' He paused and Elizabeth could hear the steady hum of the high-speed train he was on in the background.

'Yes?' she prompted.

'I'd appreciate it if you kept this confidential. It's not in my thesis and I didn't tell my professor. But I first became interested in CMP ten years ago when my older sister had a kidney transplant. Almost as soon as she woke up my parents, younger sister and I noticed significant changes in her behaviour. Not just those that could be attributed to someone being grateful for a new lease of life and making the most of it. But fundamental changes to her very personality.'

'What sort of changes?' Elizabeth asked.

'Libby, my sister, had always been overly confident to the point of being domineering and controlling. She was eldest of three and liked to get her own way. She had a successful career in marketing, and didn't mind who she trod on to get to the top. She was furious when she found out she had kidney disease and really resented the time she wasted on dialysis; she made my parents' life hell. But then suddenly after the transplant she was a different person, meek, mild, kind and gentle, softly spoken and always putting others first. It was a huge transformation, and for the better.' He gave a small laugh before continuing.

'When Libby returned to her flat she was horrified at the amount of material possessions she'd accumulated, and gave many of them away. Then she started going to church – the rest of my family and I aren't churchgoers – and after a year she converted to Catholicism. The changes in her were so startling that I began to wonder if there was any connection to the transplant. I'd already read some of the stories you see in the newspaper, as I'm sure you have, and had largely dismissed them as fanciful. But I couldn't dismiss what I'd seen in my sister so I did what you probably did and started researching online, where I found many cases. The next step was obviously to see if my new sister matched her donor. I didn't tell anyone – my family didn't talk about it – so I secretly traced the donor. She lived in Ireland. A woman in her forties who'd died of a brain haemorrhage. She'd been a Catholic nun!'

'Good gracious!' Elizabeth exclaimed. 'That's incredible.'

'Cellular memory, without a doubt. It can't be explained

any other way. No one in my family was aware of the donor's identity so you couldn't put it down to suggestion – a self-fulfilling prophecy where belief causes the behaviour. My sister had made it clear to us and the transplant team she didn't want to know the identity of the donor so I didn't tell her.'

'So you believe it is possible to transfer personality?'

'Yes, but far more research needs to be done. And it's not going to happen any time soon. Does this help with your son?'

'Yes, I think so. Although we're experiencing the opposite of what you describe with your sister.'

'In what respect?'

Elizabeth hesitated. She was talking to a stranger, but one who seemed to understand what she was going through having experienced something similar. 'All the good qualities my son had – and there were many – have gone,' she said quietly. 'His behaviour has deteriorated so dreadfully that my husband and I don't recognize him any more. Although my husband makes excuses for him.'

'I see,' he said thoughtfully. 'How very upsetting for you both. And you've ruled out the possibility of any side effects from the medication he's taking?'

'Yes, his doctor has.'

'And your son isn't depressed? A significant number of transplant patients become depressed after the operation, but it's usually within the first few weeks.'

'It's over three months since Jacob's transplant, and he's told his doctor he's not depressed. I don't see signs of depression in him either. He's out and about and doing things. More than he should be.'

'I see,' David said thoughtfully. 'I don't know what to say. There just isn't enough research to advise you. Hopefully it will pass in time.'

'Hopefully,' Elizabeth said doubtfully. 'Did you ever come across a case like this in your research?'

'Not to the same extent you are describing. And the vast majority of changes were for the better. I assumed that was because you'd have to be a decent person to carry a donor card.'

'But I'm right in saying that if personality traits can be transferred through cellular memory then it must be possible to transplant evil as well as good? As my husband says: If there's a heaven then there must be a hell.'

'I wouldn't know about that,' David said with a small laugh. 'I'm not religious. But if we accept CMP, then in theory all personality traits can be transferred – good and bad. Whether that's what's happened to your son I've no idea, but there's a way to find out.'

'How?'

'Trace the donor. Try to find out what they were like. But think very carefully before you do. I've met some families who bitterly regretted that decision. A bit like an adopted child meeting their natural parent and finding they don't match up to their ideal. And for you it's a no-win situation.'

'In what respect?'

'Well, if the donor was a bad person then you will have

to come to terms with their heart living on in your son. And if they were a good person, then you are left with the unhappy conclusion that Jacob has become bad for other reasons.'

Chapter Twenty-Five

Later that Tuesday morning, unbeknown to Elizabeth and most of the other villagers, the police had returned to Mary's home. Elizabeth only found out at 1 p.m. when she pulled into the lane and saw two police cars parked outside Acorn Cottage. She was on her way to visit Mary in hospital and had stopped off to see if there was any mail to take with her. Perplexed and concerned, she slowly drew to a halt a little behind the second police car. The front door to the cottage was wide open and a young uniformed officer stood just inside, in the lobby. He nodded when he saw her get out.

'Good afternoon.'

'Good afternoon. Is everything all right?' Elizabeth asked, as she started up the front garden path. 'I'm a friend of Mary's, the Reverend's wife. I was going to collect Mary's mail and take it to her in hospital.'

'I'm afraid you won't be able to come in here today,' he said rather officiously. 'We're treating it as a crime scene.'

'A crime scene? What crime?' Elizabeth asked, shocked.

'I can't say. We'll know more once Forensics have finished.'

'Forensics? But Mary is in hospital after a fall.'

'I don't know any more, ma'am. Sorry for the inconvenience, but we'll be here for most of the day.'

'I see,' Elizabeth said, wondering what could possibly be going on. 'And you can't tell me any more?'

'No. Sorry, ma'am.'

She threw him a polite but restrained thank-you and retraced her steps to her car. She'd phone Andrew to see if he knew what was going on, although he probably would have said when she'd left him working in the study. She decided not to do this in full view of the officer who was still watching her from the door, so she turned the car around and then drove further up where she parked out of sight. Andrew picked up at once.

'I've just been to Acorn Cottage; the police are there with a team of Forensics.'

'Whatever for?' he asked. Clearly he didn't know either.

'They wouldn't tell me. I take it you haven't heard anything?'

'No. But I'm sure Sid Jenkins will have. Someone must have let them in.'

'I'll phone him now. Is Jacob OK?'

'He's in his room. I'll check on him later. Let me know how you get on.'

'I will.'

As chairman of the parish council, Sid Jenkins would be the most likely person to know why the police had returned to Acorn Cottage. It was a few rings before he answered.

'Sid, it's Elizabeth. I've just come from Mary's cottage. I was going to collect her mail and take it to hospital with me, but the police are there. I wasn't allowed in. Do you know what they're doing there?'

'Yes, but I was told to keep it quiet.'

'Why? What's going on?'

'I'm sure it's just that Mary is confused after her fall, but she told a nurse that she didn't fall but someone hit her. The hospital notified the police and an officer interviewed her at the hospital. She said she thought she was hit, although she couldn't tell them anything about her attacker as it was dark. The police have spoken to Suzy's family and Suzy confirmed there was no sign of a break-in, that the door was locked and she had to use the key to get in. I'm sure it's nothing.'

'But the police seem to be taking it quite seriously.'

'They have to really, don't they? Supposing something had happened and they'd ignored it.'

'Yes, you're right. I wonder if I should tell Mary they're here?'

'Only if she mentions it. She might have forgotten all about it by now. They told me they'd check the place over and leave everything as they found it.'

'Good, thanks, Sid.' Somewhat reassured, Elizabeth

headed for the hospital in town. As she drove she thought back to Saturday evening; she'd seen Mary around six o'clock when she'd taken her dinner before she and Andrew had gone out to eat. Was she the last person to see her that day? If so perhaps she should tell the police? She was sure she'd locked the door and put the key under the mat. But then Julie had probably gone in after her. Julie had been popping in around eight most evenings since Mary had been ill to make sure she had everything she needed for the night. And Suzy had said the door hadn't been open and she'd had to use the key so Julie must have locked it. She was sure it was as Sid said – that Mary was still confused from her fall. She'd probably forgotten she'd even made the claim about an intruder by now. Aged 92 you were entitled to be a bit confused, especially after a nasty fall, even if it did waste police time.

Arriving at the hospital Elizabeth parked in a bay, bought a pay-and-display ticket and stuck it in the windscreen of her car. She checked her phone and left her jacket on the passenger seat before crossing to the main entrance. Maple Ward was on the second floor; Elizabeth knew it from visiting a patient there previously. It cared mainly for the elderly until they could return home or were moved into a nursing home. As she climbed the flight of stairs Elizabeth thought there was no reason why Mary shouldn't be able to return home in time, although lying in bed wouldn't help: a long spell in bed often made it more difficult for the elderly to regain sufficient mobility to live independently again.

She saw Mary as soon as she entered the ward, propped on pillows in a corner bed of the six-bedded ward. Her eyes were closed and her mouth sagged open in sleep. A large crepe bandage covered the wound on her head. Elizabeth took one of the visitor's chairs from the stack at the end of the ward and quietly set it beside Mary's bed. When she visited the elderly and found them dozing she never knew whether to wake them or let them sleep, with the possibility of them missing her visit. She put the bag of mints she'd brought for Mary on the bedside cabinet, then sat back and glanced around the ward. Two of the patients had visitors while the others slept. She found this type of ward an unwelcome and depressing reminder of how one's own advancing years might end: propped in bed, helped to the toilet by a nurse, soft food, and that musty smell of the elderly combining with disinfectant that lingered long after you left.

Mary stirred, the pressure relief mattresses reinflated around her and her jaw closed. Her hand went instinctively to the bandage on her head.

'Mary, love, it's Elizabeth,' she whispered, and placed her hand lightly on her arm. 'How are you feeling today?'

She groaned slightly, and turning her head in the direction of Elizabeth's voice, began to open her eyes.

'I've brought you some of your favourite mints,' Elizabeth said, pointing to the cabinet. Mary screwed up her eyes, trying to focus.

'Glasses,' she mumbled.

'I'll find them,' Elizabeth said, and checked the top of the cabinet and then its drawer. 'I can't see them here.' There was a fresh nightdress, a wash bag and a set of day clothes, but no sign of her glasses or their case.

'They're not there,' Mary said, still groggy with sleep. 'They're at home.'

'OK, don't worry, I'll find them and bring them in.'

'I couldn't find them. I was looking for them.' Then she peered at Elizabeth as though only just realizing who she was. 'Elizabeth?'

'Yes, it's me, dear. How are you?'

'Jacob?'

'No, he's not here. He had a big operation. Do you remember? He'll visit you as soon as he can.' She was clearly still very confused.

Mary's brow creased and Elizabeth could see pain in her eyes. 'It's all right,' she reassured her. 'He's getting better. There's nothing for you to worry about.'

'No, you don't understand.' Her bony hand clawed at the sleeve of Elizabeth's blouse. 'He was in my cottage.'

'No love, he hasn't seen you since before his operation, but he will visit you as soon as he can.'

'No. It was him. I heard him, but Elizabeth, why did he hit me?'

'Hit you!' Elizabeth exclaimed, aghast. 'Of course Jacob didn't hit you. He hasn't been near you. He's been ill.'

'I heard his voice. I'm sure it was him.'

'When?'

'Saturday night.'

Elizabeth stared at her, shaken and confused. 'Jacob was away at the weekend. You had a fall and banged your head on Saturday night. You're still confused. I brought you dinner. Do you remember that?'

Mary nodded. 'Then Julie came in, but later I couldn't find my glasses. I went to look for them in the living room. Someone was there. I heard them say, "Jesus!" like I'd startled them. It all happened so quickly but I'm sure it was him.'

'Oh Mary, don't say that please. It wasn't Jacob. It couldn't possibly have been him. He was away and he wouldn't do something like that. He thinks the world of you, as we all do. You didn't tell the police it was him, did you?'

'No. I've only just remembered.'

'Thank goodness,' Elizabeth sighed. 'Look, Mary, the police are at your cottage now, checking it over. I'm sure they'll be able to reassure you before long that no one broke in and you fell. You had a very nasty bang on your head and concussion can make us think all sorts of weird things.'

Mary's hand instinctively went to her forehead again. 'It all happened so quickly. Sorry. He probably visited me another day and I'm mixing it up. I had so many visitors.'

'Yes, that'll be it. Jacob said he was going to visit you like he used to.'

Mary nodded wearily and looked away.

'So tell me, what did you have for lunch?' Elizabeth asked, changing the subject.

'I can't remember,' Mary said.

'I'm sure it was something nice. Would you like a mint now?'

'No thank you, dear, but it was good of you to bring them. How's your dear husband? Busy as usual?'

'Yes. I left him working. He sends his love and will visit you in a day or so. Although hopefully you'll be home soon.'

The pain returned to Mary's eyes. 'I'm worried about going home. Supposing he comes back?' Clearly she really did believe there'd been an intruder.

'We'll make sure you're safe. Try not to worry. But you know Suzy said your front door was locked and she had to use the key to get in. There was no sign of a broken window so it's highly unlikely you were burgled, but the police are checking just in case.' Elizabeth hoped this would help reassure her.

Mary nodded half-heartedly. 'I told the police where I kept my money so they can check it's still there.'

'You haven't even told me that!' Elizabeth joked, trying to lighten her mood.

'It's a secret,' Mary said, with a wry smile.

But Elizabeth knew it wouldn't be much as Mary lived quite frugally. 'So is there anything else you need from home? I'll find your glasses, and also bring in your mail. Do you want a book or magazine to read?' Although there were already some untouched magazines on the cabinet.

'No thank you, dear. It's difficult to concentrate in here, and I need my glasses to read.'

'Yes, of course. If you think of anything else let one of us know.'

'I will. Thank you for coming.' Her eyes began closing and a few minutes later she was asleep.

Elizabeth waited to see if she would wake again, but when she didn't she returned her chair to the stack and left the ward.

Outside she couldn't shake off the acrid taste in her mouth, not so much from the smell of the ward but from what Mary had said. How on earth could Mary believe that Jacob would do such a thing? Break into her home and hit her? Yet a small part of her admitted that Jacob was capable of this and worse, and she hated herself for even thinking it. He was her son.

Chapter Twenty-Six

Andrew sat in the front pew of his church looking up at the stained-glass window above the altar, illuminated by the bright sun behind it. Christ, clad in a loincloth, nailed to the wooden cross, head lolling forward, with blood dripping from the nails in his hands, feet and the crown of thorns on his head. Christ dying in agony. A gruesome image but it represented what Christians believed, and served as a grim reminder that the Lord gave His only son to save humankind, although Andrew would be the first to admit it was questionable how much good His sacrifice had done. In many respects the earth was a crueller place now than it had been before. The human race was more intelligent and should know better. *Blessed are the meek, for they shall inherit the earth,* Christ had taught. Be kind and generous, and love thy neighbour. But evil proliferated. Many people seemed drawn to it. He knew, as a minister he'd seen the best and worst that people could do.

His thoughts went again to the material he'd found in his son's bedroom, and his stomach knotted to a tight ball. He'd gone up to see Jacob earlier with the intention of talking to him and suggesting that the three of them took up Dr Shah's offer of counselling. But as he'd entered the bedroom the smell of cannabis had hit him despite the window being wide open. Andrew had instantly lost his cool and had lectured him on the damage he was doing to his body and mind, how selfish he was. He'd been given the wondrous gift of a new heart – a new life – and he was abusing it, throwing it away! A young person had died to save him and he should respect that.

'I didn't fucking ask them to die!' Jacob had retorted, then he'd pushed his father out of his room.

Andrew was the same build as his son and knew he could have physically stopped him, but he'd taken the meeker, more Christian approach and hadn't put up any resistance. Then he'd stood outside the door shaken and annoyed with himself for having handled it so badly. He'd tried knocking and asking if they could talk, but Jacob had ignored him. Eventually he'd gone downstairs.

Fifteen minutes later, a cab pulled up outside. Jacob had come downstairs and without speaking or looking at him had left, slamming the front door behind him. Andrew had waited until the cab was out of sight and then done something he'd never done before. He'd gone upstairs to his son's room with the intention of searching it. It had become a no-go zone for him and Elizabeth, and while they'd always respected Jacob's privacy (as he hoped Jacob respected theirs) he now felt justified in trying to find anything that might give him a clue to Jacob's dreadful behaviour – perhaps hard drugs, mind-altering ones that had unhinged him and made him psychotic. He'd seen it when he'd visited hospitals for the mentally ill and prisons – many of those he'd counselled had very sad life stories which included hard drugs.

But as soon as he'd stepped into Jacob's room he'd seen the filth. Pages and pages of photographs printed from the internet and arranged in lines over the bed as if Jacob had intended him to see. Shocking images of women, some of them very young, subjected to the most appalling, degrading acts of sadomasochistic sex. Chained, bound, gagged, on leads, some with muzzles over their mouths with a hole just big enough to fit in a man's penis. Disgusting, sickening pictures of women being beaten, gang-raped, on all fours and forced to have anal sex. Every depravity Satan could think of was there, hard porn that could only be accessed by paying for it. He'd turned away in utter revulsion, his stomach churning and unable to believe the extent of his son's depravity.

Angry, angrier than he'd ever been before in his life, Andrew wrenched open the wardrobe doors and rummaged through but the only things inside were Jacob's clothes. He opened the drawers but, again, there was nothing obvious. In the bedside cabinet drawer he found a lighter and packet of cigarette papers beside the Dosette box containing Jacob's medication which he'd insisted on taking charge of. Keeping his gaze from the photographs on the bed, Andrew then opened the laptop on the desk. He started as the screen loaded. A close-up picture of Jacob with the devil's face filled the screen. Photoshopped to make Jacob look like the devil himself, with blazing red eyes and horns set in a face contorted by hate and rage. With it came a voice message: 'Fuck off! You don't know the password.' And a hideous laugh that could have come from the devil himself.

Closing the lid on the laptop, Andrew hurried from the room, sweating and sick to the core. The room felt like hell itself. The hot pungent air, the sickening display of photographs, and the message on the laptop that could only have been meant for him or Elizabeth. He prayed she hadn't seen it. He ran downstairs with the need to get away. Mitsy came out from under the table, wagging her tail expectantly as he pushed his feet into his outdoor shoes. With his hand trembling he opened the door and Mitsy followed him out.

The heat of the day was building now at the start of summer and he would have liked to run, forced the air into his lungs and exorcized the evilness of that room. But Mitsy was struggling to keep up and he slowed his pace as they crossed the common, his eyes fixed straight ahead and focused on the church. The village was deserted in the late afternoon and he saw no one. Arriving at the church he left Mitsy sitting obediently in the vestibule while he went through the inner door and breathed in the cold, slightly dank air of the solid stone walls and floor, familiar and comforting. He was relieved to find the church empty. He bowed to the cross, hurried down the centre aisle and dropped to his knees just in front of the altar. With his hands folded, his head respectfully lowered, and his eyes closed he prayed fervently – for guidance, deliverance, the strength and wisdom he needed to be able to deal with this.

He prayed for direction, a solution, anything that would help his family. He spoke to his God as his friend and mentor, a highly respected leader who was omniscient and would understand and know what to do. He asked Him to show him the way.

'You gave my son the gift of a new life, dear Heavenly Father, please show him how to use it and tell me what to do. I'm struggling.' He finished with the Lord's Prayer.

Andrew now sat in the front pew in quiet contemplation, hoping the answer might come to him in the peace and serenity of his church. How far away Jacob's room was now with its perversion and immorality. It almost seemed unreal and his thoughts began to calm and become more objective. What had happened to Jacob? Could it be the side effects of his medication? But Elizabeth had already raised that with the doctor. And in any event the side effects surely wouldn't produce the evil he'd just witnessed. The image of Jacob on the laptop flashed into his mind. It had been photoshopped but the picture was such a good blend, so realistic, you couldn't tell where his son ended and the devil began. He thought back to the son he'd had, and the last time he'd been in the church asking for God's help, when Jacob's life had hung in the balance, ebbing away as they waited for a new heart. God had answered his prayers then almost immediately. Elizabeth had rushed into the church, crying with joy that a donor had been found. His son as he was then had been kind, loving, respectful, playing the organ in church, and he prayed he would be returned to them very quickly.

With a final prayer of thanks he left the pew, and after bowing to the altar began down the aisle towards the door. Elizabeth would be home soon and he wanted to be with her before he had to leave again on parish business. Just to see her face, hear her voice, feel the normality of their relationship which was strong and good would give him a boost. As he neared the end of the aisle his phone vibrated in his pocket. It was a text message from Jacob. His spirits rose. God had answered his prayers again and everything would be all right. 'Thank you,' he said out loud and opened the text. Then he read the message. *Hi Dad, did you get off on the photos? You dirty old bugger! What would Mum say?* Beneath was a picture similar to one of the pornographic photographs he'd seen on Jacob's bed.

Chapter Twenty-Seven

'I told you you wouldn't get the quality stuff any cheaper,' Chez gloated, a self-satisfied grin on his face. He was standing right in front of Jacob, arrogant and tall.

'Because your fucking boss controls the whole fucking area,' Jacob hissed angrily.

'That's how it goes, man,' Chez said nonchalantly, holding and returning his stare. 'He was fucking pissed off with you, man, short-changing him. And I got the fucking blame. Had to give him the twenty quid out of my cut. Dickhead.'

'Like I care,' Jacob sneered. Chez was cockier than before, more self-assured. He fought the urge to punch the little skunk in the face, but he needed the stuff he'd brought with him.

'I think you should apologize to me, man,' Chez said. 'Say you're sorry to me for all the trouble you caused.'

'Go fuck yourself,' Jacob snapped.

Chez began to walk away.

'No. Wait!' he called after him.

Chez stopped, slowly turned, and surveyed him from the distance between them. He knew he had the upper hand. This creep was well and truly hooked, thanks to him, and he was getting through it quickly now. He was clean out and desperate, which was very good for business. Chez knew no one would supply him, not on this patch, so he could make him pay and grovel a bit. Get his own back.

'An apology then,' Chez repeated.

'Up yours!'

He turned, ready to walk away again.

'No. Wait. I fucking apologize, you cunt!'

'Say it like you mean it, man. Say you're sorry for all the aggro you caused me and my boss.'

'Sorry,' Jacob said, his hands balling into fists.

'That's better,' Chez said smugly, and slowly strolled back to him. 'I accept your apology. Now let's see your money.'

Jacob hesitated. This wasn't how Chez normally did business. Usually they exchanged the money and packet of weed in one quick furtive movement so no one could possibly see.

'Come on then man, I haven't got all day.' Chez glanced around. As usual the disused depot was deserted and littered with old half-filled skips, and piles of dumped domestic waste.

Jacob pulled the roll of notes from the pocket of his jeans and passed them to Chez. He began to count them, slowly, teasingly, making him wait. 'It's all there,' Jacob said, agitated.

Chez stopped and looked up. 'No, man, I need another twenty.'

'No, you don't. There's a hundred there like you said.'

'Yeah, but you owe me twenty from before.'

'It was underweight, you little shit.' Jacob grabbed him by his hoodie and lifted him off the ground. But this time he didn't squirm or cower as he had before, and there was defiance in his eyes, not fear.

'You owe me, man. Boss said I should get it back from you, so you learn your lesson. Or no weed.'

'Arsehole.' Jacob glared in his face. The little weasel was so puny one good blow would wipe him out. But then he wouldn't have a supplier and he needed the stuff regularly. He set him down with a jolt. 'Arsehole,' he said again. 'It better be the full weight this time.' He took the extra £20 note from his pocket and shoved it at Chez.

Chez produced the plastic bag containing the cannabis from his hoodie and threw it at Jacob's feet.

'Fuck you,' Jacob said, quickly retrieving the packet. Chez turned and giving him the middle finger began to stroll away.

Then it came again, that flash of anger, igniting him and blocking out logic or reason so that he was completely out of control. His veins coursed with searing hate and the need to wreak revenge. It had happened when he attacked Eloise and others he couldn't quite remember, and now he needed to attack Chez to assuage that burning, all-encompassing anger, hot, urgent and raw.

He went after Chez, leapt on him from behind and brought him down like a large cat felling its prey. A warning pain shot through his chest, but this guy would be easy meat just like women were. Sitting astride his back he pushed Chez's head down, ground his face into the filth and gravel. 'You little turd. Not so cocky now, are you? I think it may be your turn to apologize.'

He suddenly stopped as he heard a movement from behind him. Looking over his shoulder he saw two heavy-weight thugs, one carrying an iron bar, advancing towards him. 'You don't want to be doing that,' he said.

Chapter Twenty-Eight

Alone in the rectory Elizabeth sat in front of the computer in the study, finally convinced this was the right course of action. Indeed, she now thought it was the only course. David's advice: *There's only one way to find out. Trace the donor.* But as he'd pointed out, she'd have to live with the consequences of what she discovered. If the donor had led an evil life they'd have to come to terms with his heart living on in Jacob, and if he'd been of good character then Jacob must have become bad for other reasons, in which case she and Andrew as his parents must bear some, if not all, of that responsibility.

Taking a deep breath, Elizabeth tapped the mouse to bring the search engine onto the screen. All she knew about the donor was that it was a young man in his twenties tragically killed in a car accident. But by deduction she also knew that he couldn't have lived very far away from the transplant centre for his heart had arrived quickly and by road, and not by helicopter as would have happened had it come from some distance away. While this hadn't seemed significant at the time she now recognized its importance. It would narrow her search considerably, reducing the probability of finding the donor from highly unlikely – if the search had been nationwide – to quite likely. She planned on checking local newspapers first for reports of fatal road traffic accidents, and if that didn't produce anything she'd look at coroner's reports. However, she realized that would be like looking for a needle in a haystack as she'd no idea on which date the coroner's court had held the inquest. But she did know the date of the donor's death; it had been the night before the transplant – which was seared in her memory with other important dates like their wedding anniversary and Jacob's birthday.

Elizabeth tackled this task as she tackled most jobs, in an orderly and methodical fashion. She began by compiling a list of newspapers within a five-mile radius of Maybury, copying and pasting the links into a Word document. Most of the newspapers published weekly, but while some were free others required at least one month's subscription to view them online – the current edition and archived copies. Starting with the one at the top of the list she took her credit card from her purse and input its details, aware she'd have to explain to Andrew what she'd done before he saw their credit card statement. She hadn't told him what she was thinking of doing when he'd returned home briefly between parish business because he'd seemed anxious and preoccupied, although when she'd asked him if there was anything worrying him he'd said he was fine.

The first paper produced nothing more in the way of road traffic accidents than a car being stuck in a farmer's field and having to be pulled out with a tractor. The second two carried reports of minor collisions and a lorry becoming wedged under a low bridge. She continued with the next paper and read of a motorcyclist who'd come off his bike but had no serious injuries, and an elderly pedestrian who'd been knocked over while crossing the road. But no fatal car accidents. She widened her search to newspapers within a ten-mile radius, inputting her credit card details as necessary.

There were a surprising number of online newspapers, some of which only had a small circulation, but she checked them all. More reports of relatively minor road traffic accidents but nothing serious, no one had died. It was a macabre search. Then she found a fatality: a young woman whose car had overturned after a night out with friends. She'd had to be cut free and had died later in hospital. Elizabeth's eyes welled as she read the heart-rending words from her parents who'd said they were devastated by the loss of their beautiful, kind and generous daughter. She'd just finished university and had been out celebrating a friend's birthday. Their lives would never be the same again. The same accident was reported in a number of papers in the locality and Elizabeth paused to blow her nose and wipe her eyes. She could feel the parents' pain. They'd nearly lost Jacob and the death of a child was probably the greatest tragedy to befall anyone. She hoped that since her death they'd found some peace, although she doubted it.

Elizabeth stretched her shoulders and glanced at the clock on the mantelpiece. It was just after six o'clock and Andrew had said he wouldn't be back until seven. She didn't know what time Jacob would return, but assumed he would at some point as he was still coming home every evening for dinner. As far as she knew he didn't have a hospital appointment although Andrew had said he'd left in a cab but didn't know where he was going.

She resumed her search, opening and closing other local newspapers, and then widened her search again to include papers in a twenty-mile radius. As before she added the links to the Word document, and then began with the newspaper with the biggest circulation. Surprisingly this was free to view and she searched through the archived editions until she came to the week she wanted. The front page opened onto the screen and her mouth went dry and her pulse raced.

The headline: DEATH TRAP ROAD CLAIMS ANOTHER VICTIM.

Could this be it? She read:

Bells Lane, Shellsbury, notorious for accidents, has claimed its second victim. Shane Smith, 26, of Birch Road died from the injuries he sustained when his car struck a lorry

*in the narrow lane and overturned. He had to be cut free
of the wreckage and was taken to St Mary's Hospital. He
died three days later. The lorry driver was shaken but
otherwise unhurt. The police will not be prosecuting.*

*This accident black spot claimed the life of a cyclist two
years ago and campaigners have petitioned the council for
speed restrictions and better lighting. 'The road is full of
blind corners,' one local resident said. 'Lorries delivering to
the hypermarket take up most of the road and cars speed
along and can't see around the bends. There'll be another
one if something isn't done.'*

*The victim was one of five, and his mother Tracy Smith
said she blamed the council and the hypermarket for her
son's death and planned to sue them both. She has set up
a collection in her son's name. A spokesperson for the council
said they were considering various measures to improve the
safety in Bells Lane including introducing road humps.*

Elizabeth stared at the article and reread the first two lines.
Bells Lane, Shellsbury. Shane Smith, 26, of Birch Road. It
fitted, didn't it? She pulled up a map of the area and
studied it closely. The town where Shane had lived was
about twenty miles away, and closer to the transplant centre
than their village. Little wonder his heart had got there
so quickly, if it was him. It had to be, surely? But to be
on the safe side, aware it was too big a mistake to make
if she wasn't 100 per cent certain, she bookmarked this
web page to revisit later, and searched the rest of the paper
for any other road traffic fatalities. There were none. With

her senses tingling and on full alert, she then widened her search to newspapers in a twenty-five-mile radius from the transplant centre, where she found another road traffic fatality. But it was a woman in her fifties, and continuing her search she found no other matches. Hot, sweaty and with a slightly nauseous feeling in the pit of her stomach she searched no further and returned to the page she'd bookmarked.

Shane Smith, 26. A year older than Jacob. Now she had his name, age, and address. His heart, which they'd been encouraged to view as nothing more than a pump comprising of muscle, veins and blood like offal on a butcher's slab, was now an integral part of a once-living human being. It was Shane's heart, created in the womb of his mother and part of who he was for twenty-six years. A young man who'd doubtless had hopes, plans, aspirations for the future, and had loved and laughed, felt joy and happiness, suddenly and cruelly struck down before his life had even properly begun. Wiped out on a cold dark lane with a history of road traffic accidents. She thought of his poor mother, Tracy, and his brothers and sisters – the article said he was one of five children. A lump rose in her throat. She closed the web pages, saved the Word document, then sat back and stared at the blank screen.

A strange mixture of elation and utter wretchedness settled on her, like the anticlimax after achieving a much-coveted goal. The adrenalin-fuelled journey to find the donor had been all-encompassing. Now what? Shane's name, that of his mother and the road where they'd lived were imprinted on her mind, although what she would do with this information she didn't yet know. Write to Tracy? Try to find her phone number and call her? Or just arrive on her doorstep? But what to say? And did she really want to know? David's words rang in her ears again. *It's a no-win situation.* It had been different with his sister. Her change had been for the better, but in Jacob's case, if the badness hadn't come from the donor then it had come from her and Andrew. Damned if we do and damned if we don't, she thought. But doing nothing wasn't an option.

Chapter Twenty-Nine

For a second Jacob thought he was waking up after his transplant operation; he had the same feelings of grogginess, of drifting and not really being there, and the pain. Then as he fully regained consciousness and his eyes opened, he remembered what had happened.

'Fucking cunts!' he cursed, and tried to stand up. The ground gave way beneath his feet with a metallic echo and he fell back. 'Arseholes! Where the fuck am I?' It was dark and he felt closed in, yet he could see the sky and feel the night air. What the fuck had they done to him?

He tried to move again, and gingerly pushed himself up into a kneeling position, sitting uncomfortably on his haunches as he regained his balance. His head throbbed and he could taste blood in his mouth. He ran his tongue over his lip; it was cut and swollen. He spat and then delved into his pocket for his phone. It was still there.

They hadn't taken it; he guessed because it wasn't the latest model so had little street value. Pressing the button for the torch on the phone he shone it around. The beam picked out broken bricks, small piles of dried cement, gravel, old piping and rotting wooden planks. He was sitting on and surrounded by builders' rubble. Raising the beam slightly it fell on the rusty metal sides of a container. They'd thrown him in one of the skips at the disused depot. Bastards! Although it could have been worse, he acknowledged, he'd thought they were going to kill him.

Pointing the beam down Jacob carefully stood, got his balance on a pile of reasonably stable bricks and then picked his way over the rubble to the side of the container. Standing on the highest mound of bricks and dried cement he was now at thigh height with the edge of the container. He levered himself over the side and dropped to the ground below. 'Fuck!' he cried as his body jolted and pain shot through him. His legs felt raw and were like jelly but at least they hadn't broken them as they'd threatened to. He remembered the first few blows of the iron bar and then he must have blacked out. Wait until he got his hands on Chez. He'd teach him.

He looked at his phone. Jesus! It was 10.14 p.m. He'd been out cold for nearly four hours. There were six fucking texts from his mother, the first asking what time he would be home as his dinner was ready, then growing more and more desperate. *Where are you? Are you all right? Please get in touch. We're worried. Have you got your meds with you?* Of course I haven't got my fucking meds with me! I wasn't planning on being beaten up, he thought. He tried to laugh, but his chest hurt. He felt in his trouser pocket for his money but they'd taken it all and the cannabis he'd bought too. Bastards! Fucking wankers. He'd get his own back. Chez wouldn't be so brave without his heavies. He'd make him squirm, grovel and apologize just as he'd had to. Arseholes.

He coughed and spat, then wiped his mouth on the sleeve of his jacket. He winced as the rough material touched his split lip. His face was swollen, he could feel it, and his whole body was sore, but at least nothing felt broken. He began walking slowly across the disused depot, shivering against the cool night air. He'd had nothing to eat or drink since he'd left home that afternoon but what was he to do without any money? He supposed he could call his mother and ask her to collect him but baulked at the idea. Her questions, his explanations that she clearly didn't believe any more, and the recriminations with the Rev, going on and on about how disappointed he was with him. He really couldn't be doing with all that now. What he needed was someone placid, accepting, conciliatory and good-humoured. Rosie. She wanted him to like her; she wouldn't pry and ask too many questions.

Coming to the edge of the disused depot Jacob leant on what was left of the fence for support. He could see the lights of the town glinting in the distance. Another text came through from his mother. He left it unread and pressed Rosie's number. She'd recently bought herself another car but was she up to this? Would she do as he asked? It would be a good test of her loyalty and commitment. It was time to test her. He'd been pandering to her wishes to take things slowly for long enough. If she failed this test then that would be it. Bye-bye Rosie; he'd ditch her and move on. Women were two a penny. Look how easily he'd found her.

She answered straightaway in the quiet, self-effacing voice he liked. 'Jacob? Are you all right? It's late.' Immediately showing concern, he thought, a good sign.

'I need your help, Rosie.'

'Why? What's the matter?'

'I've been mugged.' He heard her gasp. 'They've taken my money and beaten me up. I'm outside the disused depot at the far end of the High Street. Can you come and collect me?'

'Have you called the police?'

'No. There's no point. I didn't see their faces.'

'I think you should. They can't get away with it.'

Why the fuck was she going on about, calling the police? He needed her to collect him. Didn't she understand? 'Can you come and get me?' he asked, then regretted the edge to his voice. 'Sorry. I'm in pain.'

'Yes, but shall I phone for an ambulance first?'

'No. I just want you.'

'I'll get dressed. I was in bed.'

'How long?'

'Fifteen to twenty minutes. I'll be as quick as I can.'

'Good girl. I'm counting on you. You're a gem.' He

could imagine the smile of gratitude on her face. He'd seen it before when he'd complimented her.

He ended the call and his phone bleeped with a voice-mail message from his mother. He didn't listen to it but texted: *Not coming back tonight. Staying with a friend.* Then with a feeling of self-satisfaction that he was no longer completely beholden to them he returned his phone to his jacket.

So some good had come out of what was an otherwise shit evening; he didn't have to go back to the rectory and listen to more crap, and he was working his way into Rosie's bed although she didn't know it yet. But what to do about his medication as his mother had previously asked? He could go without the vitamin and mineral supplements, but he had to take the immunosuppressants twice a day and at the same time − 8 a.m. and 8 p.m., otherwise his body would start to reject his heart. If he missed a tablet he had to take it as soon as possible and certainly within a couple of hours. It was already over two hours late and all his meds were in his room at the rectory. Then he had an idea, a rather good one. His mother had said she'd like to meet Rosie, hadn't she? Well, now she would have the chance.

He sat on the ground, using a skip as a backrest until the pale-blue Fiat came into sight. He watched it slow as it entered the uneven road of the disused depot, before he carefully stood up. Why she'd chosen such a pathetically small car and in pale blue he couldn't get his head around. He'd laughed when she'd told him what she'd bought, and had quipped that it was a woman's or old person's car. She'd gone quiet and said defensively it was the newer version of her previous car which she'd loved, so he hadn't said any more. But just as well it was dark now and the area was deserted or he wouldn't have been seen dead getting into it. As the car drew to a halt he came out of the shadows and hobbled towards it. The door opened and Rosie ran to him.

'We must get you to the hospital,' she said, breathless with worry. 'Look at you.'

'No, I'll be OK after a shower.' She linked her arm through his, peering at him with concern, then helped him into the passenger seat. He slammed the door, then shunted the seat back as far as it would go to make room for his legs. Flipping down the interior mirror he inspected his face.

'Not a pretty sight, am I?' he said as she got in.

'I think you should see a doctor.'

'No.'

'Where am I taking you then?' she asked. The interior light dimmed and went out.

'To your place. I can't let my parents see me like this. I won't give you any trouble, I promise. I'll sleep on your sofa or in the bath.'

Only the briefest of hesitations, then, 'OK.' She slid the gear into first and the car slowly pulled away. He'd never normally let his girl drive him, it felt effeminate, a loss of power and control, but needs must on this occasion. It would be the first and last time.

'I've got another favour to ask you,' he said as she drove. 'I haven't got my meds with me. I need the tablets quickly or my heart will start to reject.'

'Oh no,' she gasped. 'We can get them now. Where are they?'

'At my parents' house. It's over an hour's drive each way, which is too long. But if I phone my mother I could ask her to meet you halfway. Sorry, but it really is a matter of life and death.'

'Yes of course,' she said, even more worried and appreciating the urgency. 'We'll go there now. Which way?' She eased her foot off the accelerator, awaiting his directions.

'I can't let her see me like this, it would be too upsetting. Can you drop me off at your flat first and then go and meet her?'

Again, only a small hesitation, then, 'Yes. If that's what you want me to do.'

'Thanks. I'll call her now. She's been wanting to meet you!' He knew this would please her.

'You told her about me?' Rosie asked, her face full of hope and expectation of a future together. Women were so predictable.

'Yes of course. It's just a pity you couldn't meet in better circumstances.' He smiled. 'We'll have to make that another time.'

His mother answered immediately as he knew she would. 'Jacob, your tablets,' she said anxiously. 'Have you got them with you?'

'No, that's why I'm phoning. I hadn't planned to stay out. I'm in town with my girl, Rosie. She's offered to meet you halfway to collect them.'

A pause. 'Wouldn't it be better if you came home?'

'No, and it will take her longer to get the tablets to me if she has to drive all the way there and back.' He could see Rosie out of the corner of his eye glancing at him as she drove.

'All right. Where?' his mother asked.

'Dunsford Bridge. You know the lay-by there?' Everyone in the area knew the historic Dunsford Bridge.

'Yes.'

'Bring enough tablets for tomorrow as well,' he said. 'Just to be safe.'

'What time shall I meet her there?' she asked.

'How far to your flat from here?' he now asked Rosie.

'Five minutes.'

'She'll be there in half an hour.'

Chapter Thirty

Elizabeth concentrated on the road ahead. She knew she was driving too fast, but there wasn't much on the road this late and Jacob needed his medication quickly. Anger and concern rose in her in equal parts. How could he have been so silly as to leave the house without his medication? It had been drummed into him by the doctors and nurses at the transplant centre that it was essential he took the immunosuppressants every morning and night or the consequences could be fatal. Andrew had said he'd gone off in a taxi mid-afternoon so he'd only had his morning tablet. It was irresponsible of him to cause them so much worry on top of everything else they were having to deal with.

And where was Jacob staying tonight? Elizabeth wondered uneasily as she drove. She hadn't felt able to ask him on the phone and doubted he would have told her anyway, but she assumed it was with his new girlfriend Rosie. Elizabeth appreciated Jacob wanted to move on after Eloise, but she knew she'd struggle to accept anyone as dear and close as Eloise had been. And what was this Rosie like? Who would be attracted to Jacob as he was now? She couldn't begin to imagine. Someone like him? *Birds of a feather* . . . Jacob had said she was a nice girl with a good job in the bank, but Elizabeth doubted his perception of nice right now. Then she caught herself again. This was her son she was thinking about in this manner. Perhaps Rosie was a truly nice girl and would have a good influence on Jacob. Dare she hope? It was decent of her to drive all this way at night to collect his meds.

Elizabeth concentrated harder on driving as she left the main road and began along the poorly lit B road which would take her to Dunsford Bridge. Her thoughts turned to Andrew, who hadn't wanted her to come to this deserted spot alone at night and had offered to come too. But he'd already been in bed. Having not felt well in the evening, he'd had an early night. She'd promised to call him as soon as she arrived at Dunsford Bridge or if there was a problem. He hadn't looked well. He was drawn, tired, pale and very quiet, so she hadn't told him what she'd found on the internet; she'd wait until he was better.

She flicked her lights from full beam to dip as a lone car approached, and then onto full beam again after it had passed. A few minutes later the sign for Dunsford Bridge appeared; she knew the lay-by was just before the bridge.

She slowed, and then pulled over and into the lay-by. There were no other cars here unlike during the day when sight-seers parked and walked to the bridge to admire the view over the valley. Switching off the engine, she pressed the internal locking system. There wasn't a house in sight, just meadows, trees and the valley. She picked up her phone to call Andrew but he beat her to it.

'Have you arrived?' he asked anxiously.

'Just. She's not here yet.'

'Stay in your car and let her get out and come to you,' he warned. 'It might be a prank.'

'Prank?' she asked astonished. 'What do you mean? Jacob hasn't got his medication with him.'

'I know. Sorry,' he flustered. 'Forget I said that. Just be careful, Liz.'

'I will. Don't worry, I'll phone you as soon as I've given her the tablets.' She ended the call before he could say anything else that might worry her, for she could appre-ciate that Jacob was capable of playing a prank. He was capable of anything right now, including making her drive out here in the middle of the night as part of some perverse joke, or worse. She shuddered and drew her jacket closer around her.

A car's headlights appeared in the distance and then disappeared and reappeared as it made its way along the winding road. It finally came into full view as it slowed to cross Dunsford Bridge, and once over continued past the lay-by. Elizabeth looked in and could make out a man driving and a woman in the passenger seat. She set her gaze to the front again, staring through the windscreen into the dark cloudless night. A breeze stirred outside, whipping up some fallen leaves; it was always windy up here. A couple of minutes passed and then another set of headlights appeared in the distance, the lights on full beam, flickering in and out of view as the driver took the road slowly, unsure of where the bends were.

Elizabeth straightened in her seat, her pulse quickening, and her eyes straining as she charted the car's progress. Rounding the last bend before the bridge it finally came into view. Then it slowly crossed the bridge and indicated to pull in. She watched carefully as the car drew to a halt and parked a little way in front of her. The headlights were still on full beam so she couldn't see inside until they were switched off. She peered through her windscreen at the occupant: there was only one person in the car, and slightly built, possibly female. The interior light went on so that she could see the outline of the driver more clearly, and the passenger seat was definitely empty. She waited, her breath coming fast and shallow, until a girl got out and looked hesitantly in her direction. Elizabeth opened her car door and called out, 'Rosie? It's Liz, Jacob's mother.'

'Yes, hello,' she returned, her voice slight.

Relieved, Elizabeth took the packets of tablets from the passenger seat and went over to Rosie, offering her hand for shaking. 'Hello, nice to meet you.'

'Nice to meet you too,' she said shyly.

'Thank you for coming all this way and so late.'

'It's OK. Jacob needs his tablets.'

'He certainly does. He's told you about his transplant and how important these tablets are?'

'Yes.' Rosie smiled self-consciously.

'Good. Is he staying with you tonight?'

'Yes,' she said quietly and glanced away, embarrassed.

'As long as he's safe,' Elizabeth said. 'Here's his meds.' She handed her the packets of tablets. 'He knows when to take them.'

'Thank you.' There was a brief awkward silence. Then, 'I'd better be off. Get these to him as soon as possible.'

'Yes, of course. Well, thanks again. I hope to meet you again before too long. Perhaps you'd like to come for dinner one time?'

'Yes, I would. Thank you.' With a small, self-effacing smile Rosie turned and headed back to her car.

Elizabeth returned to her car and pressed the central locking system again. She watched as the pale-blue Fiat swung around in the road and headed back across the bridge. She had to admit she might have been wrong about Rosie. True, she'd only met her briefly, but you could tell a lot from a first impression, and Elizabeth prided herself on being a good judge of character. Rosie didn't appear to be the brash, loud girl she'd imagined her to be smug about having her son. She was quietly spoken and came across as shy and kind, and not at all worldly wise. She'd prejudged her – something she hardly ever did and wasn't proud of – and her assumptions had been false. She appeared to be a nice girl, as Jacob had said, and this worried Elizabeth for reasons she couldn't quite put her finger on.

She was about to text Jacob to tell him to treat Rosie well, but stopped herself. Whatever was she thinking of? Of course he would treat her well. Why shouldn't he? She texted Andrew instead: *Everything ok. On my way home. See you soon. xx.*

Chapter Thirty-One

Jacob lay in Rosie's bath, the hot water lapping around his shoulders, feeling much better. He'd put his clothes in her washer-dryer and had made himself a cup of coffee, which was on the bath side within his reach. It was a pity there wasn't anything stronger in the flat, not so much as a can of lager – he'd had a good look – but that could be sorted in time. He liked Rosie's flat; it was on the small side but comfortable with a decent-sized double bed, which he had every intention of spending the night in, not on the sofa as he'd said.

He felt relaxed and at home as if he'd lived here for a while. Strange the way things worked out, he thought. It was almost worth being mugged for, although if Chez thought he'd got away with it he was in for a nasty surprise. But all in good time. First things first. Tomorrow he needed to get himself wheels and find a new dealer, fast.

He was right out now and feeling the effects of withdrawing. Twitchy, nauseous, on edge. There'd be plenty of dealers in other towns away from Chez's boss's patch, he was sure, and they shouldn't be difficult to find now he knew the ropes and once he had a car.

As the water started to cool Jacob climbed out of the bath and began slowly towel-drying himself, examining the damage to his body as he went. They'd felled him from behind as he'd run so he'd taken most of the blows on his back and shoulders. That was where the pain and bruising were worst. He turned his back to the mirror so he could see. Angry welts where the metal bar had struck him or they'd kicked him ran the length of his back, his buttocks, the top of his legs, and a little round his sides. Facing the mirror again he looked at his chest; apart from the transplant scar being crimson from the hot bathwater, his front had largely escaped injury. Just as well. And his face – he leant closer to the mirror – now the dried blood had gone it didn't look too bad. None of his teeth were missing or loose and the swelling to his lip and cheekbone had been helped by the bag of peas Rosie had taken from the freezer to use as an ice pack. It now lay defrosting on the floor by the bath. His head was still aching, although the paracetamol Rosie had given him had taken the edge off it and he could take some more later.

Knotting the towel around his waist he left the bathroom and sauntered into the kitchen to check on his clothes. The dial showed the machine had finished the wash part of the cycle and was now on dry, but still had forty minutes to run. He'd forgotten how long these things took. The last time he'd used a washing machine had been at university. Once he'd returned home his mother had taken over his laundry again. Weird to think he'd actually been to university. He couldn't picture himself doing that, it seemed like a different person. Not just the passing of time, but why would he have ever wanted to attend university and read business studies? He couldn't imagine it, any more than he could imagine returning to the office where he'd worked. Picking up the remote for the television, he settled on the sofa, put his feet on the wooden coffee table and began flicking through the channels. All he needed now was a drink and a joint but that wasn't going to happen tonight.

A few minutes later he heard the door to the flat open and close. Then Rosie's voice, bright and sparkly despite the hour. 'Hi, I'm back. Got your tablets!'

She appeared in the living room and stopped dead. 'You've made yourself at home then.'

He looked at her. 'Yes, was that all right?' He wasn't sure if she was niggled. You couldn't tell with women, so he took his feet off the coffee table, switched off the television and, standing up, kissed her. 'Thank you so much. I don't know what I would have done without you.'

'I'll get you some water so you can take the tablets,' she said, appeased, and went into the kitchen.

'How was the dragon?' he called.

'Jacob! She was fine.' She returned with the glass of water and sat beside him on the sofa. 'She's asked us to dinner.'

'God! You're in favour. She's spotted a future daughter-in-law.' She smiled, pleased, as he knew she would. It was exactly the sort of thing women liked to hear.

It was easy to get her into bed after that. Of course he let her go through the motions of bringing a pillow and cover to the sofa, but when he groaned and said he couldn't get comfortable, she relented and said he could sleep in her bed.

'But just sleep,' she emphasized.

'Of course. I promise I'll keep to my side of the bed. It's late and we both need some sleep. You look exhausted. Thanks again for letting me stay and collecting my pills.' He could be so fucking reasonable.

Then once he was in her bed wearing only his freshly laundered boxer shorts it was a short step to reaching out and touching her and then she was putty in his hands. He knew it was months since her last relationship – she'd told him – so underneath her initial prissy reluctance she was gagging for it. She couldn't come fast enough, and, for him, ejaculating gave him some relief from the twitchiness and irritability of withdrawal.

The following morning to his relief he found he didn't have to spend long gazing lovingly into her eyes and telling her what she wanted to hear as she had to be up early for work. One quick fuck and he let her go. She brought him coffee in bed as she got ready and told him to help himself to breakfast, then kissed him goodbye and left.

'Goodbye, see you later,' he called after her. 'Thanks again for everything.'

Alone in the flat and with time to kill, he felt obliged to check her wardrobes and drawers to make sure she was telling him the truth and there was no sign of another bloke. You couldn't be too careful with women, especially independent ones like Rosie who were self-sufficient, with a job and a flat of their own. But he couldn't find anything to suggest there'd been a guy here so leaving everything as he'd found it he showered, dressed and then booked a cab for 9.15 a.m.

He was feeling good, despite the soreness from the beating; in control again and more at ease in this flat than he'd ever felt at Eloise's house. In the kitchen he threw some eggs into a frying pan with a large lump of butter. There wasn't any bacon or sausage – Rosie didn't eat much meat – but he found a can of baked beans and emptied that in too. He made toast in her toaster, some more coffee, and then, pleased with his effort, carried the plate and mug into the living room where he settled on the sofa in front of the television.

He'd just finished when a text came through saying the cab he'd booked had arrived outside. Leaving his dirty mug, plate and cutlery on the coffee table he picked up his jacket and with a mounting feeling of well-being left the flat.

'I need to stop off at a cash point on the way to Grange Motors,' he told the cab driver as he got in.

'No worries, mate. I have to fill up with petrol, there's a cash machine at the filling station.'

He sat back and enjoyed the journey; he was really looking forward to seeing Gary and his boss Craig again after the last time. He could have caught the bus; the showroom wasn't far. But a cab was far more comfortable and in keeping with his style. The driver pulled up onto the forecourt of Grange Motors soon after 9.30. Jacob paid him, added a decent tip and then strolled up the forecourt and in through the glass doors of the main entrance. The showroom had only just opened and he was the only customer. He spotted wanker Gary straightaway and Gary saw him. So too did his arsehole manager Craig. Clearly anticipating trouble, it was Craig who came over, drawing himself to his full height and touching the middle button on his jacket as he approached.

'Can I help you, sir?' he asked straight-faced and eyeballing Jacob.

'I want to buy a car,' Jacob said.

There was a short pause as Craig snorted air in through his nostrils before speaking. 'If I'm not mistaken, I believe you were in not that long ago and we discussed your situation then.'

'And my situation has changed,' Jacob said. 'I want to buy a car, a decent one, and I'll be paying with cash.' He could see wanker Gary watching from the other side. 'Using my debit card,' he added. 'The money is in my current account. Check if you like.'

Another short pause. 'That won't be necessary.' No, of

211

course he couldn't risk losing business. 'What type of car did you have in mind?'

'Not sure yet, I was hoping you could help me choose.' He was going to make him work for his money.

'And your budget?'

'Around fifteen grand,' Jacob said and watched his reaction. A definite shift in attitude.

He signalled to Gary to come over, explaining that as the manager he wasn't involved in actually selling the cars but left that to his staff, which suited Jacob fine. Wanker Gary would be doing the work and showing him some respect while he did it.

'Would you take care of this gentleman?' Craig said to Gary as he joined them. Gentleman was it now, Jacob thought. He liked the sound of that. Just showed what a bit of money could do. 'His budget is fifteen grand,' Craig said. 'He's not sure what he wants so show him around.' Then turning to Jacob, 'If you can't find what you're looking for on the forecourt we can check online with our other garages, then arrange to have the car brought here.'

'Excellent,' Jacob said, enjoying his new-found attentiveness; rather different from last time!

Craig gave him a comradely tap on his shoulder and returned to his office from which he could see most of the showroom and some of the forecourt outside.

Jacob stood squarely in front of Gary and looked at him expectantly. Gary was clearly struggling and would probably rather have been shovelling pig shit than selling him a car.

212

'Well?' Jacob asked.

'What type of car are you looking for?'

'Not sure yet, so do as your manager told you and show me some.' He saw Gary's mouth twitch as though a retort was trying to get out. 'Pardon?'

'Nothing. This way,' he said stiffly and led the way outside and to the first row of cars on the forecourt. 'Do you have any idea of the make, model, or engine size you want?' he asked.

'No.'

'Do you want petrol or diesel?'

'Not sure yet,' Jacob shrugged.

'Manual or automatic?'

'Open to either really.'

'Any preference in colour or the number of doors?'

'No, not yet. So tell me about them and then I can make up my mind.' He was going to enjoy this. There must be a hundred cars on the forecourt and he began walking around the first.

Gary hesitated, guessing he was probably being made a fool of but aware if he was there was nothing he could do about it. With his face set in an expression of salesman's professionalism he began telling Jacob about the car he was now looking at. Once he'd finished, Jacob shrugged.

'It's not really what I want,' he said, and moved to the next one. 'What about this one?'

Gary went into his spiel again and talked about the make, model, engine capacity of the car and why it was a popular choice. As before Jacob showed interest until he'd finished and then with a shrug said, 'Nah, not for me,' before moving on to the next.

So they continued along the first row of cars and then began on the second row, when Jacob suddenly stopped; something had caught his eye.

'Isn't that the car I wanted when I was in here before?' he said, pointing to one in the row behind.

'Yes. Would you like to see it?' Gary asked enthusiastically. 'It's in your price range.'

Jacob thought for far longer than was necessary as Gary waited expectantly. 'Nah, I don't think so. You've got plenty of others here for me to see.'

Gary's irritation was palpable but to his credit he concentrated on his sales pitch and explained in a fairly amicable tone the selling points of the car Jacob was now showing an interest in. He listened, nodded and then asked a couple of questions as though he might really be considering buying it, but then shrugged and said, 'Nah, it's not for me.' And moved to the next.

Presently he grew bored with simply looking at the cars and said he wanted to test-drive his favourites.

'I'll need to see your driving licence,' Gary said, clearly hoping he hadn't brought it with him.

With a self-satisfied flourish Jacob produced his licence. The look on Gary's face was priceless as he took it to the office to be photocopied. An hour later he'd test-driven three cars and it was nearly twelve o'clock. He'd been here for two and a half hours and was tired of wanker Gary. He was hungry and had yet to find a new supplier for his weed. He'd had enough fun for one day, so he pointed to the car he'd originally wanted on his first visit to the garage. 'I'll take that one,' he said.

'The one you chose last time?' Gary asked incredulously, looking at him. Jacob nodded. 'But I asked you at the start if you wanted to see it.'

'Yes, but I hadn't decided then. Give me a good price and the deal is done. Come on, cheer up mate, just think of your commission.' And slapping him heartily on the back, Jacob led the way inside. He was even with Gary now, which left just Chez to sort out.

Chapter Thirty-Two

It felt good being behind the wheel again, very good indeed. It was a powerful motor and in his favourite colour, black – black bodywork, seats, dashboard and upholstery, which seemed to add to the power and a sense of control. Black was definitely his colour now.

He'd got a good deal too, the price lowered by another £500 after he'd pointed out that the car hadn't exactly been snapped up as it had been there at his first visit. Gary hadn't had the authority to lower the price so he'd done the deal with the manager. Yet even as he'd finalized the deal he could see they both doubted he really did have the money. So when the bank called back to verify the purchase – standard practice on any transaction over £5,000 – he got a huge kick from seeing the looks of thinly masked surprise on their faces. That showed them!

Gary had come onto the forecourt to give him the keys and see him off, and before he'd driven away Jacob had lowered the window and said, 'You need to get rid of all your shit, man. I can smell it from here.' He saw Gary give him the middle finger in his rear-view mirror so he slammed the car into reverse and drove back, making Gary jump out of the way. Great fun. The wanker. He'd left in a blaze of tyre noise and burning rubber, his image and credibility restored. Now to get his weed.

He stopped off at the fast food drive-thru, bought a burger, fries and a Coke and ate them as he drove. He felt he'd had a satisfactory morning and the day promised to get better. As the road widened into a dual carriageway between the towns he put his foot hard down on the accelerator to see what the car could do. She met the challenge: eighty, ninety, ninety-five miles per hour. The adrenalin rush from the speed raised his mood further. He had to swerve to avoid an oncoming motorbike. 'Up yours!' he yelled out of his window.

Yes, the car was performing well. Big, powerful and dark was the new him, it matched his image and street cred. Rosie would be impressed. Women liked powerful dominant men, even independent women like Rosie. He hadn't asked if he could stay with her. He'd just assumed that's what would happen. She'd be fine with it after last night. He smiled at the thought of banging Rosie again; he'd done a good job, despite his injuries, and he'd do even better tonight. Make her scream and beg for more, unlike Eloise who didn't know what she was missing. Silly cow.

Throwing the empty food cartons out of his car window, Jacob ramped up the music and drove like a bat out of hell. Ten minutes later he slowed the car as he entered the outskirts of the town and speed cameras appeared. He continued to Southdrive estate, a well-known hot spot for drugs, crime and the disaffected. He parked on the edge of the estate and waited. A woman with three kids walked past, then an old guy with a dog, not the type of people he was looking for. But it wasn't long before three teenage boys sauntered towards him, low-rise jeans, hoodies and obviously NEETs – not in employment, education or training. Perfect. He watched them approach, then as they neared the car he lowered his window.

'Hey.' They paused. 'You know where I can buy a smoke?'

They looked at him carefully, standing a couple of feet from the car and clearly trying to decide if he was a plain-clothes cop. 'Why?' the tallest and probably the eldest asked.

'I'm looking for some.'

'What makes you think we know where you can get it? It's illegal, man.' They laughed.

Jacob laughed too. 'I'm sure smart boys like you know where I can buy a smoke. I'm clean out.'

The eldest looked around, checking for anyone watching. 'OK. Come with us.'

Jacob shook his head. 'Nah.' They would know he had

money on him if he'd come to buy and could mug him just as Chez had. 'Bring it here. I can wait.'

The lad shrugged, said something under his breath to the others, and then they all walked away. Jacob wasn't sure if they were going to get him the stuff or not. If they didn't return he could always ask someone else, there'd be plenty selling on this estate. But five minutes later they reappeared, now with a fourth guy. He pressed the internal locking system as they approached the car and then lowered his window again. The new guy stepped forward.

'Taco,' he said, offering his hand for shaking through the open window.

'Jay,' Jacob said.

'You want a smoke?'

'Yes. I'm out.'

Taco lifted his jacket to show him the goods, and a minute later the deal was done.

'Good doing business with you,' he said, shaking his hand again.

'And you,' Jacob said.

They walked away, quickly disappearing back into the estate. Jacob tucked the packet under his seat and drove off in a screech of tyre rubber. It had gone well, he thought. Easy-peasy. He had enough for a week and Taco's number for next time. He'd also paid £10 less than he had been paying Chez; not that the price mattered, it was the quality that counted, and Taco had promised it was good, pure stuff.

* * *

He drove from the town and, once in the countryside, parked in a lane and rolled a joint. As he sat with his window down inhaling the smoke he began to feel in a better frame of mind for going back to the Rectory. He didn't plan on staying long, just long enough to collect fresh clothes, his meds and a few things he needed. But it was likely that at least one of his parents, perhaps both, would be in. That was the problem with having parents who didn't work 9 to 5. Just as well he didn't have to stay long.

His head was buzzing now and the view from the car window shimmered with a new-found vibrancy. Yes, it was good stuff as Taco had promised. Life was good. He took his time finishing the joint and then threw the butt in the ditch and set off, driving fast along the twisting country lanes, so fast that he felt he could fly. The thrill of it was intense, almost orgasmic; the ultimate climax where he came forever. Oncoming drivers couldn't always see him because of the dips and bends in the road so they had to brake and swerve at the last second.

'Get out the way, you fucking prick!' he yelled, sounding his horn. 'Idiots!' Didn't they know he was competing in a cross-country rally? He was the best in his field – in his race of one.

He laughed out loud, gripped the steering wheel and kept the speed up. He could see the look of admiration on the faces of those he passed as he rounded another bend with the minimum drop in speed. You couldn't let up for a moment if you wanted to stay ahead of the rest, in the lead. And that applied to life in general, he thought. Stay on top and you commanded respect, but take your foot off the pedal and you were done for – a nothing.

Time compressed and it seemed he'd only been driving a minute or so before he was approaching his village, although it must have been half an hour. Ignoring the thirty mph speed limit and the 'Please drive carefully through the village' sign Jacob sped on, sending road chippings flying up the fronts of the cottages he passed. Just as well Mummy and Daddy couldn't see him now!

With a screech of tyres he turned into Rectory Lane and came to an abrupt halt outside the rectory. His mother's car was parked there but not the Rev's. A few seconds later, having heard his car arrive, her face briefly appeared at the living-room window. He got out as the front door opened.

'Are you all right?' she asked anxiously.

'Yes. Why shouldn't I be?' He began up the path.

'You took your tablets very late last night. Have you had a check-up at the hospital?'

'Yes,' he lied. It was easier than saying no.

'You've got a car,' she remarked as he stepped in and past her.

'Apparently. I've come back to get some clothes and more tablets, then I'll be off again.'

'You're not staying?' she asked.

'No.' He started towards the stairs.

'Where will you be? I mean if we need to get hold of you.'

'At Rosie's, but you have my mobile number.' He went upstairs and into his room.

Elizabeth waited for him in the living room, anxious and on edge, until he returned downstairs, his bulging holdall slung over his shoulder and keys in his hand. 'Jacob, I need to talk to you,' she said.

'What? Can't it wait? I'm in a hurry.' He glanced at her, with a look of derision. She felt shaky inside, but pushed on.

'It will only take a moment. I need to ask you something.'

'Go on then.'

'Can we sit down?' She'd been hoping for time to have a proper discussion.

'No. What is it? If it's about the car, I got a bank loan.'

'No, it's not.' Although it had crossed her mind how he'd been able to afford the car without an income. 'Jacob, have you ever considered tracing the donor? Do you have any thoughts on the subject?'

'What are you talking about?' he asked, and might as well have added, 'You silly cow,' for the scorn on his face.

'The donor. Your heart donor. Have you thought about tracing him?'

'No. Why?'

'Some people who have transplants want to trace their donors. Meet their family, thank them, and find out what the donor was like.'

'So?'

'Is it something you want to do?'

'No. I couldn't give a shit,' he said with disdain.

'So you don't feel strongly one way or the other?' She needed to know. It was important. 'We've never really discussed it.'

'He's dead, for fuck's sake. End of story as far as I'm concerned.'

'There's no need to swear,' she felt obliged to say.

'Is that it then? Is that what you wanted to talk about?'

'Yes. Say hello to Rosie for me.'

He hesitated and for a second Elizabeth thought he might be going to kiss her cheek as he always used to do when he left the house, but the moment passed, and raising his eyes in exasperation he went off, slamming the front door behind him.

With a slight feeling of relief that she'd finally broached the subject, Elizabeth moved to the window and, standing back so she couldn't be seen, watched him get into the car. His body, the way he stood and held himself seemed different now. He appeared to walk with his legs slightly further apart, his arms a little more out from his sides as though pumping himself up to seem as large as possible, as she'd seen thugs do in the street. But at least she now had the answer she needed, and felt exonerated in tracing his donor. She'd decided that morally she should find out Jacob's views first. Had he said under no circumstances should the donor be traced then she'd convinced herself that would be the end of it. If he'd shown great enthusiasm for tracing the donor and meeting his family then she'd have been prepared to share her findings with him, and suggest they visit the family together. But now she could take the next step alone, and her disquiet increased. For one way or the other she'd have the answer she sought. Jacob had either become evil through cellular memory in his transplanted heart, or she and Andrew were responsible. She wasn't sure which was worse.

Chapter Thirty-Three

Jacob had just finished taking Rosie for a ride in his new car, showing it off and showing her what it could do. She'd looked a little surprised when he'd arrived on her doorstep with his holdall.

'You're staying then?' she'd asked.

'Of course. You don't get rid of me that easily.' He'd said it with such roguish charm that she couldn't refuse. He'd kissed her, and then deposited his holdall just inside the door. 'Come on, I've got something to show you.'

'But I've just got back from work and I'm about to make dinner,' she'd protested.

'Leave it. We'll pick up a takeaway later.'

Taking her by the hand and allowing her to grab her handbag which contained the keys to her flat, he drew her down the stairs. 'What is it?' she asked, her face a mixture of excitement and apprehension.

'Wait and see.'

Outside he'd proudly showed her his new gleaming motor parked by the kerb and told her to get in. She said all the right things to begin with, and he'd enjoyed her admiration. But once they were out of the town and away from the speed cameras she became edgy as he opened the throttle and showed her what his beauty could do. She told him to slow down, that he was driving too fast, like his mother or Eloise might have done. Heaven forbid she was going the same way and felt it was all right to criticize him. He might have to put her in her place like he had them.

He hadn't slowed, not one little bit, and she'd grown quiet, and was no longer praising him or his car, which irritated him. Women were so fickle; they could change in an instant. He headed back to the flat making sure she understood he wasn't happy – his face set, his hands gripping the wheel, ignoring her. Then she'd said, 'Someone I knew died in a car accident and going fast makes me scared.'

'Boyfriend?' he'd asked with a niggle of resentment that she'd had to mention her past and spoil his fun. That was women for you. Always digging up the past and confiding. He'd thought Rosie might have been different but clearly he'd been wrong.

Then she'd touched his arm and apologized. 'I'm sorry. I shouldn't have said that. It's just me being silly. I didn't mean to criticize you. Forget I said anything. It's a fantastic car and you're a great driver.'

So perhaps it would be OK after all?

Back at the rectory, Elizabeth and Andrew were talking as they ate dinner, making everyday conversation. Elizabeth had slipped in as casually as she could that Jacob was staying at Rosie's and had taken out a bank loan to buy another car. She omitted to say that it looked quite new and therefore expensive so the bank loan was likely to be quite large. Even so, Andrew had raised his eyes to the ceiling and said, 'Well, I hope he can afford the repayments.'

Elizabeth had never got around to telling him of Eloise's mother's phone call and her shocking claims that Jacob had raped her daughter. Andrew always seemed so anxious and preoccupied that she hadn't wanted to add to his concerns, and with Rosie on the scene it was starting to slip into the past. She didn't want to go stirring up trouble; Andrew would be devastated if she told him. It was possible that Eloise had been jealous and exaggerated as Jacob had claimed. Best to let it rest, she decided.

Neither had she told him about her latest internet search which had revealed the donor's identity. She knew if she did tell him he would try to persuade her not to go as he'd taken Dr Shah's view that it wasn't possible for a transplanted organ to pass on personality. Elizabeth needed encouragement to take the next step, not someone trying to dissuade her. What Andrew didn't know couldn't harm him, so keeping the conversation on safe ground she asked about the church restoration fund, a subject on which he spoke often and with great animation.

As usual they took their coffee into the living room so they could watch the evening news. A few minutes after settling into their respective armchairs the landline rang and Andrew answered it. Elizabeth pointed the remote at the television to silence it.

'Hi Sid. How can I help you?' Andrew asked amicably.

Elizabeth glanced over. It was late for Sid Jenkins to be phoning about routine parish business. She watched Andrew's expression grow serious as he listened to what Sid was telling him. Then, 'No. Surely not?' And his brow furrowed. He fell silent and listened again, then, 'Dear me, what a shock.' Another pause then, 'No indeed. I will. Thanks for letting me know. Goodbye, Sid.'

He met Elizabeth's gaze, his expression serious.

'It seems Mary's cottage may have been broken into after all.'

'No!' Elizabeth gasped. 'What makes you say that?'

'The police have been in touch with Sid; the money Mary claims was hidden in her cottage has gone. However, she's a bit confused and keeps changing her mind about how much she had and where it was hidden, so the police are being cautious at present. It may be that in the end it turns out there wasn't any money, but for now they're treating it as a burglary.'

'Oh dear. Mary was confused when I visited her in hospital. She thought that Jacob had been to see her at the cottage on Saturday, until I told her he'd been away for the weekend. Then she realized it must have been another day.'

'I didn't know he still went to see her,' Andrew remarked. 'That's decent of him.'

Elizabeth nodded non-commitally. 'How much does Mary think has gone missing? Does she have any idea?'

'From what Sid said it could be thousands but the sum keeps changing. It's upsetting all the same, even if it turns out Mary is mistaken. We may need to put in some extra help when she comes home if she's very confused.'

'Yes, absolutely.'

'And Sid said to tell you that the police have finished at the cottage now so if you want to collect her glasses and mail it's fine to go in.'

'Good. I'll go tomorrow.'

Which effectively postponed visiting the donor's family for another day.

Chapter Thirty-Four

At one o' clock the following afternoon Elizabeth left the rectory to go first to Acorn Cottage and then on to see Mary in hospital. She'd take her mail, hopefully her glasses if she could find them, and buy her some of her favourite sweets and magazines from the hospital gift shop, although unless she found her glasses the magazines wouldn't be much use.

The lane was empty and as Elizabeth parked outside the cottage she thought it already looked a little abandoned, its warmth and vitality coming from Mary's presence. She went up the garden path and took the key from under the mat to open the outer door. If Mary had been burgled then they'd have to think about having a key safe box with a code installed; it had never been considered necessary before.

Elizabeth replaced the key and then opened the inner

door, never locked – which again they might have to reconsider – and stepped into the cottage. Sunlight shone through the small latticed windows but there was a musty smell, since the cottage was not being properly aired each day. She opened one of the windows in the living room and then looked around. The room appeared as it always did – no sign of the police having been here and nothing out of place, although Mary's walking frame, usually by her side, was standing by the doorway that led to the back hall. Mary would need that when she was discharged, and Elizabeth made a mental note to mention it to Sid (self-appointed trustee of Mary's business and that of many of the other villagers), so that whoever collected Mary from hospital would take it with them.

Looking around the rest of the living room Elizabeth saw that the fruit bowl on the sideboard contained a couple of overripe bananas which were adding to the mustiness. She took them into the lobby to throw away on her way out. Then she set about searching for Mary's glasses, but there was no sign of them, just the glasses case on the coffee table where it always was. She continued through to the kitchen where Mary's mail had been left in a neat pile on the work surface, but no glasses. She checked the cupboards and drawers and then the fridge, for if Mary was becoming confused and in the early stages of dementia she might have put them in there. But apart from milk and eggs, which would need replacing before Mary returned, there wasn't much else. She checked inside the oven and then took the mail into the living room where she placed it on the sofa to take with her later.

Next she went through the small rear hall and into Mary's bedroom. The fragrance coming from the small china bowl of potpourri on her dressing table pleasantly personalized the room, leaving Mary's mark. Her library books were also on the dressing table, but not her glasses. Elizabeth felt a pang of sadness as she looked at the old-fashioned bed, exactly as Mary had left it on Saturday night when she'd gone in search of her glasses, then tripped and fallen in the dark. Like most of those in the village she doubted anyone had broken in and knocked Mary unconscious, not from what Sid had said about her being confused.

Elizabeth began making the bed, as she did so checking the glasses hadn't become concealed in the pillowcases or between the sheet and blankets – Mary refused to give up her blankets for a duvet. Then she got down on her hands and knees and looked under the bed, but there was nothing there except a few dust motes and a spare pair of slippers. Straightening, she checked the chest of drawers and wardrobe, then opened the top library book and saw it was due back in two days – as were the others. She carried them into the living room and placed them on the sofa beside Mary's mail to take with her.

Elizabeth continued into the bathroom, which smelt stale, so she squirted some disinfectant down the toilet, sink and bath, then checked the bathroom cabinet for the glasses. There was nowhere else they could be in the bathroom so she returned to the hall and went into the second bedroom. Mary only used it for storage and it appeared she hadn't been in here for ages, so with a quick glance around she closed the door and went to the third bedroom. This room was seldom used and contained a single bed and a dressing table – no sign of the glasses.

Back in the living room Elizabeth gave a perfunctory last check around to see if she'd missed anything obvious, but wherever they were, the glasses were well and truly hidden. She now resigned herself to ordering two replacement pairs from the opticians, one as a spare to stop this happening again. In the meantime she could offer Mary her own over-the-counter spare pair of reading glasses.

She closed the window and crossed to the sofa to pick up her handbag, the library books and mail, then with a final glance around the room went to the inner door. As she opened it the smell of overripe bananas hit her, even more pungent in the confines of the warm sun-filled lobby. She picked them up, locked the front door, then took them to Mary's dustbin, which was always kept out of sight down the side of the cottage. As she dropped them in she caught a flash of glass glinting in the sunlight and looked closer. Moving a bag of rubbish out of the way, she gingerly reached in and took out Mary's broken glasses. Both lenses were smashed and the frames bent. Well, that solved the mystery, although it was worrying that Mary had completely forgotten she'd broken them.

Sid was right. She would need extra support if she was going to be able to return to live in her cottage.

As Elizabeth drove to the hospital Rosie and Eva were on their lunch break, enjoying a proper meal by way of a little celebration rather than their usual sandwiches.

'Your last day tomorrow,' Rosie sighed regretfully. 'I'm really going to miss you. Work just won't be the same. We have such a laugh.'

'I'll miss you too, but we'll get together regularly. I count you as one of my closest friends.' Eva shifted in her chair and rubbed her baby bump. 'One thing for sure, I couldn't have continued coming into work much longer. I've been going home in the evening and just sleeping. Syed has been telling me for some time to finish.'

'You've done well,' Rosie said. 'Don't forget to wear your best dress tomorrow for the presentation.'

'Don't remind me,' Eva said pulling a face. 'It's nice of them to arrange the collection but I could do without having to make a speech. How embarrassing.'

'You'll be fine. Just say thank you. And when the baby is born make sure you text or phone me straightaway.'

'I will, but you'll come and see me before then, won't you? I've still a month to go.'

'I hope so.' She smiled and both women paused to continue eating the quiche and salad they'd ordered, before Eva said, 'Enough about me. How is Prince Charming? You've gone all quiet and secretive. Tell me all.'

Rosie smiled coyly. 'He's fine.'

'Just fine! Miss Super-cool. You look like the cat that's swallowed the mouse.'

'If you must know, Jacob's moved in.'

'Really? You didn't say anything. That was quick.'

'It's only been a few days.'

'And you're all right with that?' Eva asked slightly seriously. 'Sorry. Daft question. Of course you're happy with that or you wouldn't have let him.'

'I didn't really have much choice,' Rosie said with a smile. 'He just turned up with his bag. But it's OK. I've met his mother, she's lovely, and has invited us to dinner. Although I think there's some friction between Jacob and his father; being a reverend they don't always see eye to eye on things.'

'That's understandable,' Eva said, taking a sip of her sparkling water. 'But what about Jacob's health? You're not going to end up looking after an invalid like my mum did.' Eva's father had suffered from a chronic lung condition and had died when Eva was a child.

Rosie shook her head. 'After a transplant you can live a normal life. You have to take tablets and have check-ups but it's not a problem.'

'Good. So he can go back to work?'

'Yes, in a few months, although he's thinking of changing his job.'

'I thought he had a good job?'

Rosie shrugged. 'He didn't like it. It's up to him.'

'So it's still the honeymoon period then?' Eva said, pressing her for more detail. 'You haven't discovered any nasty habits yet, like picking his nose in the bath?' They laughed.

'No, but I am going to have to teach him to clear up after himself. I think his mum must spoil him because he leaves all his dirty plates and mugs around for me to deal with.'

'Start as you mean to carry on,' Eva said with a smile. 'I wish I had with Syed!'

'I will. I'm wiser this time,' Rosie said. She saw Eva glance at her questioningly, but as before when she'd let similar comments slip Eva didn't press her. 'I've already made it clear he has to smoke outside and not in the flat,' she added.

'I didn't know he smoked?' Eva said, popping another mouthful of the quiche and salad into her mouth.

'Not ordinary cigarettes, he smokes cannabis for medical purposes. It helps with the pain and discomfort after a big operation. It's legal in many other countries. His parents know,' she added as if that made it acceptable.

'I'm pleased for you,' Eva nodded. 'He always seems very pleasant when he comes into the bank, but do take it slowly. Give yourself time. There's no rush.'

'I know.'

'You must both come for supper one evening after the baby is born. Bring out his paternal side.'

'And I thought you'd just told me to take it slowly!' Rosie exclaimed, laughing.

Chapter Thirty-Five

'That's kind of you,' Mary said as Elizabeth set the sweets and magazines on her bedside cabinet. She was now sitting in the hospital chair beside her bed and looked much better. The head bandage had been replaced by a large plaster and there was some colour in her cheeks.

'And I brought all your letters but I think most of them are circulars. Shall we go through them now?'

'No, thank you, dear. Leave them on there.' She tapped the bedside cabinet. 'I'll see to them later. It will give me something to do.'

Elizabeth did so and then leant in closer so that Mary could hear but not the rest of the ward. 'I found your glasses. They were in the dustbin. I saw them when I threw away some overripe bananas.'

'What were they doing there?' Mary asked, genuinely surprised.

'I assumed you'd put them there. They're broken. They can't be repaired.'

'It wasn't me,' Mary declared adamantly. 'I would have remembered. Perhaps the police or one of my visitors trod on them by accident.'

'I think they would have said,' Elizabeth said in a conciliatory tone. 'But never mind, you can borrow mine until I can get yours replaced.' Elizabeth passed her spare pair to Mary, who put them on and tentatively looked through the lenses.

'Thank you dear, but mine were bi-focals.'

'I know, but at least you'll be able to read your magazines and mail until I can get you a new pair. I'll phone your opticians and order a repeat prescription today.'

'Yes, I'll need them when I go home.'

'I was thinking of getting two pairs so you'll have one pair as a backup.'

'How much will that cost?' Mary asked, concerned. 'I haven't got much money. He took it all. Didn't they tell you?'

'Yes.' Elizabeth placed a reassuring hand on Mary's arm. 'Don't worry. We can sort out payment later.'

'Perhaps he smashed my glasses?' Mary suddenly said, her eyes widening.

'Who?'

'The man who broke into my cottage and robbed me.'

'And then bothered to put your glasses in the dustbin?' Elizabeth asked sceptically.

'Perhaps he broke them and someone else threw them

away.' Clearly Mary still believed she'd been burgled and Elizabeth wasn't going to enter into a discussion on it. The police or Sid would put her straight once the investigation was complete. Mary was obviously feeling better; she was more like her old self again, quick-witted, sharp and wanting to have the final say. It was what gave her character.

'That would fit,' Mary said, not willing to give up the subject easily. 'He smashed my glasses so I couldn't identify him. The police asked if I could give them a description but of course I couldn't see him. I just heard his voice. I couldn't be sure how much he'd taken. I've saved up all my life and it's all gone. I told them I thought it was about twenty thousand pounds but I couldn't be sure.'

'Twenty thousand!' Elizabeth exclaimed incredulously. 'You didn't have that much in the cottage, Mary, surely?'

'I did,' she said defiantly. 'I hid it under the mattress. I thought it was a good hiding place. But the police lady said it would be one of the first places a burglar would look.'

Five hundred pounds of savings Elizabeth might have believed, but not £20,000. 'Would you like one of your sweets?' she asked, changing the subject again.

'No, thank you dear. I've just had lunch.' She looked at Elizabeth carefully. 'You don't believe me, do you? I can understand why. You don't want to believe ill of your own.'

'Whatever do you mean?' Elizabeth asked.

'Well, I think it must be someone from the village who

knew where I kept my key. Perhaps one of those townies who moved in.'

'Mary, you mustn't say things like that. It's dreadful to accuse someone of stealing. Let's leave it to the police.'

'Yes, good idea. I'm sure they'll find him. It was obviously someone who needed money desperately. Pity he didn't just ask. I would have lent it or even given it to him. He didn't have to hit me; that was vicious. I don't know what the world is coming to.'

'Mary's convinced her cottage was broken into and the burglar took twenty thousand pounds!' Elizabeth told Andrew as they ate dinner that evening. 'She's also saying she thinks it was someone in the village. When you think of everything we do for her, to then be accused of such an awful crime, it's hurtful.'

'She's still confused and in shock by the sound of it. I'm sure she didn't mean it.'

'She's told the police it was a young man, maybe one of the new arrivals from town. But at least she hasn't mentioned Jacob being there on Saturday evening again.'

'Even if she does it can be easily disproved. I know he and Eloise aren't together any more but I'm sure she'd tell the police he was with her if necessary. I guess we'll all be needing alibis at this rate!' He smiled and then looked thoughtful. 'What time did Jacob get in on Saturday night?'

'I don't know, I was asleep. Why?'

'Oh, it's nothing.' He shook his head and resumed eating.

Elizabeth studied her plate, aware that if Eloise was contacted by the police then the allegations she'd made about Jacob were bound to come out. 'I'm sure it won't be necessary to speak to Eloise,' she said. 'I doubt the police will take Mary's allegations seriously, will they? I mean, who keeps twenty thousand pounds under their mattress and lives as frugally as Mary does?'

'Exactly. I'll try to pop in and see her next week. I haven't had a chance this week.'

Once they'd finished, Andrew excused himself to go to his study. He'd been out all day and hadn't had a chance to catch up on his voicemail messages or even open his mail, of which there was always plenty. Elizabeth cleared the table and began washing the dishes, uncomfortably aware that the list of things she hadn't told Andrew was growing, and the longer the list grew and the more time elapsed, the more difficult it was going to be. Just as she'd finished washing the last pan Andrew came into the kitchen, face set and holding an opened letter in his hand.

'I don't believe this! I really don't! It's the last straw.'

'What?' she asked, immediately concerned. It was unlike him to be angry.

'Our credit card statement! Nearly five hundred pounds on internet downloads.'

Elizabeth went cold. She'd never told him about her internet search for Jacob's donor. There never seemed to be a right time. But surely it hadn't cost that much? None of the newspaper subscriptions had been more than £15, she was sure of it. But then she hadn't kept a check on

241

how much she'd spent, she'd been too involved in the search. 'I'm so sorry,' she said, ready to explain.

'It's not your fault,' he snapped. 'I should have realized. Bad enough he watches that filth, but to use my credit card! Can you imagine if this came out – the reverend paying for his son to watch porn!'

'Jacob?' Elizabeth asked.

'Yes of course. Who else?'

Only slightly relieved, she took the statement he now thrust towards her and began looking down the long list of transactions. 'All those I've marked in red are his,' he said as she read.

It was impossible to tell from the company names what exactly the websites were – Holdings Ltd, Connections, but the amounts were similar: £45, £50, £49.99. In between these she saw the much smaller deductions for the newspapers she'd accessed plus their other credit card purchases.

'Those are mine,' she admitted, pointing.

He nodded absently. 'Every single one of those I've marked is a porn site,' he said, his voice tight. 'What's the matter with him?'

Elizabeth shook her head and her thoughts flipped back to the time she'd entered Jacob's room with his medication and had caught a glimpse of the porn he'd been watching on his laptop.

'I gave him that card to use at university,' Andrew reminded her, annoyed. 'I'd forgotten he still had it. He used it sensibly for three years – all the time he was away.

So what's got into him now? I'll put a stop on the card immediately and when he starts work he can repay me. He needs some form of sanction. And I'll speak to him when I see him. He's sick and needs professional help!'

Chapter Thirty-Six

'You must be desperate, man, calling me after the pasting boss man arranged for you,' Chez said.

'I am,' Jacob admitted. 'So don't piss me around.'

'Boss man would be angry with me if he found out I was supplying you again.'

'So don't tell him. I'll make it worth your while. Come on, mate. I'll pay you over the odds if you sell me the stuff tonight.'

'It's late, man.'

'You're never in bed at eleven on a Friday night! Meet me in half an hour and you'll be tucked up again by midnight. I'll give you an extra twenty quid.'

'Make it forty and the deal's done,' Chez said.

'I'm broke, man,' Jacob said, not wanting to agree too readily and arouse Chez's suspicion. 'Thirty.'

'Forty or there's no deal. I've got better things to do than hang around old dumpsters.'

Jacob sighed. 'OK. Forty. You're a hard man.'

'I'll be there!' Jacob could hear the anticipation in his voice.

'Thanks, man.'

Jacob headed back into the block of flats. Payback time was fast approaching and it felt good. The little shit needed to be taught a lesson. Using the key Rosie had given him he let himself into the flat. She was still on the sofa watching television as she had been since they'd had dinner and sex earlier. Friday night was for relaxing, she had told him; he could dig that. But as he entered the room she cut the sound on the television and looked at him accusingly. What the fuck was the matter with her now? Jesus! Women were hard work.

'Your mother just texted me,' she said, raising her phone so he could see the screen. 'She's asking when you last visited Mary Hutchins. Who is Mary Hutchins?'

'I didn't know you had each other's mobile numbers,' he said, ignoring her question as he read the text.

'You gave us each other's numbers when I had to get your tablets.'

'Oh, right. Yeah. I'd forgotten. Anyway, I have to go out now, and when I come back I expect to find you in bed. I'll be in the mood for more sex.' He found violence and the thought of it a great turn-on, violent sex even more so.

'Jacob!' Rosie said, rising to the bait and standing to face him. 'Who is Mary Hutchins?'

God. Women were so predictable. Nosy bitch. 'Why? You jealous?' Pity he didn't have more time – he could have wound her up even more.

'No. But we're living together, I think I have the right to know.'

He cocked an eyebrow. 'Mary is an old bird in her nineties who lives in the same village as my parents, you daft cow.'

Rosie looked embarrassed. 'I'm sorry. I didn't know. But don't call me a cow, I don't like it.'

'I don't like being called a cheat and a liar.'

'Sorry,' she said again. He picked up his jacket, ready to go out.

'What shall I tell your mother?' God, her voice was whiny.

'I'll deal with it. See you later and make sure you're ready for me.' He knew she would be. She was in the wrong so she would be wanting to make it up to him. Friday night was promising to be very good indeed.

Outside, Jacob got into his car and sped off in a screech of tyre rubber, very excited. He'd thought when he'd first met Taco that he might be the kind of guy with connections, and he'd been proven right. He'd arranged to supply the thugs for tonight and had told Jacob to set it up for a time when the pubs were emptying so it looked like a pub brawl. Taco had also said not to give Chez much notice so he didn't have time to bring anyone with him, and to find himself a watertight alibi just in case. Rosie would vouch for him if necessary and he'd only be out for three-quarters of an hour – not much longer than it took to smoke a joint. Besides, he wanted to watch the fun. He was paying for it after all. He couldn't wait. He'd get there early and park so he had a good view.

Ten minutes later, Jacob slowed the car as he entered the disused depot, switched to sidelights only and crawled noiselessly across the yard, looking for a place to park. He found a spot that would be perfect and reversed in beside two large skips from where he would be able to see, but not be seen. Giving the wipers a flick to clear the windscreen he switched off the engine and turned off the sidelights. The interior light faded and went out. He was now in complete darkness. He pressed the interior locking system and looked through the windows. The only movement at present came from rubbish being blown across the yard. His black car blended in well with the shadows. Now all he had to do was watch and wait, and his excitement grew. Three hundred and fifty quid this had cost him – one hundred for each of the three guys who were going to do the job and fifty quid to Taco for arranging it, so it better be good.

Ten minutes later three guys walked into the depot, heavily built, dressed in dark trousers and tops. They stood for a moment looking around and pointing, apparently debating where they should hide. Jacob glanced at the clock on the dashboard. There was still fifteen minutes before Chez was due to arrive, and he never arrived early as he didn't want to draw attention to himself by being seen hanging around. Not that there would be anyone here to see him but he was a creature of habit. After some discussion the guys produced black balaclava helmets and headed off in three different directions and secreted themselves in three separate locations. That was clever, Jacob thought. Chez would effectively be covered from all sides and cut off if he tried to escape. They clearly knew their stuff. Taco said they were professionals; that's what he was paying for.

His heart was racing now, going like the clappers as the adrenalin built. He could have done with a joint to calm him down but for obvious reasons that was out of the question – the smell, smoke and glow from the lighted tip would give him away. He'd just have to be patient, he told himself, and rubbed a small mark off the steering wheel, then gazed out of the windscreen. The rain had eased but his vision was blurred by the residual rain on the glass. He resisted the temptation to turn on the wipers. Later, once the action had started and it didn't matter if he was seen, he would.

The minutes ticked away and at 11.25 with five minutes to go his phone vibrated with an incoming text. Shielding the screen under his jacket so the light wasn't visible from the outside, he opened the message. As he guessed, it was from Chez; he always texted ahead of his arrival. *Five mins. Be ready.* Oh yes he was ready all right, so too were the other guys. His heart threw in an extra few beats as if

248

appreciating what lay in store. Nothing like the expectation of a good beating, followed by a good fuck, to get the juices going. He put his phone away and watched the clock on the dashboard as the countdown began in earnest. Five minutes, four, three, two, one, and then Chez appeared. The scraggy little runt was dressed in his usual jeans and blue hoodie. It didn't really need three guys to take him down, but Taco had insisted. He said it was how the boys worked, in case the guy brought mates with him. It also meant they could get the job done faster, more easily and efficiently.

Jacob's breath was coming fast and shallow now as he sat motionless, watching Chez through the misted windscreen. He saw him glance around as he took up his usual position, expecting Jacob to immediately appear as he had before. His right hand was resting on the outside of his jeans pocket where he kept the packet of weed, ready to take out, so the deal could be done as quickly as possible. Jacob could see he was edgy at having to wait. But it was only a few seconds that he had to glance around, frustrated and doubtless annoyed that Jacob hadn't immediately appeared. Then he saw the first figure come out from the shadows a little way in front of him and he craned his neck forward, staring into the darkness and trying to identify Jacob. His head flipped to the side as he caught sight of the second guy coming from the right. He remained where he was as it took another second for him to register what might be happening. Then it dawned on him and Jacob laughed as he turned, ready to run, but too late. The third guy was already behind him and punched him hard in the face. Ouch. He must have felt that. He was down and the beating really began.

Jacob flipped on the wipers for a better view. Chez was on the floor, pathetically trying to cover his head with his hands as he was kicked around like a football. Three sets of large booted feet were laying into him, his face, head, body, legs, kicking him hard without pause. He was jerking all over the place, and then he was still. God, that was quick, Jacob thought. It had only taken a few minutes and it was all over. He would have liked a rerun in slow motion. But now what was happening? One of the guys had taken what looked like a miniature bottle of spirits from his jacket and was unscrewing the top. The other two turned Chez onto his back and forced his mouth open. The guy with the bottle tipped in the contents. 'Very clever,' Jacob said, impressed. Make it look like he's been drinking, a pub brawl Taco had said. Then, dusting themselves off, they removed their balaclavas and strolled out of the yard. All over and done within five minutes. It was time for him to leave.

Jacob started the car's engine and, using the sidelights only, drove slowly towards Chez's body. Stopping a little in front of him he left the engine running and got out. He took the few steps to his side. God, what a mess. His face was unrecognizable, barely human, with big lumps and splits that were oozing a crimson mixture of what looked like blood and tissue. His mouth had split wide open and some of his teeth were on the outside of his cheek. Yuk. Jacob looked away and then down to Chez's pocket where he kept the weed. Moving his belt up, he took the packet. No point in wasting it. He was about to leave when another thought occurred to him. Chez still owed him for all the times he'd overcharged him or had sold him underweight.

Keeping his gaze from the mangled face and ignoring the gurgling sound now coming from Chez's throat he checked his other jeans pockets and then his hoodie. A used tissue, disgusting; Jacob threw it on the ground. Then he found what he was looking for, a roll of bank notes. It was a thin roll, only sixty quid. Clearly Chez hadn't done much business tonight. Satisfied there was no more, that they were even now and his pride and dignity had been restored, Jacob returned to his car. He drove forward slowly, up and over Chez's body, the resulting bump and squelch reminiscent of roadkill. The sweet taste of revenge made his heart lurch again, causing a sharp pain in his chest.

Chapter Thirty-Seven

Elizabeth received two text messages on Saturday: one from Jacob replying to hers, and saying he hadn't visited Mary in ages. He asked why she wanted to know and that she should text him, not Rosie, in future. Elizabeth didn't respond. She had the answer she needed, and the reason she'd texted Rosie and not Jacob was because he hardly ever replied. The other one was from David asking her how she was getting on with her search, which was thoughtful of him. She answered straightaway saying she'd managed to trace the donor but was now working up the courage to visit his family. *To be honest, I'm not sure I want to know*, she wrote.

He texted back: *I know it's a difficult decision, and a very personal one. Good luck whatever you decide.*

Since Andrew's suggestion that Jacob could be mentally ill and that that could be the reason he was behaving so dreadfully, Elizabeth had harboured doubts about contacting the donor family. Andrew could be right, in which case her time would be better spent trying to find her son a good psychiatrist rather than visiting the donor's family. But to pursue that she'd need Jacob to agree to see a psychiatrist, and that would be impossible with his present attitude, even if he came home long enough to discuss it, which he hardly ever did. She could imagine the scene if she or Andrew suggested a consultation. Perhaps she could enlist Rosie's help? But she hardly knew the girl, and it was a difficult subject to bring up without the intimacy of a close relationship. 'Is my son behaving oddly? Nastily? Different from how he used to? Could you help me persuade him to see a psychiatrist?' And of course Rosie wouldn't know he was behaving differently as she hadn't known him before.

In any case, she doubted Rosie would side with her against Jacob, even if it was for his own good. But she seemed a nice girl who would know right from wrong so she guessed Jacob was behaving reasonably well with her or she surely wouldn't have continued their relationship and allowed him to stay there. This thought brought her back to the point that she and Andrew could be to blame. They'd brought him up. But then again, she was sure Jacob hadn't been like this prior to his operation. And so her thoughts continued, round and round in a never-ending spiral of debate and indecision, which kept her awake at night and distracted her during the day, and could probably only be addressed by visiting the donor family.

On Sunday morning Elizabeth went to church as she did most Sundays and prayed for guidance. Andrew's sermon was about the power of prayer and she knew it wasn't a random choice for she was aware that recently he'd been spending a lot more time praying than he usually did. His words resonated with her as personal and poignant although he looked at the whole congregation as he spoke. Prayer was our telephone line to God, he said, who provided a sympathetic, non-judgemental ear. If we listened He offered guidance to us to make the right decisions. It allowed us to forgive others and redeem ourselves. Prayer was a great healer and could show us the way forward. God was a good listener but we shouldn't be selfish in our requests. 'I doubt the Lord would divulge the winning lottery numbers to any of us, no matter how sincere our prayer,' Andrew said with a smile, sending a titter of laughter through his small but loyal congregation. They appreciated the occasional jokes in his sermons.

As they all prayed Elizabeth was particularly devout in asking for guidance and forgiveness, especially in respect of Jacob. After the service she mingled with the small groups which as usual gathered in the churchyard for a chat. The weather was good and no one seemed in any hurry to leave. The talk was mainly about Mary, and the likelihood of what she was claiming to be true. A number of the villagers had now visited her in hospital and had their own version of what had happened, part of which was what Mary had told them, and part their own interpretation. Speculation was running rife again.

'Fancy her having all that money stuffed under the floorboards,' Bert said. 'Who would have thought it!' The place where the money had been hidden varied, as did the amount – anything from £5,000 to £50,000.

'Where did she get it from?'

'Savings I guess.'

'Pity she didn't spend it on a good holiday or having central heating put into the cottage. But who would do such a dreadful thing?'

Elizabeth listened without comment as Sid tried to curb the gossip, and repeated that nothing was certain yet and they should wait until the police had finished their investigation and told them for definite what had happened. Then Maggie, one of the newcomers to the village, said she felt her two sons were under suspicion as it was a young man who had committed the crime, and there hadn't been any crime in the village before. Sid was quick to reassure her that *if* a crime had been committed – and it was a big *if* – they weren't under any more suspicion than anyone else.

'But the police think it's definitely a young man from our village,' Bert's wife Sandra said.

'No, that's hearsay,' Elizabeth finally put in. 'And to be honest all this talk doesn't help. Mary is very confused. As Sid said, it might turn out that there was no robbery at all.'

'Perhaps she lent the money to someone and forgot,' someone suggested.

'And hit herself on the head?' Bert said.

'She certainly wasn't confused when I saw her,' Sandra persisted. 'She knew what day of the week it was and was convinced she'd been burgled. I'm keeping all my doors locked until they catch him. Shocking when you're not safe in your own home.' Everyone agreed with that.

Elizabeth said her goodbyes and walked away from the gathering deep in thought. Perhaps Andrew's next sermon should be on the power of the tongue and the harmful effect of gossip. Maggie wasn't the only one with sons and if the police were pursuing that line of inquiry then at some point they could want to see Jacob.

Chapter Thirty-Eight

On Monday morning Jacob sat in the outpatients department of the transplant centre waiting to see a doctor. He wasn't in the best of moods. The nurse who'd done all the preliminary checks – blood test, urine, ECG, and so on – had given him a telling off for missing his last two check-ups. He didn't like bossy women disrespecting him and could have easily slapped her. Now he was having to wait to see the doctor, which was annoying. Prior to this he'd had an argument with Rosie. She'd said she couldn't come with him as she daren't take any more days off work.

'Stuff your work!' he'd shouted. 'I should come first!' This had led to her looking hurt and saying it was her job that paid the bills and if he felt like that then perhaps he should consider moving out. So he'd apologized – the thought of living at the rectory again overrode his indignation at having to say sorry. She still wasn't completely happy as she dressed for work so he ate more humble pie and confessed he was worried about his health, which was making him tetchy as he thought there might be something seriously wrong. That had done it. She'd become all loving and concerned, but had still gone into work, telling him to text her as soon as he'd seen the doctor.

While he'd been waiting the old Rev had phoned and left a message on his voicemail saying he needed to speak to him urgently. He'd cancelled his credit card. Arsehole. Jacob could guess what had brought that on. Well he could go and fuck himself. He'd get a credit card of his own, and in the meantime he had money in the bank. So all in all it hadn't been the best of mornings and now he was having to wait to see the doctor because he didn't have an appointment. Since all the excitement on Friday night when he'd watched Chez being beaten up he'd been having pains in his chest and felt hot and clammy, possible warning signs that something was wrong.

Thirsty and with his blood sugar levels dropping from replacing breakfast with a joint, he went into the main reception area where he got a Mars bar and a can of Coke from the vending machine. He returned to his seat and was still drinking when the nurse called him into the consultation room to see the doctor.

'Good morning, Jacob, have a seat,' he said, glancing up from reading his medical notes. 'I'm Dr West, one of the team here. We've met before.'

'Hey,' Jacob said and sat back in the chair, legs spread. He finished off the Coke as the doctor read, then crumpled the can and threw it into the bin where it landed with a sharp metallic twang. The doctor looked up.

'So how are you? We haven't seen you for a while. The nurse said you've been experiencing some chest pain.'

'Yes. It started on Friday night. And I feel hot and sweaty sometimes too.'

'Have you been taking your medication?'

'Yes.'

'At the set times?'

He nodded.

'Any other symptoms?'

'No, just the pains and feeling hot.'

The doctor looked again at the folder which contained the results of his most recent tests.

'Your blood pressure is up,' he said. 'I'll adjust your medication, although that wouldn't necessarily account for your symptoms.' Jacob could see he was worried. 'Your urine sample showed possible signs of an infection. We'll send it to the lab for further testing, but in the meantime I'll start you on a course of antibiotics. How is your diet?'

'Fine,' Jacob said with a shrug.

'Plenty of fresh fruit and vegetables and not too much meat?'

Jacob nodded. He wished he'd just get on with it and tell him he was all right.

'Alcohol?' he asked. 'How often do you drink?'

'Just the occasional beer.'

'What's occasional?'

'One beer a week,' he lied.

'That shouldn't affect your immunosuppressants but cut it out completely if possible.' Jacob met his smile stony-faced. 'OK. I'll examine you now.'

Jacob knew the procedure like the back of his hand and took off his jersey. The doctor put his stethoscope in his ears and placed the metal end on various points on his chest and asked him to take deep breaths in and out. Then he had to sit forward so he could do the same to his back.

'I fell off a ladder,' Jacob said before the doctor had a chance to remark on the bruises on his back from the beating Chez's boss had arranged. They were fading now but still visible.

'Whatever were you doing up a ladder?' the doctor asked.

'Putting up a light fitting for my girlfriend,' Jacob said.

'Very admirable, but please be more careful in future.' He finished listening to Jacob's back and then asked him to lie on the couch.

'That's fading nicely,' he said, referring to the operation scar on his chest that ran nearly the length of his sternum. Using the palm of his hand he began gently pressing Jacob's stomach and around his sides. 'There's no sign of fluid build-up so we won't increase your diuretics. It all seems normal. You can get dressed.'

Jacob gave a sigh of relief and climbed off the couch. He returned to his chair and put on his jersey as the doctor wrote.

'As you probably know there is only so much I can tell from examining you and the routine tests we run here. So you will need to have another biopsy. You're due for one anyway, overdue in fact. I'll try to book if for this afternoon if possible, if not tomorrow at the latest. You don't feel nauseous, dizzy or short of breath, do you?'

'No.'

'Why have you missed so many appointments?' He looked at him seriously.

'Work commitments.'

'They must allow you time off to attend your hospital appointments. I can give you a letter if necessary,'

'I'll tell them,' Jacob said.

He paused, scrutinizing Jacob in a manner he didn't appreciate.

'These check-ups are very important,' he emphasized. 'I am aware that once you recover from the actual operation and feel so much better you may not see the need for continuous monitoring. But the risk of the organ being rejected, whilst it diminishes with time, is still there. These check-ups are as important now as they were at the start, as is having a healthy lifestyle. I see you've stopped attending your physio programme. Are you exercising at home?'

'Yes.' Fucking Rosie was very good exercise Jacob thought, unable to hide a smirk. It beat going to the hospital gym any day.

'OK,' the doctor said, making a note on the file. 'If you take a seat outside a nurse will advise you when we can do the biopsy.'

Jacob nodded and stood. The doctor watched him go. There was something he didn't like about that young man; his manner was hostile and arrogant. Cocky. The sort of patient who thought he knew better than the doctor, until it was almost too late. He turned to his computer and brought up the schedule for the special procedures room to see when it was next free to book it for the biopsy.

Chapter Thirty-Nine

Elizabeth sat in her car, concentrating on number 33 Birch Road. She was parked on the opposite side of the road a little way up from the house and had a clear view. She'd been there for nearly an hour now watching, waiting for any sign of movement, but so far there'd been nothing. She guessed Shane's siblings were probably at school and his mother Tracy could be at work. But she continued waiting just in case. If she did see Tracy entering or leaving the house she knew what she would do; quickly get out of the car and intercept her with a polite, 'I'm so sorry to bother you but could I possibly talk to you about Shane?' She knew what Tracy looked like from her profile picture on Facebook and if it wasn't convenient she'd ask if she could come back another time as it was very important.

She thought the poor woman might break down and

cry at the mention of her son, and Elizabeth would comfort her until she felt well enough to continue. She pictured Tracy inviting her into her house where over a cup of tea she'd tell her all about Shane. Elizabeth would thank her and commiserate with her at her loss but wouldn't tell her the real reason she needed to know: that through cellular memory her son could be responsible for Jacob's behaviour. It would be too cruel, for regardless of how bad Shane had been in life – if indeed he had been bad at all – he was still her son. And meeting Elizabeth might help Tracy come to terms with her loss and see that her son hadn't died in vain. If she was a practising Christian then they could say a prayer together before she left.

Birch Road was a mixture of social and private housing as was most of the 1950s estate, and as usual it was clear from the outside which was which. Tracy's house was mid-terraced and had the standard external appearance of social housing. It was slightly run down, suggesting the family didn't have much money. The window frames and front door were in need of painting if not replacing, and the net curtains that hung at the windows were badly faded. The front garden was an old crumbing concrete drive with straggling weeds and rubbish that had been blown in from the street, in sharp contrast to many of the neatly tended gardens of her neighbours. Unloved and uncared for, Elizabeth thought, but then the poor woman had lost her son a year ago so she was unlikely to be concerned about the niceties of a pretty front garden.

When Elizabeth had set off from home she hadn't known the number of Tracy's house, since the newspaper had stated only Birch Road, but she'd assumed – rightly as it turned out – that her tragedy would be known in the street and someone would know where the poor woman lived. The first door she'd knocked on had been answered by an elderly gentleman. 'I've come to see Tracy Smith,' Elizabeth had said. 'I'm sorry, I must have the wrong number.'

'Number thirty-three,' he'd replied without hesitation. Elizabeth had thanked him, and driven further up the street to Tracy's house.

It was now 3.30 and Elizabeth thought that if Tracy's other children were of school age then they would be returning home soon. But another half-hour went by and no one appeared. Elizabeth was growing stiff from sitting in the car for so long. She stretched her legs as far as she could. Five more minutes and then she'd knock again on the front door to make sure no one was in, possibly put a note through the letterbox with her mobile number asking Tracy to phone, and then leave. She couldn't stay here indefinitely, although whether she would ever summon the courage to return and try again, she wasn't sure.

A few minutes later, as Elizabeth was about to start the engine, two women appeared, walking down the street towards her. Dressed similarly in leggings and blouse tops they were laughing and talking loudly. As they arrived outside number thirty-three one of them turned into the drive and calling, 'See ya,' continued up to the front door. Before Elizabeth realized what was happening and that this could be Tracy, she'd let herself in and the front door had closed behind her.

Lambasting herself for not acting sooner, Elizabeth got out of her car and ran across the road and up the crumbling drive, her mouth dry and her stomach tight. There was no doorbell so she clattered the letterbox. As she did she heard a deep female voice shout from inside, 'Don't give me your lip, you little cow! I fucking told you if you stayed in bed all day again, you'd be out on your ear. Now pack your stuff and get the fuck out.'

Then the front door suddenly opened. 'Yes?' the woman demanded. 'What do you want?'

'Tracy?' Elizabeth asked, shocked. She didn't look anything like her Facebook photo, which had clearly been taken when she'd been younger and showed her with her hair styled and her face made up.

'Who's asking?' she demanded. A teenage girl crossed the hall behind her, disappearing into one of the rooms. Tracy turned to shout at her. 'Get a move on you lazy slut.' Then she returned her attention to Elizabeth. 'If you're from the council I've already told you lot you'll get the fucking rent money as soon as I've got it. I can't magic it out of thin air, much as I'd like to.' She gave a thick mucus-filled laugh, suggesting she was or had been a heavy smoker.

'No, I'm not from the council,' Elizabeth said, her voice unsteady. 'Are you Shane's mother?'

'Maybe, why? He can't be in any more trouble. He's dead. You the police?'

'No, I'm not. I'm sorry, I know he's dead. Could I come in so we can talk?'

'Say what you have to say there. I'm busy.'

This wasn't what Elizabeth had imagined when she'd pictured meeting Shane's family, not at all. The woman was so aggressive that she felt intimidated, almost scared of her, but she'd come this far so she tried to hold her nerve. 'My name is Elizabeth,' she began. 'I'm sure you know this, but when Shane died his organs were used for a transplant. My son received his heart.'

'Well, bugger me! You don't say!' the woman exclaimed. 'Well I never! Yeah, I'm his mother, or was.' Some of her aggression had softened a little, but it was soon replaced by mirth. 'The hospital phoned and asked about his organs. Don't tell me they've stopped working and you want a refund.' Her laugh broke into a bronchial cough and Elizabeth waited until she'd recovered before continuing.

'I'd like to learn more about Shane,' Elizabeth said hoping she might be invited in.

'Like what?'

'What he was like as a person. His hobbies, his likes and dislikes, hopes for the future, his career.'

Tracy was laughing raucously again. 'Are we talking about the same bloke? The only hobby Shane had was breaking into people's homes. And as for his career? Well, that was very specialist.' She couldn't contain her laughter. 'Secure children's home from the age of eleven, then a

267

young offenders' institution, and when he was old enough, adult prison. That was his career!'

Horrified, Elizabeth waited until the woman's laughing and coughing had subsided before she asked, 'So Shane spent most of his life in prison?'

'Yeah, best place for him. Not sure why they let him out. He tried to move back 'ere when he came out the last time but I sent him packing. I mean, he hit me before so I don't think I was being unreasonable.'

Elizabeth stared at her, bewildered and dismayed, not only by what she was learning about Shane but that any mother could speak so unkindly of her son. 'Did he take drugs and drink a lot of alcohol?' she asked, remembering some of the information she'd been hoping to find out.

Tracy eyed her suspiciously. 'Are you a reporter?'

'No. I've said, my son received Shane's heart.'

The girl appeared again in the hall behind Tracy, now dressed and with a bag over her shoulder. 'I'm going,' she said with attitude.

'Good riddance, you little cow. And don't come back,' Tracy retorted.

Elizabeth stood aside to let the girl pass. She couldn't have been more than fifteen.

'Bitch!' the girl called over her shoulder, lighting a cigarette as she went.

'Fucking kids! Why do we have 'em?' Tracy said loud enough for the girl to hear.

'She's your daughter?' Elizabeth asked, horrified.

'Yeah, one of 'em. The other three did the sensible

268

thing and got pregnant so the council housed them. But that one is just fucking idle. Shane was me only son.'

'I'm sorry,' Elizabeth said, feeling she had to say something.

'Well, shit happens, don't it. But we weren't close. In fact, I hadn't seen 'im properly for years, although I didn't tell the vicar that. He helped me with the collection.' She paused and eyed Elizabeth carefully. 'Perhaps you'd like to donate as your son got me boy's heart? I mean you didn't have to pay for it.' She gave a guttural laugh.

Elizabeth couldn't believe what she was hearing and deeply regretted coming. She just wanted to get away, but fearful of how Tracy might react if she just turned and left she took a £10 note from her purse and handed it to her.

'Make it twenty and we'll call it quits,' Tracy said without any embarrassment.

Elizabeth took out another £10 note and gave it to her. 'Goodbye.' She turned and walked away.

'Cheers love. Nice to meet you. If you want to know more about him visit the girl he shacked up with. God knows what the fuck she saw in him apart from his dick.'

Trying to block out the awful woman's words and laughter Elizabeth hurried down the path as Tracy's front door slammed shut behind her. She got into the car and clutched the steering wheel, her hands knuckle-white. She stared straight ahead, her stomach churning. Why had she ever come? She was aware that people like Tracy existed but their paths rarely crossed with hers. Selfish, greedy, uncouth, without a decent bone in their bodies. She appeared to have no maternal feelings whatsoever and by the sound of it had sent all five of her children packing as soon as she could.

What life experience had shaped her and made her what she was? Elizabeth couldn't begin to guess. From what Tracy had said, Shane had been no better than his mother and indeed may have been a lot worse. Did this information help? Not one bit. For while it might have absolved her and Andrew of responsibility for Jacob's behaviour, it left no clear solution. It wasn't as though there was a vaccine that could reverse the effects of cellular memory. Now Elizabeth would have to come to terms with Tracy's son's heart living on in Jacob. And from what David had said, where cellular memory had occurred, the longer the organ was in the recipient's body the more that person resembled the donor, like that girl in Brazil whose blood group had changed. The transplanted organ now seemed like a giant, malignant parasite that had infiltrated and taken over the host and there was absolutely nothing they could do about it.

She wouldn't be telling Andrew this but she needed to tell someone and there was only one person who would understand: David. *Have just met donor's mother. Wish I hadn't! Definitely CMP. Thanks for your help. Liz x*

He replied almost immediately. *I'm so sorry. Phone if you want to talk. David x*

Then before she drove away another text came through from him. She left the car's engine running while she read it. *Evidence suggests that where there is a strong presence of CMP there is a greater risk of organ rejection. So make sure your son attends all his check-ups.*

Just for a moment Elizabeth thought that possibly the organ being rejected wasn't the worst-case scenario, then she caught herself. If Jacob's heart was rejected there was nothing else the medical profession could offer and he would slowly die. She didn't really want that, did she?

Chapter Forty

'Mary is being discharged from hospital tomorrow,' Andrew said, as he and Elizabeth were having dinner.

Elizabeth looked at him and nodded. 'Good.' She'd eaten very little and was toying with the rest of her food.

'Sid's wife is going to collect her and see her settled into the cottage. I said you'd look in.'

'Yes, of course.'

Andrew paused from eating. He too seemed quiet this evening. 'What isn't such good news is that the police are going to interview all young men in the village.'

'Why?' Elizabeth asked, startled. 'They must believe what Mary is telling them?'

'Sid didn't know any more than that. But Maggie has taken it badly, unsurprisingly. There aren't that many lads in their twenties in the village and two of them are her sons. Sid reassured her it is procedure and that they have to eliminate all the young men in the village from their inquiries. He pointed out they'd be seeing Jacob too.'

'Will they?' Elizabeth asked, unable to hide her concern.

'I'm assuming so. They can hardly not see him just because I'm a reverend.'

'When will they want to see him?' she asked.

'I've no idea of the date or time. Sid didn't say. Why?' He met her gaze.

'Jacob's not here often.'

'No, so they'll have to see him at his girlfriend's flat. It's not a problem, is it?'

'I haven't got her address,' Elizabeth said defensively. 'Just her mobile number.'

'I suggest you find out her address quickly. It will look suspicious if the police come here looking for Jacob and we say we don't know where he is.'

'Will it?' Elizabeth asked, the colour draining from her face.

'Liz, it'll be fine. Just phone the girl and get her address. Are you all right?'

She managed a weak smile. 'Yes, just a bit tired.'

By the end of the week Elizabeth was starting to feel less anxious. She'd had a busy, productive few days going about the routine business that being a reverend's wife entailed. This had included organizing activities and outings for their local women's guild, charity fund-raising events, leading the Bible class, updating the rotas for looking after the church, and taking care of any other parish business Andrew asked her to. It helped being able to focus on matters apart from Jacob, although it didn't take much for her to suddenly be transported back to that meeting with Tracy.

She visited Mary on Wednesday, taking her some home-made soup and her new glasses. Mary was delighted to be home again and happy to see her. She'd stayed for over an hour during which time there'd been no mention of being robbed or a police inquiry, and the key remained under the mat. Elizabeth thought it was probably only a matter of time before Mary remembered what she'd done with the money, or that (more likely) she'd spent the little savings she had. Then the whole business would be put to rest.

Now Jacob wasn't living with them many of Elizabeth's negative thoughts and feelings about him were starting to wane, replaced by more pleasant memories of the son she used to have, to the point where she'd managed to convince herself that he probably wasn't as bad as she'd been thinking, and his relationship with Rosie was allowing him to sort out his life and turn a corner. She'd left him a voicemail message asking them both to come to dinner, and mentioning that the police were visiting all young men in the village to eliminate them from their inquiries, and as he wasn't home very often could she give them Rosie's address? Jacob didn't return her call, which was a disappointment, so she'd telephoned Rosie and they'd had a pleasant chat. She explained about the inquiry and Rosie had given her her address without any hesitation. Jacob had forgotten to mention the invitation to dinner so Elizabeth repeated it.

'Saturday or Sunday, any weekend. Let me know what suits you best.' Rosie thanked her and said she'd phone or text as soon as she'd spoken to Jacob.

'He's not there then?' Elizabeth asked.

'He's just popped out. He won't be long.' She omitted to say for a joint as Jacob had told her it now worried his mother.

'OK. See you soon, love.'

Yes, Rosie was a lovely girl who was clearly doing Jacob a power of good. Furthermore, Elizabeth was now starting to wonder if Shane really had been the bad boy his mother had made him out to be. More likely it was Tracy who was bad. Having witnessed the way she'd treated her teenage daughter – swearing at her and throwing her out on the streets – it put a different interpretation on what she'd said about Shane. Elizabeth wondered what Shane's girlfriend would say about him if asked. She probably had a very different opinion having lived with him. Elizabeth was trying to take the view that Shane had been rejected and probably abused by his mother, had then unsurprisingly got into trouble as a lad, but had gone on to make good, and was in a committed relationship when he'd died. Tracy had said he was 'shacked up with a girl'.

Elizabeth thought that she'd like to talk to the girl, who would probably confirm what she now believed. She checked the newspaper articles online again for any mention of Shane's partner or girlfriend, but either she'd declined to be interviewed (unlike Tracy who'd relished the media exposure) or the press hadn't been aware of her. The only way to identify her and find out where she lived would be to go back to Tracy and ask her. Elizabeth recoiled at the thought. Then as she was vacuuming the living room on Saturday afternoon she realized there was another way she could contact Tracy: message her through Facebook.

She switched off the vacuum cleaner and sat down in one of the fireside chairs to log in to Facebook through her phone. Tracy's privacy settings were on the minimum so there was no problem in sending her a direct message. After much thought and many attempts at getting the wording right she sent: *Dear Tracy. I hope you are well. Thank you for talking to me last week. I'd like to speak to Shane's girlfriend to learn more about him. Could you send me her contact details? Kind regards, Elizabeth.*

It was possible Tracy didn't know where the girl lived, but even with just her name Elizabeth should be able to find her on the internet. Most young people had an online presence. Having logged off from Facebook she sent a text message to Rosie reminding her about the invitation to dinner.

Chapter Forty-One

Jacob entered the block of flats, stepping over the pile of local newspapers and circulars dumped in the hall by the newspaper delivery lad who was too lazy to deliver them to each flat. Usually, and like most residents, he left them there for someone else to deal with, and the pile grew until eventually someone chucked the lot in the bin and the pile started again. But today the headline caught his eye. He picked up a copy that hadn't been trodden on and stood in the lobby reading it.

YOUNG MAN VICIOUSLY ATTACKED

A young man was repeatedly kicked in the face and head and run over by a car during a sustained and vicious attack at the disused depot by a group of two or more assailants. Oliver Cambridge, 22, also known as Chez to his friends, was found on Monday by a group of council workmen. He has sustained life-threatening injuries and is now in a coma at the Royal Infirmary. Detectives are trying to establish a motive for the beating, which they believe happened at around midnight on Friday. They are appealing for anyone who may have information to come forward. His mother, a solicitor, has been continuously by his bedside.

Detective Constable Pamela Small said: 'At this time we have not established a motive for this attack and I am appealing to anyone who might have witnessed the incident to contact the police immediately. I'm particularly anxious to speak to any who may have been in the vicinity at the time the pubs closed and may have seen the attackers running away.' Anyone with information is asked to contact the police on . . .

Jacob looked up, a smile hovering on his lips. Oliver Cambridge, what a posh name and his mother a solicitor! Well, well. Who would have thought it? The little skunk hadn't been dragged up in the gutter but had been given a chance of a decent life and had thrown it away. What had happened served him right. He had it coming to him. What an embarrassment he must have been to his mother. Jacob had probably done her a favour getting rid of him. But hold on, just a minute, he was getting ahead of himself. He hadn't got rid of him completely. The article said he was in a coma with life-threatening injuries. What were the chances of him waking up and telling the police who was responsible? Shit! He looked at the date on the newspaper – last Thursday – then chucked it on the floor with the others. Perhaps there was more news since the paper went to press. He remained in the lobby and Googled: *man attacked in disused depot*. A number of links came up and clicking on the first he read: *Oliver Cambridge, 22, died yesterday, a week after being viciously attacked by two or more assailants at the council's disused depot. Police are appealing* . . .

Relieved, and with his smile spreading, Jacob pocketed his phone, not bothering to read the rest of the article, and headed up the stairs two at a time to the flat.

'Your mother has texted again about dinner,' Rosie said as he let himself in.

She obviously wanted to go and he was in a good mood. 'OK. Next weekend.'

'Really?'

'Anything for you.'

She eagerly picked up her phone. 'Saturday or Sunday?'

'Saturday or we'll have to go to church with them on Sunday.'

'I don't mind going,' Rosie said animatedly.

'I do.' He flopped on the sofa beside her.

'And my mother wants to meet you,' she said, as she texted a reply to Elizabeth. 'So I've suggested she pop in later.'

'Tonight?' Jacob asked, unable to hide his irritation.

'Yes.' She looked at him seriously. 'Jacob, I know you were angry with me about giving your mother this address, but my mother is always welcome here.'

He shrugged. 'OK. I'll meet her, but not for too long. And before she arrives I've got time to give you a good shag.' He pulled her on top of him and, unzipping her jeans, roughly pulled them off.

At the Rectory Elizabeth had just taken a call from Maggie and she was worried.

'The police are on their way here,' she said anxiously to Andrew. 'They've just left Maggie's.'

Andrew glanced at the clock on the mantelpiece. 'Saturday evening. Must be overtime,' he replied cynically.

'They arrived at Maggie's without any warning. She was about to serve dinner. They said early evening is a good time to find young people in before they go out.'

'I suppose that makes sense.'

'Maggie said they asked her lads where they were on the night of the break-in. But they've also told the boys to go into the police station to be fingerprinted.' Her stomach had tightened to a knot.

'Why?' Andrew asked, shifting in his chair. Mitsy looked up from where she lay on the floor beside him.

'So they can be completely eliminated from their inquiries I suppose.'

'All right. So we'll just tell them Jacob is living with his girlfriend and give them her address. If they'd phoned us we could have saved them a wasted visit.'

'Do you think it's as simple as that?' she asked, fighting to keep her voice steady.

'Yes. Why shouldn't it be?'

Elizabeth began plumping the cushions and giving the living room a quick tidy as a displacement for what she was thinking and feeling. Her mouth was dry and her pulse raced. She needed to calm down. There was nothing to worry about. Jacob hadn't done anything wrong. She'd invite the officers in, offer them a coffee, and explain he wasn't here. They might not even want to come in or see him.

Chapter Forty-Two

'The reverend's kid in my school was a right hell-raiser,'
DC Evans said as they pulled into Rectory Lane. 'I went
to his house a few times, my parents knew his. He was
like Jekyll and Hyde. As good as gold when his parents
were there but away from them all hell ripped loose. You
name it, he did it. Much to the embarrassment of his father
he even spent a spell in care. I suppose that's what happens
when the reins are too tight, you buck against them.'

'You're very philosophical tonight,' PC Mandy Taylor
quipped as she parked the unmarked police car outside
the rectory. 'But from what we know Jacob is squeaky
clean, and of course he's been very ill.'

Evans nodded. 'We'll see. It might turn out it isn't a lad
after all. It's only Mary's word and at ninety-two everyone
under sixty appears young. She thought I was in my twenties.' They both laughed as they got out of the car.

Evans led the way up the path and pressed the doorbell. It was a pleasantly warm evening and still light, but it was the end of a very long day. A fourteen-hour shift and he was looking forward to going home. 'Soon be finished,' he said, more for his benefit than Mandy's. She *was* in her twenties and ran on unlimited adrenalin.

The front door was opened by a woman Evans took to be the Reverend's wife. She had a dog at her side. 'Mrs Wilson?'

'Yes.'

'Good evening. I'm DC Charlie Evans and this is my colleague PC Mandy Taylor. I think you're probably expecting us.' He knew how news travelled through these villages so someone was sure to have told her they were on their way.

'Yes, come in,' Elizabeth said, opening the door wider. 'Come through and have a seat.'

'Thank you. I assume you know why we're here? The inquiry into the burglary at Acorn Cottage.'

'Yes. This is my husband, Andrew,' she said as the entered the living room. The dog went over to him.

'Pleased to meet you,' Andrew said, standing and shaking their hands.

'And you, sir,' Evans said.

'But I'm afraid you've had a wasted trip. My son isn't here.'

A little abrupt, Evans thought, but smiled convivially. 'May we sit down?'

'Yes of course,' Elizabeth flustered; she was forgetting her manners. 'Can I get you both a drink?'

'No thank you. We won't keep you long,' Evans said for them both.

As they sat on the sofa Elizabeth took an easy chair and Andrew swivelled his armchair round so they were all facing each other. The PC took out a notepad and pen.

'Would you like my son's address?' Elizabeth asked, trying to be helpful. 'He stays with his girlfriend much of the time.'

'Yes, please,' Evans said.

Elizabeth picked up her address book from the coffee table and in a steady voice slowly read out the address of Rosie's flat as the PC wrote it down.

'How long has Jacob been living there?' Evans asked.

'A few weeks,' Elizabeth replied.

'Before or after the break-in at Acorn Cottage?'

'After. He had a different girlfriend back then.' She could have kicked herself as soon as the words were out of her mouth. It made Jacob sound shallow, fickle, a womanizer who regularly changed girlfriends, which wasn't true. 'We're going to meet her soon,' she added, trying to repair the damage. 'They're both coming here for dinner next weekend.'

Evans nodded. 'And the name of his present girlfriend?' he asked.

'Rosie,' Elizabeth said. 'Sorry, I don't know her surname.' This omission seemed to add to the casualness of her son's relationships.

The PC wrote something down.

'Either we or one of our colleagues in town will visit him. As you know we're speaking to all the young men in the village as part of our inquiry into the robbery at Acorn Cottage.'

'So the cottage was definitely broken into?' Andrew asked.

'Mary seems rather confused,' Elizabeth added quickly. 'We thought there was some doubt.'

Evans looked from one to the other. 'Acorn Cottage was burgled but I'm not sure about broken into. There's no sign of a break-in, which is why we think it could be someone who knew there was a spare key under the front doormat.'

Elizabeth's hand shot to her mouth. 'You really believe someone in the village would do such a thing?'

'It's one line of inquiry, yes,' DC Evans said. Elizabeth wanted to ask what the others were but didn't dare. Everything she was saying sounded wrong, as if she or one of her family was guilty.

'But surely the doormat is the first place any intruder would look for a key?' Andrew asked.

'Agreed. If you knew the cottage was there, and that it was inhabited by an elderly lady with savings,' Evans said. 'It's not exactly on the main street.'

'Which seems to rule out a passing opportunist,' the PC added.

'But I can't believe that anyone in our village would rob a frail old lady,' Andrew said. 'I just don't believe it.'

'I know it's difficult and of course, she wasn't just robbed. She was assaulted too – hit over the head with a large object.'

'So she definitely didn't fall then?' Elizabeth asked clutching at straws. Clearly there was a lot in the inquiry that seemed to have already been confirmed.

'She was hit with a heavy metal object,' Evans said. 'We've yet to find the weapon. But returning to Jacob, so we can eliminate him from the inquiry, where was he on the night of the break-in?'

'At his girlfriend's house,' Andrew said.

'Present or previous girlfriend?' Evans asked in a deadpan voice.

'His last girlfriend,' Andrew replied before Elizabeth had a chance. 'Her name is Eloise and he was going to stay the weekend.'

'Going to?' Evans queried.

'They had an argument and Jacob returned home earlier than expected.' Elizabeth winced; Andrew's comment seemed to add to the poor image they were conveying of their son – not only did he change girlfriends regularly but he argued with them too.

'It was his first proper relationship,' Elizabeth said, trying to minimize the damage. 'They met at university so it wasn't likely to last. They didn't argue much at all, but decided to go their separate ways.'

Evans nodded, possibly in agreement. 'Do you have Eloise's address please?'

'I'm not sure I do any longer,' Elizabeth said, keeping

her gaze away from her address book. 'I'd have to try to find it.'

'The young lady's surname and the town where she lives will be enough,' Evans clarified.

'Davies,' Andrew said as Elizabeth hesitated. 'And she lives in Sommersville. I'm sorry, I don't know the postcode off by heart.'

'Thank you. And Jacob is still off work sick at present?'

'Yes,' Andrew said. 'He had a heart transplant. It's a long road to full recovery.'

'I'm sure it must be,' Evans said.

'My cousin had a kidney transplant,' the PC offered. 'Nearly five years ago. He's fine now but it's sad someone had to die for him to live.'

Andrew nodded while Elizabeth looked at her.

'So what time did Jacob arrive home on that Saturday night?' Evans now asked.

'It was around midnight,' Andrew said. 'Liz and I had been out for dinner. Liz was in bed and I was in the bathroom getting ready when I heard her car pull up.'

'Her car?'

'Jacob was borrowing Liz's car until he could afford his own.'

Evans nodded as the WPC wrote. 'And did you see him come in?'

'No, as I said I was in the bathroom getting ready. I went straight to bed.'

'So neither of you actually saw Jacob that night?'

'No, but I heard him come up to bed,' Elizabeth said,

thinking she was doing the right thing by Jacob. 'He must have tripped over Mitsy – our dog. She often sleeps at the foot of the stairs. I heard Jacob on the stairs. Andrew was snoring.'

'Do you know what time that was?'

'Yes. My bedside clock showed two-thirty.'

'So what would Jacob have been doing between arriving home and going to bed? Do you know?'

The silence seemed to grow as Elizabeth realized what she'd done. Far from helping Jacob she'd made matters worse. There was a two-and-a–half-hour gap. 'Making a hot drink, I suppose. He usually had one when he came home.'

Evans nodded as the PC continued to write. 'Could we have a look at his room now? And then we'll leave you in peace.'

Elizabeth felt hot and uncomfortable. Maggie hadn't said anything about the police looking at their sons' rooms. It seemed Andrew felt the same.

'Is it necessary?' he asked. 'I feel it's an invasion of my son's privacy as he's not here.'

'It would be helpful,' Evans said. 'But we could always come back another time.'

With a poorly disguised sigh Andrew stood. 'We may as well do it now.'

'His room will be messy,' Elizabeth warned, also standing.

'Show me a lad's room that isn't,' Evans said affably.

She and Andrew led the way upstairs and into Jacob's room, then they stood to one side as both officers began looking around. It felt awkward, unnatural, all being in there when they'd been going to such lengths to avoid Jacob's room. 'He likes a smoke then,' Evans commented casually, sniffing the air.

'I don't know,' Elizabeth said. 'We give Jacob his privacy. He's an adult.'

'Sometimes,' Andrew said, aware it was ludicrous to suggest they couldn't smell the stale cannabis. 'It helps with the pain from his transplant.'

Evans nodded; he had begun opening and closing various drawers and doors, his well-trained eye sweeping the contents as he went. He didn't have a search warrant so if they objected he'd have to stop, but he doubted they would.

'Nice view,' the PC said, glancing out of the bedroom window.

'Yes,' Andrew said stiffly. 'This room has the best view in the rectory.'

'I see he's studious then?' Evans said, referring to the shelves of Jacob's books from university.

'Yes, he got a first at university,' Elizabeth said proudly. 'He had a promising career before he fell ill.'

'But he's recovering now?' Evans asked, glancing over.

'Yes.'

'Has he got his laptop with him?' Evans now asked, having seen the printer on the desk.

'I think he must have,' Andrew said.

Evans nodded and took a final glance around the room.

'Thank you. We're all done here.' He led the way back downstairs.

Once in the living room, he thanked them again for their cooperation. 'Enjoy the rest of your evening.'

'Thank you,' Andrew said. Elizabeth stood beside him as he opened the front door.

The officers stepped out. 'Are both these cars yours?' Evans asked, nodding to the two cars parked outside.

'Yes,' Andrew said. 'That one's mine and that's my wife's.'

'So Jacob has his own car now?'

'That's correct,' Andrew said.

'Good night. Thanks again for your time. I hope Jacob makes a full recovery soon.'

Andrew nodded and closed the door.

DC Evans and PC Mandy Taylor didn't speak again until they were in the car.

'So what are they hiding?' she asked.

Evans gave a low laugh. 'Indeed. Good question. Privacy my arse. Not so squeaky clean now, is he? Smoking dope and downloading porn. You saw the printouts at the bottom of the wardrobe?'

'Yes, dumped there in a quick tidy-up?'

'Possibly. And he has his own car, yet he's off on long-term sick. Perhaps Mummy and Daddy bought it for him, but I didn't get that impression. He was borrowing his mother's until he could afford a car of his own so I'd like to know where he got the money from.'

'You should have asked,' Mandy said with a smile. 'It's not like you to hold back.'

'All in good time. We'll visit Jacob first and see what he has to say for himself.'

'His poor parents,' Mandy sighed. 'They seemed very anxious, especially his mother.'

'Yes, but don't feel too sorry for them. Whatever Jacob has done I'm pretty sure they have their suspicions and are covering up for him.'

'She didn't want us to speak to Eloise, that's for sure,' Mandy said. 'If she had his most recent girlfriend's address in her address book then surely she would have the old one's? Even if she'd crossed it out. Jacob was seeing her for all the time he was at uni.'

'Exactly. You're not just a pretty face, are you?' Evans said. 'Sorry, strike that sexist remark from the record.'

'I will,' she laughed. 'Don't worry. I can take a joke.'

Chapter Forty-Three

'Why didn't you want them to have Eloise's address?' Andrew asked as they returned to the living room and sat by the hearth.

'I couldn't see what good it would do. I mean, they don't see each other any more and it's just raking up the past.' She stared into the grey empty grate.

'But Eloise can confirm where Jacob was that Saturday night – before he returned here. The police are being very thorough. We need to be honest.'

'But supposing Eloise is still angry with Jacob for finishing with her?' Elizabeth said not meeting his gaze. 'She might say something horrible about him.'

'Like what?' Andrew asked puzzled.

Elizabeth shrugged. 'I don't know.'

'If you're worried give Eloise a ring and explain about

the robbery, and that the police are eliminating all the young men in the village. I'm sure she'll be reasonable. Probably best to phone her or it might come as a shock if the police just arrive.' He looked at her carefully. 'What is it, Liz? There's something else worrying you.'

She finally looked up and met his gaze with a small nod. 'The first time I visited Mary in hospital she was convinced it was Jacob's voice she'd heard. That he was the one who broke into the cottage and hit her.'

'And you told her it couldn't possibly be him.'

'Yes, and that he was away. But why would she say such a thing?'

'She was confused,' Andrew said. 'Jacob used to visit her. He's the lad she knows best in the village. She'd had a blow to the head and saw you sitting there. All those disjointed memories got jumbled up.'

Elizabeth gave another small nod. 'She hasn't mentioned it again.'

'There you go. She'll have forgotten she ever said it. Try not to worry. Mary's old, bless her, and she had a dreadful shock. I'm still not convinced she was burgled, but the police have to do their job.'

Elizabeth managed a small muted smile and Andrew picked up the unread newspaper. How she would have liked to tell him what Eloise's mother had said and unburden herself, but that couldn't be so easily dismissed. Eloise wasn't old and confused, she was a young, intelligent woman, sensitive and caring, and not known for hysteria or making things up. To share what had happened was to voice the unthinkable – that their son was now so evil he had attacked and raped his girlfriend.

'Why don't you give Eloise a ring now?' Andrew asked, glancing up from the paper.

'I'll leave it until tomorrow. I need to think what to say and I'm rather tired.'

'OK, love. I'm sure she'll be fine. You always got on very well.'

'Yes,' Elizabeth agreed absently, and picked up one of the weekend supplements to give the appearance of being occupied.

Elizabeth went to bed early that night with a headache, but she didn't sleep well. DC Evans's voice juxtaposed with Eloise's mother's in a diatribe of accusations and blame, not just towards Jacob but to her too for concealing the truth. In between their condemnations were her ill-conceived replies to Evans's questions. It would have been better if she'd said nothing for all the good she'd done Jacob. But she wasn't sure Andrew had done much better with his responses. Lying there unable to sleep in the dead of night she was sure they were separately and jointly culpable, not only for their son's behaviour but the web of lies and deceit that was now their life.

She began practising what she was going to say to Eloise, running through it in her mind over and over again, changing words, sentences, then starting all over again. None of it sounded right. Should she ask Eloise how she was and make small talk or get straight to the point? Or start by apologizing for Jacob? Not so long ago she'd have been able to chat easily to Eloise but now the words she needed failed her.

Elizabeth was up early in the morning, more exhausted than when she'd gone to bed. It was Sunday, Andrew's busiest day. She cooked him breakfast, and as soon as he left to take the first communion at eight o'clock she psyched herself up to telephone Eloise and get it over with. But the call went through to her voicemail. She was probably still in bed on a Sunday; Elizabeth didn't leave a message. If Eloise still had her number stored in her phone she'd see the missed call had been from her and hopefully phone her back.

When she'd heard nothing by nine o'clock Elizabeth phoned again and this time it rang out. Had Eloise recognized the number and not answered? Then before she left for the mid-morning service – the one she usually attended and which Eloise and Jacob had accompanied her to – she tried yet again. This time when the call went through to voicemail she left a message. 'Eloise, it's Liz, Jacob's mother. I hope you are keeping well. I need to talk to you about something important. Could you phone me back please? I'm going to church now but will be home by lunchtime. Thank you, love.'

She waited to see if Eloise would return her call straight-away, but when she didn't she left her phone on the table and went to church.

She heard very little of Andrew's sermon; her thoughts kept returning to the conversation she needed to have with Eloise. After the service she didn't mingle with the groups of parishioners but went straight home and checked her phone. Nothing from Eloise but a text message from David: *Thought this might interest you. The best case yet of cellular memory.* It was followed by a link to an online article. She'd read it later; Eloise was her priority for now.

She made herself a cup of coffee and then sat at the kitchen table, sipping it and wondering when she could reasonably phone Eloise again. Her thoughts went to the congregation still outside the church chatting in their small groups, discussing the police's visit to the village the night before, and more specifically discussing Jacob. Everyone was sure to know. She could guess at their speculation, made even more exciting because he was the Reverend's son. She'd felt that with Evans's visit too – that his interest had been piqued by Jacob's father being a reverend, because from what Maggie had said his visit to her sons had been short and perfunctory. Perhaps she was imagining it, unless of course Jacob was their prime suspect. Her head was throbbing again and she took two painkillers with the last of her coffee, then went through to the living room where she sat down in an armchair and closed her eyes.

Andrew was out for most of the day on parish business and Elizabeth wasn't expecting him home until the early evening. Slightly refreshed from a short nap she checked her phone and then set about some housework, the volume on her phone set to loud so she could hear it as she moved around. An hour or so later she sat down again to read the online article David had sent about cellular memory.

It was a scholarly article and some of the scientific data was difficult to understand but the findings were clear. David was right to enthuse, it was the best reported case yet that she knew of. The partner of a man who'd received a transplanted heart had been pregnant, and when the foetus was tested for the gene that had caused the father's heart defect it was found that their DNA didn't match. He couldn't possibly be the father of the unborn baby. He accused his partner of having an affair but she adamantly maintained she hadn't. More tests were run on him and the present results compared with those before the transplant. Not only had his blood group changed but there were significant changes in his DNA too. His DNA prior to the transplant matched that of the baby. More follow-up work needed to be done, the article said, and while this wasn't conclusive proof, all the indicators were that cellular memory was responsible. The implications for the future of transplant work were far-reaching, it concluded.

Elizabeth resisted phoning Eloise again until three o'clock when she thought she must have listened to her voice message by now. With her hand trembling and her heart racing she pressed Eloise's number, and this time after a couple of rings Eloise's small voice answered, 'Hello Liz. What do you want?'

'Thank you for answering. How are you?'

'All right,' Eloise said, her voice flat.

'I need your help. I'm sorry things ended badly between you and Jacob but I have to ask you something.' She knew she was gabbling but she needed to get it out quickly. 'The last time you saw Jacob there was a robbery in our village at Acorn Cottage – Mary, you knew her.' She paused but Eloise didn't respond. 'The police think it might have been a lad in his twenties so they are visiting all the young men in the village and checking their alibis. Jacob was with you for part of that evening so we've had to give them your contact details. I'm not asking you to lie, but could you not mention the other stuff, the things that your mother told me? It will reflect badly on Jacob.' She stopped, hot and uncomfortable. Eloise would under-stand, wouldn't she?

'They've already contacted me,' Eloise said in the same small voice. 'DC Evans phoned me yesterday evening.'

'Oh, I see. And what did you say?'

'I said Jacob was here and gave them the time he left.'

'And you didn't say anything else?'

'No.'

Relief flooded through her. 'Thank you, thank you so much. I am grateful.'

'Don't be. I didn't do it for you or him, but for me. I'm trying to forget what happened, erase it from my mind, and if I told the police I'd have to make a statement and it would all come back to me. I couldn't cope with that. I'm barely coping now. I was off work for three weeks after he attacked me. I daren't go out for fear he might be waiting for me.' Her voice broke. 'He hurt me so much. I don't think I'll ever get over it. He's ruined my life. I should have ended it the first time he hurt me but you persuaded me to see him again. Now I've got to live with the consequences. I won't ever trust anyone again. He's a monster, a cold heartless monster,' she cried. 'I pity you and Andrew, but don't phone me again. I want to believe he never existed.' And the line went dead.

Elizabeth sat with the phone in her hand and then, resting her head on the chair back, she wept openly.

Chapter Forty-Four

'Are you sure it's OK for me to phone now?' Rosie asked.

'Yes, of course. It's good to hear from you. I was just watching daytime television,' Eva admitted with a guilty laugh. 'But with only a week to go before my due date I'm indulging myself. How are you? How's the bank?'

'Pretty much the same as usual. It's sunny so I thought I'd come out for a walk and phone you before I have my sandwiches.' She left the busy High Street and went down a side street to talk.

'Yes, it's a lovely day,' Eva agreed. There was a short silence. 'So how is Prince Charming? Any luck with house-training him?' She laughed.

'Not really.' Rosie fell silent. She needed to talk – to confide – and Eva was her closest friend, but where to begin? 'There's some things I need to talk to you about,' she said at last, but her eyes immediately filled and her breath caught. She turned away from the man coming towards her so he couldn't see.

'Rosie? What's the matter? Are you all right?' Eva asked, immediately concerned.

'Not really.' She stifled a sob. 'I'm in a real mess, Eva, and I don't know what to do.'

'What, with Jacob you mean?'

'Yes. It's my fault. I should have spent longer getting to know him like you said, but he was desperate for somewhere to stay and he seemed so nice.'

'And he's not nice any more?'

'No. Well, sometimes, but at other times he's really nasty and I'm afraid of him. I do my best to please him but nothing seems to work.'

'Oh Rosie. He hasn't hit you, has he?'

'Yes but it was my fault and he apologized after.'

'Rosie, that's not good. There is never a reason to hit someone.'

'I know,' she said defeated. 'And after the last time I swore I'd never let another man treat me the way Shane did, but I have! It's happened again.'

'I didn't know Shane hit you?' Eva said shocked.

'Yes, a lot. But I couldn't talk about it, not even to you. What's wrong with me that's it's happening again?' She blinked back fresh tears.

'There's nothing wrong with you,' Eva said firmly. 'Other than that you're too trusting. You need to tell him to leave straightaway. It's your flat. I don't understand why you haven't already if things are that bad.'

'I can't. I've tried to talk about it but he gets so angry. He scares me. He's got a bad temper.'

'Have you told anyone else? Your mum? You're close to her.'

'No. Mum met him. She dropped by the other weekend. He didn't want her to come but he was polite to her. But when I spoke to her after she admitted she didn't like him. She said there was something in him that she found unsettling.'

'Could you confide in her now? I'm sure she could help you. I'm not much use in my present condition.'

'I don't want to worry her. And what could she do? She'd tell me to get rid of him, but it's not that easy. I gave him a key when he first moved in. I'd no idea he'd be like this. And there's other stuff as well. Worse.'

'Like what?' Eva gasped, unable to imagine anything worse than a woman being afraid of and hit by her partner.

'There's a lot of stuff going on that doesn't make sense. We went to his parents for dinner last Saturday. You know his father is a reverend?'

'Yes, you said.'

'They seem really nice people but Jacob hates them. He's so rude to them and they seem to take it. There was an awful atmosphere. After dinner I helped his mum, Liz, with the dishes. While we were talking she commented that it was nice Jacob and I were getting on so well, and then asked if he treated me well?'

'You think she might suspect?'

'I don't know. But what could I say? I just nodded.

And then she said she was surprised my bank gave Jacob such a big loan to buy the car when he didn't have any income. But they didn't, Eva. I checked. He hasn't taken out a bank loan. He talked to me about applying for one soon after we met, but then he didn't need it because he inherited from his grandmother. I suppose he could have got a loan from somewhere else but why, when he had money from his inheritance? Then later she tells me that an elderly lady in the village was burgled, and it would have upset Jacob, as he used to visit her and treated her like a grandma as his own grandparents died when he was very young.'

'Oh no! You think it's possible that's where the money came from?' Eva asked, horrified.

'I don't know. I don't want to believe it. But there's so much about him I don't know any more. When I think back to when he first came into the bank, he was so charming, I fell for him. He's not the same person and I've no idea what to do.'

'You need to make him go,' Eva said. 'And perhaps you should tell the police about the money?'

'I can't. He'd be furious. And maybe I've got it all wrong. Perhaps it's me. I can't think straight any more.'

'It's not you, Rosie,' Eva said firmly. 'Believe me. But I think you need to get away from him so you can think clearly and decide what to do. Why don't you stay here for a couple of nights? Syed won't mind. We often have his friends and relatives to stay.'

'That's kind of you but I can't. Jacob wouldn't like

it and I'd have to go back and face him at some point.'

'Well, come here after work tonight for a few hours then. I'll make you some dinner.'

'Thanks but no. I need to deal with this. I'll have to go soon, it's nearly the end of my lunch break.'

'Oh Rosie, I'm so worried for you.'

'Don't be. You've got enough with the baby due next week. I'm sorry I put this on you, but I feel as if my head is bursting. I know I have to talk to him and I will tonight. As soon as I get home.'

'All right, but phone or text me after to let me know you're OK.'

'Yes. Thanks, and sorry for all of this.'

'Don't apologize. Take care and phone soon.'

'I will.'

Chapter Forty-Five

DC Evans was feeling rather self-satisfied. Although he hadn't been able to check Jacob's bank account – it required a court order to do that – he'd done the next best thing: identified the car he'd bought. With Jacob's name and address it had been straightforward policing, requiring only an online search as all car dealers were obliged to inform the DVLA of the details of the cars they sold and their new owners. He'd checked with the garage and the car hadn't been bought on finance but a debit from Jacob's bank account. It wasn't a cheap motor – £14k, and he'd bought it the week after the break-in at Acorn Cottage.

The manager had been very helpful and had mentioned that the guy who'd bought it – a Jacob Wilson – had been in before and had become aggressive when he'd been refused credit. He admitted he'd been surprised when the transaction had gone through.

Evans couldn't wait to share this news with PC Mandy Taylor but she was on annual leave for the week. He was now being driven by another officer, Linda Simpson, and he knew better than to comment on her appearance. Mandy had known him long enough to excuse his well-intended compliments and faux pas, but he hardly knew Linda and she might not be so forgiving. She'd been drafted in from the town to cover maternity leave and they were now on their way to visit Jacob. He'd been filling her in on the background to the case as they went, culminating in his hope that this would lead to an arrest. It was on days like this that he was able to acknowledge how much he enjoyed his job, deriving immense satisfaction from it when a line of inquiry led to a crime being solved.

'And if I find out Jacob's parents have been withholding information I'll have them for obstruction, Reverend or not,' he continued. 'They were very vague about the missing two-and-a-half hours when his father heard Jacob arrive home but not go to bed. Plenty of time to walk to Acorn Cottage and rob Mary Hutchins.'

'They haven't found the weapon used then?' Linda asked as she drove.

'No, not yet, but when they do I'd put money on Jacob's fingerprints being on it.'

'So what turned a previously decent lad into a thug?' she asked, glancing at him.

'Drugs at a guess. His room stank of weed. If he's upped his usage to crack cocaine it will have done his head in and be expensive to maintain. Twenty grand was taken from Acorn Cottage so my guess is fourteen went on a car, which left six to pay off any debt he owed to his suppliers and keep his habit going for a while.'

She nodded as she pulled into Highland Grove, a road of low-rise privately owned flats.

'Which block?' she asked.

'Hill Court, flat seventeen,' Evans replied.

'Just a minute, I've been here before,' Linda said as she parked outside the flats.'

'What, to the block or the flat?'

'What's the name of the girl he's living with?'

'Rosemary Jones. She's clear. No previous.'

'Rosie. Yes, I'm almost certain that was her name. I'll know for sure when I see her.'

They walked the short distance to the main entrance then up the stairs to the first-floor landing. 'Yes, it's the same flat,' Linda said, recognizing the door. 'Her last boyfriend was Shane Smith. He was in a serious road traffic accident about a year ago. I was one of the officers who came to break the news.' They paused on the landing. 'She was a nice girl as I remember but Shane was a nasty bit of work. Lot of previous. Bad stuff, GBH etc. He hadn't been out of prison long when he moved in with her. What does she see in these guys?'

'Search me,' Evans said.

He gave the bell a good hard push. It was 4.30pm so even someone with a drink or drug habit should be up by now, unless of course he was out, or his parents had tipped him off. There was no reply so he pressed again, keeping his finger on the bell for longer, then supplemented it with a good hard knock on the wood with his fist. If you made enough noise and they were in they usually answered. Another good ring and thump and true to form the door opened.

'What the fuck!'

'Jacob Wilson?' Evans asked, flashing his ID card. He nodded. 'DC Evans, and this is PC Linda Simpson.'

'What do you want?' Jacob demanded. Barefooted, unshaven with tousled hair and a creased shirt hanging over faded jeans, he could easily have just fallen out of bed.

'We'd like to talk to you about the robbery at Acorn Cottage in Maybury,' Evans said.

'Why?'

'We're eliminating all the young men from the village.'

'How did you know I was here?'

So his parents hadn't tipped him off then? 'Your parents gave us your address. I assume that isn't a problem? We'd like to ask you a few questions.'

'I'm busy,' Jacob said, and began to close the door.

'So are we,' Evans said, placing his foot in the door to stop it. 'Here or at the police station?'

Jacob threw open the door with unnecessary force and disappeared into the flat. Evans and Linda followed him in. Down the short hall and into the one main room, tidy except for the empty beer cans and pizza box. Jacob picked up the remote and, silencing the television, flopped onto the sofa. 'Well, what do you want?' he demanded.

There were no other chairs in the room so Evans perched on the wooden coffee table in front of Jacob while Linda stood to the side of the sofa. 'How are you?' Evans asked convivially.

'Fine.'

'A heart transplant is quite something.'

Jacob shrugged. 'If you say so. Can we get on with this? I'm busy.'

'Certainly, sir; you'll be aware of the robbery at Acorn Cottage?'

'Obviously. The whole village knows about it.'

Evans nodded amiably. He wasn't easily antagonized; you couldn't afford to be in police work. 'One line of inquiry we're looking at is that the person who broke into the cottage was a young man, probably in his twenties. We're trying to eliminate all the young men of that age who lived in the village or visited it regularly at the time.'

'I was away the night it happened,' Jacob said. 'Trying to patch things up with my ex.'

'So I believe. I've spoken to the young lady.'

What did she say?' he asked uneasily.

'Eloise confirmed you were with her for some of that night,' Evans said. 'Why? Did you expect her to say something different?'

'No. And that was all?'

Evans nodded and threw him a small reassuring smile

to put him at ease. 'So what time did you arrive at your parents'?'

'I can't remember exactly.'

'Approximately will do, sir.'

'Some time after midnight, I guess.'

'Could you be a bit more precise? Was it just after midnight, or nearer one or two or o'clock? Or later?'

'Just after midnight,' Jacob said.

'Thank you. Then what did you do?'

'I went to bed of course. It was late.'

'Straight to bed?'

'Yes, I was tired.'

'So what time do you think it was when you were in bed?'

Jacob shrugged. 'Around twelve-thirty I guess.'

Evans felt a warm glow of satisfaction. First lie. Give him enough rope and he'd hang himself, as the saying went.

'Is this your laptop?' he now asked, touching the closed laptop beside him on the coffee table.

'No. Mine broke, that's Rosie's, my girlfriend's. I'm using it to job-hunt.'

So perhaps he had been warned after all? Evans considered. But the owner of the laptop could easily be identified as could all the online activity and downloads, once he had enough evidence to charge him and take it away. 'I understand you used to borrow your mother's car. Do you have one of your own now?'

Jacob nodded.

'Did you buy it with a loan?'

There was a pause and Evans watched Jacob carefully as he searched for the right answer. 'Sort of.'

'Sorry, sir? Did you take out finance to buy the car?'

'No. My girl lent me the money,' Jacob replied.

'For the whole cost of the car?'

'And some extra to see me through until I have a job.'

Definitely forewarned Evans thought, exchanging a glance with Linda. 'So how much would that be in total?'

'Around twenty thousand pounds.'

'Wow. That was very generous of her!'

'I guess she must like me a lot,' Jacob said cockily.

'And she'd be happy to confirm she lent you all that money if I were to ask her?'

'Of course. You can ask her soon. She'll be on her way home from work now. But I'm forgetting my manners. Would you like a drink?'

'No thank you,' Evans said stiffly. He didn't like being made a fool of.

Chapter Forty-Six

Rosie felt physically sick as she ran through what she was going to say to Jacob when she arrived home. Without a doubt he'd be in and waiting for her; he always was at this time. She'd have to say what she needed to at once or she'd lose her nerve and another day would pass. But how to approach him? He was always so irritable and angry that one wrong word or misconstrued look could send him over the edge and into a temper. She feared his anger as much as she feared his love-making, which had become brutal and selfish, an animal act where he showed her no consideration or love at all. Fucking is what he called it, and that's exactly what it felt like.

Eva had been right when she'd said she mustn't let it go on any longer and she needed time alone to sort herself out. Perhaps if she put it that way to Jacob – as though it was her problem – he wouldn't take it so personally.

She tried to rehearse the words she wanted to say. 'Shane, I'm sorry but I think I rushed into our relationship. It's not you, it's me . . .' She stopped, horrified, realizing what she'd done – substituted Shane's name for Jacob's. Her eyes welled.

She'd invited two men into her life who'd abused her. Whatever was wrong with her? Shane had said she was one of those women who secretly liked being kept in their place by a bloke. She'd dismissed it at the time but now history was repeating itself and she was starting to believe it. The two men she'd fallen for had turned out to be vicious, aggressive brutes, and while with hindsight she thought she should have seen it coming with Shane and his history, Jacob had been raised in a good home with kind, loving parents. He'd gone to university, had a good job and had never been in prison. Was it possible she was the magnet, a catalyst for abuse? She honestly didn't know.

With her mouth dry and her stomach churning, she pulled into the residents' parking area at the rear of the flats, saw it was full, and drove out again to park on the road. Jacob was definitely in; his car was in her bay. How she wished she could have taken up Eva's offer and stayed the night with her and Syed, or even spent just a few hours talking to her friend, but it would incite Jacob's anger if she was late back, and at some point all this had to be faced. Perhaps telling him wouldn't be as bad as she anticipated.

She climbed heavily out of the car. Perhaps he'd be

pleased she was finishing their relationship, maybe he wanted that too but hadn't liked to say. Yet even as she had the thought she doubted it. He appeared to be very comfortable living at her flat and seemed to get off on humiliating and hurting her. Her eyes welled again and she blinked back the tears as she entered the building and went up the stairs.

It was important he didn't see how scared she was, as he feasted off it. She must keep the anxiety from her face and her voice steady while she said what she had to. *Shane.* No! *Jacob!* Don't make that mistake! *Jacob, I need to talk to you* . . . Her pulse raced as she tried out the words in her head. *It's nothing you've done. I'm sorry, but I'm just not ready for another serious relationship.* No, she couldn't say 'another' – it might spark his jealousy. *I'm sorry, I'm not ready for a serious relationship, I should have thought about it before I invited you to stay.* But of course she hadn't invited him, he'd just arrived. But then again she could have said no at the time. It would have avoided all this but then he hadn't been like this then— Stop! she told herself. Stop overthinking it, just go in and say what you have to.

With her hand trembling and nausea building in her stomach, she slid her key into the front-door lock. As she did the door suddenly opened from inside, making her jump. Jacob appeared. He never usually met her at the door; he was usually either lying on the bed or on the sofa when she came home from work. Perhaps he was going out?

314

'Hello, love. How are you?' he asked, smiling. 'Have you had a good day?'

She looked at him carefully. What was his game? 'It was OK,' she said, going in and trying to raise a smile.

'We've got visitors,' he said buoyantly. So that was the reason. 'The police are here. They want to talk to you, just to confirm something.'

'About the robbery in the village?'

'Yes, sort of. Did you know they were coming?'

'No,' she lied and followed him into the living room.

'Good afternoon. I'm DC Charlie Evans,' the male police officer said, standing.

'Hello,' Rosie said quietly.

'And this is my colleague PC Linda Simpson.' Rosie returned her smile with a vague feeling of having met her before.

'Can I get you a drink?' Jacob asked her attentively.

'No thank you.' It crossed Rosie's mind, but only briefly, that if she told the officers now how he treated her and asked for help they could perhaps escort him from the flat. But the very thought made her legs tremble. He'd return as soon as they let him go and there was no telling what he'd do to her then.

'Here, love, sit down,' Jacob said.

She did as he said, placing her handbag on the floor beside her. DC Evans perched on the coffee table a little in front of her and Jacob took up position beside him, looming over them. As she glanced at him she saw the unmistakable warning signs in his gaze – be careful or else.

'We won't keep you long,' Evans said. 'I'm sure you want to relax after a day at work.'

Rosie nodded and wondered why exactly they wanted to speak to her. Elizabeth had said the police would need to speak to Jacob to eliminate him from their inquiries, but she couldn't help; she hadn't known Jacob well at the time of the robbery and had never met the elderly lady whose house had been broken into.

'Can I ask you how long you've worked at the bank?' Evans asked. Jacob straightened beside him, drawing himself to his full height.

'Five years,' she said. 'Since I left school.'

'You obviously like your work and are good at it or you wouldn't have stayed so long.'

'Yes, I suppose so,' Rosie said, wondering why this was relevant.

'And you receive a reasonable salary for all your hard work?'

'Yes. Although I'd like more.'

'Wouldn't we all,' Evans said with a smile and the PC laughed.

'Do you rent this flat or have a mortgage?' he now asked.

'I rent it,' Rosie said, 'although I'd like to buy my own one day.'

He nodded. 'And you run a car?'

'Yes. It's not new though. I bought it second-hand.'

'With a bank loan?'

'No, I saved up for it. It's only small.'

'And buying your car presumably took all your savings?' he asked, the flow of his questions continuing lightly.

She was about to say most of them, but saw Jacob gave a small shake of his head.

'Er, no, not all my savings,' she said.

'Can I ask how much you had left?' Evans asked.

Jacob was staring at her, clearly wanting her to say something, but she'd no idea what.

'I'm sorry,' she said, flustered. 'I don't remember. But why do you want to know all this? You surely don't think I broke into that old lady's house and stole her money?'

'No, of course not,' Evans said. 'I'm just trying to make a few things clearer in my own mind. Could you tell me approximately how much savings you had left after you bought your car?' He saw her glance at Jacob who was standing behind him, out of his line of vision. Linda wouldn't be able to see his face either.

'I'm not sure,' Rosie said.

'Roughly,' Evans said. 'Did you have five hundred pounds left, five thousand, fifty thousand or more?'

'Oh no, not as much as that,' she said incredulously.

'It was twenty thousand,' Jacob put in.

'Thank you. I was asking Miss Jones,' Evans said tightly over his shoulder. Then to her: 'Is that correct?'

She nodded without meeting his gaze.

'That's a lot of money,' Evans said. 'Where is it now?'

'I've told you, she lent it to me,' Jacob said.

'Did you?' Evans asked Rosie, leaning slightly towards her with a quizzical look.

'Yes,' she said quietly, keeping her eyes down.

'Why did you lend Jacob all that money?'

She didn't need to look at Jacob to know the answer. 'It was for a new car,' she said. Her lie hung in the air. When she dared to look up she saw him smile and nod.

'That was very magnanimous of you,' Evans said. 'You bought a second-hand car for yourself and gave Jacob all the rest of your savings so he could buy himself a new car!'

She felt her cheeks flush and nodded dumbly.

'She's good like that,' Jacob put in smugly.

'Obviously,' Evans said. 'Just one more thing and then we'll leave you in peace.' Rosie forced her gaze to meet his. 'How did you give Jacob the money? Bank transfer?'

She knew the answer as Jacob had been asked a number of questions when he made the deposit to check it wasn't laundered money. 'Cash,' she said.

'Really?' Evans asked, astounded and clearly doubting her. 'I'd have thought someone who works in a bank would have had their savings invested, and use a direct debit to transfer money.' He looked at her. Hot and uncomfortable, she didn't know what to say. 'Where did you keep all that money? Surely not in this flat?'

She knew it was ludicrous and he wouldn't believe her but Jacob nodded. 'Yes, I'm sorry, that's what I did,' she said. Why didn't she just blurt out the truth and tell them everything? She knew why, and Jacob's threatening, narrowed eyes confirmed it.

318

Evans stood and drawing a deep breath through his nose, said, 'Thank you for your time, Miss Jones. There's my card.' He placed it on the coffee table. 'If you think of anything you'd like to tell me please phone, and just a reminder that perjury carries a prison sentence.'

She didn't move or say anything.

'Will that be all?' Jacob asked cockily.

'For now,' Evans said.

'I'll see you out then?'

'Goodbye, Rosie,' Linda said. As she passed, she lightly touched her shoulder. 'You know where we are if you need us.'

'Thank you,' Rosie said, and at that point she suddenly remembered when she'd seen her before.

Chapter Forty-Seven

DC Evans and PC Linda Simpson began their descent of the stairs. 'It's the same girl,' Linda said. 'And I'd put money on her being in another abusive relationship.'

Evans gave a curt nod, annoyed with himself for not having handled the interview better. 'She's lying to protect him. But why? A nice girl like that.'

'She's scared of him. I could see it in her face. You left your card so perhaps she'll get in touch when she's had a chance to think about it and he's not around.'

'Perhaps,' Evans said doubtfully. 'But if she sticks to her story there's not much we can do. His parents and ex-girl-friend are providing an alibi for the night of the robbery and if that doesn't change we're buggered. With unlimited police resources I'm sure I could nail him, but there's only so much time I can put into this – a relatively small robbery with assault. So unless more evidence comes to light this is going to have to go on the back burner for now, much as it grieves me.'

Linda nodded thoughtfully.

Inside the flat Rosie heard the front door close and a few seconds later Jacob was in the living room. Fist raised and eyes blazing he came towards her. She cowered on the sofa and covered her head with her hands, impotently trying to protect herself from his blows.

'You silly cow!' he shouted. 'If you hadn't given my mother this address they wouldn't have known I was here.'

'Don't keep hitting me,' she cried. 'I want you to go, now!'

'I bet you do!'

She fended off another blow and then breaking free made a run for the door. But as fast as she was off the sofa Jacob was faster. Grabbing her hair he pulled her back.

'Get off me,' she screamed, trying to kick him.

'Shut up, bitch.' He slapped her face and raised his hand again. 'Stay still if you don't want another one.'

She glared at him. 'You stole that old lady's money. I know you did. It wasn't an inheritance.'

'But you're not going to tell anyone, are you?' he snarled, bringing his face right up close to hers. 'Not if you know what's good for you.' His eyes were staring and deranged as he spat the words in her face. 'You're a cold-hearted bitch, just like my mother! It was her fault my father left. She drove him away.'

'What are you talking about?' Rosie cried. 'Your father didn't leave your mother. He's at home.'

'Don't lie to me!' He hit her again. She felt a tooth slice into her bottom lip and immediately tasted blood. 'Stay there and don't move while I think what to do. Move an inch and you'll regret it.'

He straightened and began pacing the room, his eyes darting around, manic and preoccupied, as if considering various deluded options. She stayed still on the sofa, trying not to draw attention to herself and fearing him more than ever. Gone was any semblance of the Jacob she'd known who'd walked into the bank. In his place stood a monster

She saw her handbag on the floor by her feet, open with her phone tucked just inside. If he turned his back for long enough or left the room briefly she'd quickly grab the phone and conceal it in her clothes. Then if she couldn't get out of the flat to phone for help she could pretend she needed the bathroom, lock herself in and phone for help from there.

'I can't trust you at all,' he said, pausing from pacing to look at her. 'That's a big problem for me. I know how my dad felt now. But I can't walk away from you like he did with my mum. You know too much.'

She was about to correct him and say something real-istic about his father, but she saw his gaze go to her bag and her heart sank. She didn't try to stop him, there was no point. In an instant he'd reached into her bag and grabbed the phone. 'What's the PIN?' he demanded.

She hesitated, only for a second. But it was long enough

322

to incite his anger further, and his fist crashed into the side of her head, making her cry out in pain. 'It's the seventh of July, my birthday,' she said, her hand going to her head. 'Zero seven zero seven.'

He laughed cruelly. 'Pity you won't be celebrating it this year.'

Fear overwhelmed her as she watched him sit on the coffee table in front of her where Evans had sat. He entered the PIN and began scrolling through her text messages. 'Why's my mother texting you and asking if you're all right?' he demanded.

'I don't know,' she said honestly.

'Yes you do!' Before she had a chance to protect her face he'd slapped her hard, making her cry out. 'Tell me, bitch!'

'I don't know! I really don't. She texts each day to ask if I'm all right and I reply yes.' Which was true. 'I honestly don't know why your mother keeps texting.' Her last message had been that afternoon and normally Rosie would have texted back – *I'm fine, thanks. How are you?* But today she'd been so anxious and preoccupied by what she had to say to Jacob she hadn't responded.

'And she phones you,' Jacob said accusingly, checking her call log. 'Why? What have you been telling her?'

'Nothing. She just wants to know if we're OK. And she said we should go to dinner again soon.'

He laughed caustically. 'I don't believe you.'

Fearing another blow or worse she jumped up from the sofa and made a dash for the door again. He was on her in a flash. Grabbing her collar he dragged her back and into the kitchen where he pulled a knife from the block.

'Do what I say or else, understand, bitch?' he hissed, pressing the tip of the knife to her throat.

Eyes wide in terror, she nodded.

Keeping the knife pressed to her neck he pushed her into the living room and onto the sofa. 'Stay there.' He sat on the table again, placing the knife beside him. 'I think it's time you replied to Mummy's text.'

He pressed the keys of her phone and read the message aloud as he wrote, a smug, self-satisfied grimace on his face. '*Hi Liz. We're fine thanks.*' He sent the text. 'Now let's see who else you've been gossiping with.'

Rosie watched, sick with fear as he continued scrolling down, checking her messages. 'Eva. Well no surprise there. You two were always gossiping at the bank.' Rosie took some small comfort that she and Eva usually spoke on the phone so there should be no incriminating texts.

Apart from the last one. 'What does this mean?' he demanded. '"Text or phone once you've told him." Told me what?'

Her stomach churned 'She's asked us to dinner,' she lied, trying to keep her voice steady. 'I said I'd text to let her know.' Did he believe her? She held his gaze. Thankfully he did.

'We'd better tell her then. '*Sorry, Eva,*' he read out as he composed the message. '*We won't be able to make it. Jacob has made other plans for us. Thanks anyway.*' He looked at her. 'Does that sound right? Is that the sort of thing you'd say?'

Rosie nodded, praying he wouldn't see through her lie, and that Eva would realize there was something badly wrong and get help.

Head slightly bowed as he concentrated, he continued going through her messages, checking for any signs of her unfaithfulness or disloyalty. She looked at the knife beside him on the table. She'd found him going through her phone before which was why she'd locked it with a PIN. Not that there was much to discover. Since he'd moved in she hadn't seen her friends, but he bent and miscon-strued innocent words so he could accuse and punish her. She started as her phone vibrated with an incoming call.

'Well, well, if it isn't Eva,' Jacob said smugly. 'What a surprise!'

Rigid with fear, she held her breath as he answered the call on speaker. 'Hi Eva, how are you?' he said brightly.

Rosie heard her friend pause. 'Is that Jacob?' she asked tentatively.

'Yes. Who else could it be?'

Another pause then, 'Is Rosie there?' She could hear the tension in Eva's voice and hoped Jacob couldn't hear it too.

'She's in the bath,' he replied good-humouredly. 'Can I give her a message?'

'No, it's OK. Just ask her to call me when she's finished.'

'Will do. And thanks for the invite. Sorry we can't make it.'

Rosie froze, expecting Eva to ask, 'What invite?' But she didn't. Would she suspect something was wrong? 'Just ask her to call me please,' she said, and the line went dead. Jacob was looking at her suspiciously.

'You know, I think you've been lying to me.' His eyes narrowed in accusation. 'I think you've been telling me things that aren't true. And you know what the best punishment is for lying? Cut out your tongue.' He picked up the knife.

'No!' she screamed, and made another dash for the door.

He was after her, the knife clattering to the floor, then he was on her, grabbing her arms and forcing them behind her.

'You're hurting me,' she cried.

'Not as much as I'm going to.'

Dragging her up from the floor he frogmarched her down the hall and into the kitchen where he forced her onto one of the two kitchen chairs that stood either side of the small table. 'Stay there or I really will cut your tongue out. Then your ears and eyes. "Hear no evil, see no evil and speak no evil."' He laughed. 'That's what women need to learn.'

She sat where he'd put her, her mouth dry with fear. He retrieved the knife from the floor in the living area and then placed it on the work surface within his reach. Next he opened what she called her 'bits and bobs' drawer and took out a ball of string and duct tape. Returning to the chair he forced her hands behind her and tied her wrists to the chairback, then came round to the front and pulled out a length of duct tape which he took to her mouth.

'No,' she cried. 'Don't do that. I won't say anything. I promise.'

'Too late,' he pronounced. 'Do you want your mouth stuck open or closed? I'd recommend closed. It's marginally more comfortable, I saw it in a film.'

Without waiting for a reply he pressed the tape over her mouth, then wound it around her head twice, before cutting it with the knife. Her eyes filled and she concentrated on trying to breathe.

'Bound and gagged just as a woman should be,' he laughed. 'Now I can think what to do with you.'

Chapter Forty-Eight

It was nearly seven o'clock and Elizabeth was sitting in one of the hearthside armchairs, dreading the long evening that stretched ahead of her. Andrew was out of town at a meeting with the Bishop and other clergy and wasn't expected back until ten o'clock at the earliest, probably later. She'd had dinner on her lap while watching the early evening news and had then taken Mitsy for a short walk before the rain had set in. Although she should have been used to being alone with Andrew often out on church or parish business, it was becoming increasingly difficult with so much on her mind. At least when he was here he offered some diversion so she couldn't just sit for hours and torment herself. Exhausted from not sleeping, she was constantly anxious and on edge so that any space in the day or night was quickly filled with thoughts of Jacob, and Eloise's words ringing in her ears.

Of course Eloise had been within her rights to blame her. If she hadn't encouraged Jacob to see her that weekend – even lending him her car – it would never have happened. That she had acted in good faith, unaware that he'd harmed Eloise before, didn't alleviate her conscience one little bit. Even though Eloise hadn't reported it to the police, Elizabeth had to live with the knowledge that her son was a rapist.

She picked up her phone again and opened Rosie's text. *Hi Liz. We're fine thanks*. Had the police visited Jacob yet? She thought Rosie would have mentioned it if they had. She'd used the term 'we' so Jacob must be with her and she'd said they were both all right, which she had to accept. Perhaps it wouldn't happen again. Perhaps Rosie was suffi- ciently different from Eloise that whatever it was that had turned Jacob into a sadistic rapist wouldn't resurface. But even as she had the thought she knew that it was unlikely, and that her reasoning was one step from blaming the victim, which was completely unacceptable. Jacob had committed one of the vilest acts possible, traumatizing and scarring Eloise for life. Of course he could strike again – hence all her texts and phone calls to Rosie.

Closing Rosie's text, she scrolled to David's with the link to the article detailing what was probably the best reported case of cellular memory so far. She read it as she had before with a cold, sinking resignation, for although it added to the pool of research, it didn't help her as she'd thought it might. Indeed, it compounded her feelings of hopelessness, for here was irrefutable proof that what was happening to Jacob had happened to others.

Even more depressing was that there was no chance of the donor recipient ever reverting back.

With mounting feelings of despair, Elizabeth closed the article and clicked on the new message icon which had appeared while she'd been reading. She now saw it was a Facebook alert, advising her that Tracy Smith had messaged her. She logged in and read the message, trying to make sense of Tracy's poor spelling and grammar. *Hiya. How ya doin? Sory I aint been in touch. Got banned from ere for bein f*ing threatening and abusive. Lol. Hav to behave meself now. Lol. Heres the stuff u wanted about the girl Shane waz wiv. I got it off her bank statement that waz in his pocket when he died. Now I wonder what he waz doin with her bank details! Lol That's me boy!*

Elizabeth recoiled from the foulness of the woman and her admiration that her son had been stealing from his girlfriend. But then her hand shot to her mouth as she read the name and address of Shane's girlfriend. Rosemary Jones, 17 Hill Court, Highland Grove. It couldn't be. Surely not. She quickly scrolled back through Rosie's text messages to the one she'd sent giving her address. It was the same. It was the same girl. She could barely get her breath. The bile rose to her throat as the realization dawned: Jacob's girlfriend had been Shane's too.

Chapter Forty-Nine

'What's the matter with you?' Jacob snarled. 'I thought I told you to keep still.'

Rosie tried nodding again towards the bathroom, her brow creasing, trying to make him understand. She needed a wee. She'd come home straight from work and the police had been here so she hadn't had a chance to use the bathroom. She nodded again and finally he understood.

'Later. I'm busy.' He laughed.

He was standing a little way in front of her, trying to reach someone on his phone. It had been busy for some time and he was becoming increasingly agitated and angry each time he tried, cursing someone called Taco. Rosie watched him, terrified, but aware she needed to try to be calm and rational – like she was at the bank – to think of a way to call for help or escape.

He was becoming even more delusional and deranged,

talking about things in his past that had never happened and making no sense at all. She feared him more than ever. The string was cutting painfully into her wrists where he'd tied her to the chair and her mouth was sore from the duct tape. Every time she moved her head, the sticky tape stretched her skin and pulled her hair. She tried to push it from her mind and concentrate on planning her escape. He'd have to untie her hands to let her use the bathroom and once in there she could quickly lock the door, rip the duct tape from her mouth and scream for help from the bathroom window. The window was too small and the flat too high up to escape from, but it overlooked the road. If she screamed loud enough and waved a towel out of the window surely someone would hear her? She prayed they would, and that the lock on the bathroom door was strong enough to keep Jacob out as he fought to get in.

'About fucking time!' he cursed as he finally made contact with Taco on the phone. There was a reply that Rosie couldn't hear. 'Yeah, whatever,' he said dismissively, pacing the room. 'Look man, I need you to arrange something, like you did before at the depot.' He paused, listening to the reply, then, 'No, it's a woman.' Another pause, then, 'Call me when you know, but don't piss me around. I need it doing tonight.' Finishing the call, he lowered his phone and looked at Rosie.

There was a glint in his eye as he spoke that made her blood run cold. 'The thing is, you know too much,' he said as though rationalizing his decision. 'I can't trust you.

I'm sure you'll tell the police at the first opportunity. You're too honest for your own fucking good, and I'm not going back to prison again. I've spent too much of my fucking life there already. I don't see that I have a choice.'

She shook her head, unsure of what he was talking about, but trying to indicate that she wouldn't tell if he let her go. He ignored her. She tried again, a small muffled cry.

'All right! I know you want a pee,' he said, annoyed.

Jamming his phone into his jeans, he came over and untied her hands. Once released, her aching arms fell limply to her sides and she rubbed them to recover the circulation. He came round to the front and pulled her roughly to her feet, then began tying her hands again in front of her body.

'No!' she tried to cry from beneath the tape, and pulled away.

He shook her and snarled in her face. 'Do you want a pee or not?' He was perspiring heavily, beads of sweat stood on his forehead. She nodded. 'Well keep fucking still then.'

She stood still, petrified, as he retied her hands in front of her. Then, grabbing her roughly by the arm, he pulled her towards the bathroom and pushed her in. 'You've got two minutes!' He drew the door to, but placed his foot against it so it couldn't be completely closed.

Rosie looked helplessly at the window and the partially closed door, and knew her plan had failed. Her eyes filled and her legs trembled. She caught sight of herself in the mirror over the handbasin, bound and gagged, debased and humiliated. How had she allowed this to happen? It seemed macabrely unreal, as if she were playing a part in a low-budget horror movie. But the image in the mirror was real, as was the string binding her wrists and the tape over her mouth. What was he planning to do with her next? Pass her on to the person called Taco? She'd seen stories on the news and in magazines about women who'd just vanished, possibly sold into slavery abroad, or murdered and their bodies never found. She didn't doubt that Jacob was capable of anything. If only she could persuade him to take the tape off her mouth she might stand some chance of talking him out of whatever he was planning. But gagged and tied she was helpless and at his mercy

'Hurry up!' He banged on the bathroom door.

Crossing to the toilet, she struggled to lower her pants, used the toilet and then flushed it. He immediately came in, his eyes on the phone in his hand. Without looking at her he grabbed her arm and pulled her from the bathroom into the kitchen where he sat her roughly on the chair again, leaving her hands tied. He moved away, more interested in his phone. If she kept very still and didn't draw attention to herself perhaps he wouldn't notice he hadn't tied her to the chair? Then with her hands in front maybe she could do something, but she'd have to be careful. She'd only have one chance. He was so agitated and volatile that anything could ignite his anger.

She sat very still and watched him as he concentrated

on his phone, texting and then trying to call. Her phone was on the worktop where he'd thrown it. It had vibrated a couple of times with incoming text messages but he'd been too preoccupied to notice it. But now it was vibrating again for longer, indicating an incoming call. He snatched it up.

'Eva again! What the fuck!' He cut the call, letting it go through to voicemail, then studied her call list. 'And my mother's been messaging. Aren't you popular tonight.' She held her breath as he read the recent texts, praying they didn't contain anything incriminating that would make him more angry. A few moments later he threw her phone back onto the worktop, where it landed with a clatter, and looked at his own phone again.

Whoever he wanted to get hold of, it was clearly urgent and she could see his agitation increasing as he kept trying. If he turned his back for long enough or left the room perhaps she could get to her phone, run to the bathroom, lock herself in and, if she could get her hands free, summon help. Perhaps. But what if she failed? *Don't think about it.*

He was pacing the room again with his phone to his ear. She watched him carefully and tried to calm herself and concentrate on what she needed to do. The call must have connected for he was listening now to what the person was saying, and he clearly didn't like it. She saw his face grow tense and pale. She sat very still, her plan formulating.

'You're fucking joking me!' he cursed. 'He doesn't do

335

women! What sort of pussy is he? So find me someone who does, and quickly. I need her gone tonight.'

Rosie turned ice cold as she realized what he was doing. There was no doubt now that he was talking about her, arranging her disappearance or even murder. How long did she have? Probably not long. He'd said tonight. She needed to act quickly if she stood any chance of saving herself. He ended the call and then checked his messages. Seizing the opportunity, she jumped up from the chair, ran to the bathroom and got in, but not with enough time to bolt the door. It flew open and his anger was obvious, even before the first blow.

Chapter Fifty

Fate, coincidence, or could Jacob have been drawn to Rosie? What were the odds of them meeting by chance? Elizabeth had no idea. The likelihood of a transplant recipient accidentally meeting and then forming a relationship with the donor's girlfriend must be very slim, although they lived in the same county so the odds were increased. Or had it nothing to do with chance? Had Shane's DNA, now carousing through Jacob, sent him on a trajectory to Rosie? If you accepted cellular memory then it was certainly possible. Elizabeth shuddered at what she was having to come to terms with.

Should she tell Rosie that Jacob had Shane's heart? No, not now, perhaps never. She needed to think about it more. But first and foremost she needed to make sure Rosie was safe. With her breath coming fast and shallow she pressed Rosie's mobile number again. As before it rang twice and then went through to voicemail. Keeping her voice light, she left another message.

'Hi, love. Hope you're OK. Just a reminder to give me a date when you're both free to come to dinner again. Hope all is well with you.' She paused, feeling she needed to say something more but unsure of what, then said goodbye.

She tried as she had before to picture Rosie's flat with Jacob there. The two of them relaxing or having fun together. But she couldn't, not at all. It had been easy with Jacob and Eloise, they'd been a couple for years and she'd seen them together many times. And of course back then Jacob had been her son, the young man she'd brought up and knew, not the changeling she now saw. She couldn't imagine this Jacob with any decent woman, and not for the first time she prayed he was treating her well and being kind to her. Surely he must be or Rosie would never have agreed to him continuing to live with her? Unless of course the poor girl didn't have any choice, like at the end of his relationship with Eloise, when he'd kept her hostage and raped her. But that was ridiculous, Rosie had been to work today. She'd checked.

Mitsy stirred beside her and Elizabeth absently ruffled her fur. The clock on the mantelpiece now showed a quarter to eight. It was possible Rosie and Jacob were watching television or listening to music so hadn't heard the phone. Or perhaps Rosie was reading or taking a bath and her phone was in another room? Or maybe it was on silent and she hadn't checked it. There were any number of possible reasons why Rosie hadn't replied but none eased Elizabeth's concern.

At 8.15 when there'd still been no word, Elizabeth couldn't bear it any longer and telephoned Rosie again. If she answered this time she'd apologize for disturbing her and say she was just a bit worried she hadn't heard from her and was she OK? That was reasonable, wasn't it? Not overbearing or paranoid?

But Rosie didn't answer. It went through to voicemail again and Elizabeth left yet another message. It was difficult to keep the tremble from her voice. 'Hi, love. It's Liz again. Sorry to bother you. Just wanted to check you received my messages, and everything is all right. Could you phone or text me please? Sorry to be a pain.' She waited for a moment to see if Rosie would pick up but she didn't.

At 8.45 when there'd been no reply she tried once more, with the same result. She didn't leave a message this time, as there was nothing more she could say without sounding obsessively anxious. Perhaps they were out at the cinema and Rosie hadn't checked her phone? There were other plausible reasons for her not answering, but there were more worrying alternatives too and these now dominated and took control.

Ten minutes later Elizabeth collected her bag and jacket and went out to her car. The sun was just starting to set so it was still light. Perhaps she was being neurotic. She barely knew Rosie, but if there was a slim chance she wasn't all right she needed to check. She'd never forgive herself if something had happened and she'd ignored her instincts after what had happened to Eloise. She entered Rosie's postcode into the sat nav and then fastened her seat belt, and with mounting apprehension started the engine. If she arrived to find they were both contentedly watching television or similarly occupied and oblivious to her messages she'd admit she'd been worried and apologize profusely for overreacting.

Placing her phone on the passenger seat within view and the volume set on high she drove through the village. If Rosie phoned while she was driving she'd pull over, take the call, and assuming she was all right, go home. There'd be no need to admit she was on her way over, worried sick that something bad might have happened to her. She'd never mention it, not even to Andrew, for sometimes decisions that seem rational when deeply concerned about a loved one can appear ridiculous in the cool light of day when the danger has passed. She would keep this to herself as she did many things connected with Jacob now.

She gripped the steering wheel and concentrated on the road ahead. The sun continued its descent. The sat nav fell silent as she drove along the main road that would eventually take her into the town. Her thoughts scattered and re-formed, going from absurd speculation to what she actually knew. But then what she knew was disturbing enough.

Twenty minutes later she passed the transplant centre where they'd spent so much time when Jacob had been ill, and then entered the outskirts of the town. The sat nav sprang into action again, issuing a series of instructions to turn left and right. Five minutes later she turned into Highland Grove and heard 'you have reached your destination'.

Elizabeth parked as close as she could to the Hill Court flats. Now she'd arrived, her intention seemed even more ludicrous and also inappropriate. Parents of adult children didn't just arrive on their doorsteps in the late evening, especially when they were living with a partner. It wasn't the done thing. But then she hadn't come all this way for nothing, and fear for Rosie's safety once more overrode any concern about etiquette or making a fool of herself. Taking a deep breath, she quickly pressed Rosie's number, expecting it to go through to voicemail again.

To her utter amazement it was answered by Jacob with a terse, 'What do you want?'

'Jacob,' she said, completely thrown.

'Yes, it's still me,' he replied sarcastically

'How are you? I've been trying to contact Rosie but she's not picking up. Is everything all right?'

'Yes, why shouldn't it be?' he asked sharply. 'You keep phoning, but she's out and she's forgotten her phone.'

'Oh, I see. I'm sorry,' she stammered. Relief flooded through her and she felt an absolute fool for not considering the most obvious reason. 'I'm sorry to trouble you. Please tell her I rang.'

'Yeah, OK.'

'Let me know when you'd like to come to dinner,' she added, but he'd already ended the call.

Elizabeth sat for a moment, gazing through the windscreen. The sun had set now and the streetlamps were on. Thank goodness she hadn't gone straight up to the flat. He hadn't known she was outside, so the only evidence of her complete over-reaction was all the phone calls and messages she'd left on Rosie's phone. Clearly Jacob had been annoyed by them but then he could have answered her phone earlier or texted telling her Rosie was out. But that was how he was towards her now, thoughtless and curt. Of course she'd apologize to Rosie when she next spoke to her, but for now she needed to go home.

She reset the sat nav to the Rectory and started the engine. The voice on the sat nav told her to 'turn around where possible'. The road was full of parked cars so she'd have to make the turn further up using the entrance to the residents' car park. She pulled out and around the cars parked in front and then began a three-point turn. As she did she saw a light-blue Fiat just like Rosie's parked between two larger vehicles further up. And while neither the make nor the model were uncommon, the colour was. When Liz had admired it, Rosie had agreed it was different, and said it had taken her ages to find it as she'd wanted one the same colour as her old car, Betsy.

Elizabeth completed the turn and began slowly down the street towards the T-junction at the end of the road. There were many plausible reasons why Rosie's car was parked there when Jacob had said she was out. It was quite possible that wherever Rosie had gone was within walking distance, or a friend might have given her a lift, or maybe she'd taken a bus: all perfectly logical explanations. Having badly misinterpreted the situation once tonight, Elizabeth wasn't about to do so a second time.

She continued to the end of the road and turned left as the sat nav directed. But instead of driving straight on she pulled in and stopped. Jacob had been curt to the point of rudeness, but then he often was with her and Andrew, so she shouldn't read too much into that. There'd also been an underlying tension in his voice, probably because he was having to speak to her. There was no reason why Rosie shouldn't be out with her friends and it was feasible, although not likely, that she'd forgotten her phone. Yet that was what was niggling her. Most young people she knew were glued to their phones and if they did leave home without them, they quickly realized their omission and returned to collect them. Indeed, even she and Andrew (and most of their generation) had got into the habit of taking their mobiles with them if they went out.

Elizabeth waited for a car to pass and then made a U turn. The sat nav complained and she switched it off. She turned into Highland Grove again and parked in the spot she'd just vacated, her pulse racing. Switching off the engine, she sat for a moment trying to calm herself before pressing Jacob's number. He would see her number come up on the caller display. He answered immediately. 'What is it this time?'

'Jacob, don't be angry, I'm parked outside.'

'What the fuck! You're outside! Why?'

'I need to talk to you about something urgent. I'm coming up, OK?' And before he had a chance to say no she cut the call.

Chapter Fifty-One

'One sound and you're dead,' Jacob threatened, dragging the chair with Rosie tied to it into the bedroom. 'Understand me?'

She nodded, petrified and aware he meant it. Since beating her in the bathroom and retying her to the chair he'd grown increasingly violent and agitated. He'd sworn at Taco on the phone and threatened to kill him. He kept giving little coughs and patting his chest as though trying to get his breath. Now his mother had arrived, causing him to panic. He went out of the bedroom and slammed the door shut behind him.

Her face was sore from where he'd hit her and the string around her wrists was even tighter now. He'd tied her legs to the chair as well to make sure she couldn't make another run for it. But Liz was outside and on her way up. It was a lifeline of hope; she couldn't believe it.

Whatever had brought her here so late in the evening? Perhaps one of her texts or phone calls had been to say she was coming, for Jacob hadn't let her see her phone. But he'd told Liz she was out. She'd heard him. So she'd need to make her aware she was here: draw attention to herself, signal.

She glanced around the room for anything she could use to make a noise. Whatever she did she'd only have one chance and then he'd be in to silence her for good. She couldn't throw something at the door or window. Even if she could pick it up with her hands tied behind her back it would be impossible to move her arm into a position where she could produce enough force to throw it and make a noise. Then she saw her make-up purse on the chest of drawers. Inside was a pair of nail scissors. If she could reach them would it be possible to cut through the string with her hands tied behind her? She'd no idea but she had to try. If Liz stayed long enough and kept him talking maybe she would have a chance.

Digging her feet into the carpet she began pushing the chair backwards, inching the legs over the carpet towards the chest of drawers. The doorbell rang. She stopped still, listening, her senses on full alert. She heard Jacob curse his mother as he went to answer the door. Then Liz's voice, familiar and kind. 'Hello, love.' She kept perfectly still, listening and waiting until they were in the living room. Then she continued her piecemeal journey towards the chest of drawers, hoping and praying Jacob wouldn't come in to check on her.

Chapter Fifty-Two

Elizabeth glanced around the compact neat living space and through to the adjoining kitchen.

'There's Rosie's phone,' Jacob said rudely, thrusting it under her nose. 'I told you she was out.'

'I know, I believed you,' she said, trying to keep the tremor from her voice. 'It's you I've come to see. Could I have a glass of water please? I'm very thirsty.' She took a step towards the kitchen.

'I'll get it,' he said, brushing past her. 'You stay there.'

When did he start issuing orders that she obeyed? But she remained where she was and watched him. He looked ill. There was a sickly pallor to his skin which she hadn't seen since he'd been on the transplant list waiting for a donor, and he was perspiring heavily although it wasn't that hot in the flat. His breathing sounded laboured too.

'You haven't got a chest infection have you?' she asked.

'You know the immunosuppressants lower your body's resistance.'

He ignored her and returned with the glass of water, which he thrust into her hand.

'Thank you, can I sit down?'

'Suit yourself.'

She perched on the sofa. 'Are you all right?' she tried again, genuinely concerned.

'Why shouldn't I be?'

'You don't look well. Have you been keeping your hospital appointments? You know how important they are.'

He shrugged dismissively. 'What's it got to do with you? You don't care.'

She flinched. His comments still hurt even though she now knew it wasn't him talking. She took a sip of water and set the glass on the table. 'Jacob, there's something I need to tell you. Something I've found out – about transplants. Can you sit down please so we can talk?' He was standing a little way in front of her, shifting agitatedly from one foot to the other. It was making her more anxious.

'I'm OK here,' he said bluntly. 'Say what you have to quickly, I need to go out later.'

'Really? It's late.'

'To collect Rosie.'

'Oh, I see.' She took a breath and summoned her courage. She knew what she had to say was going to anger him, but she had to tell him and make him aware so he could hopefully stop himself from doing more harm.

'I've been doing some research,' she began, 'and although it's not proven a hundred per cent, there's a lot of evidence to suggest that some people who receive transplants take on the mental and physical characteristics of the donor. It's called cellular memory.' She paused and looked at him for a reaction. The old Jacob with intellectual insight and understanding would make the connection, but he was just staring at her.

'So?' he demanded.

'I think that's what has happened to you.'

His lip curled into a ridiculing smile. 'What? That I've become someone else? Don't be so daft.'

'Yes, sort of.'

He began laughing, loudly and derisively. Then he stopped as quickly as he'd begun and his eyes narrowed accusingly. 'You gotta be joking me. If I'm rotten it's your fault, because of the way you treated me. You never showed me any love or affection. Not one bit. You treated me and my dad like shit. You're an evil bitch and I'd say you got the son you deserved.' He grinned humourlessly.

Now she knew where his words had come from, they weren't the shock they might otherwise have been. She swallowed, trying to keep calm. 'Jacob, what you are saying is not true of our family, but it is true of the donor's. Listen to me please, you have to understand what's happening to you.'

She stood and took a step towards him. She needed to make him realize. 'I'm not the only one who believes this, there is a lot of research. I've been reading articles and talking to a doctor who researched cellular memory in depth for his PhD. He's confirmed it does happen. There are many documented cases. Cellular memory is the way cells hold and transfer memory in their DNA. A girl in Brazil found her blood group had changed after a liver transplant, and in another case a man's DNA changed completely after a heart transplant. So in many ways they were more like the donor than their previous selves.' He sneered but she continued.

'It doesn't happen in all cases and some changes are quite minor, like changes in food or music likes and dislikes, but others have experienced astounding changes – some for the better and some for the worse. I'm sure that's what's happened to you, Jacob. Try to remember what you were like before the transplant and compare it to how you are now.' She stopped, breathless.

'It's an excuse!' he said, without giving her words any consideration.

'No it's not.' She placed her hand on his arm and he shook it off. 'I've traced your donor. I've spoken to his mother. He was called Shane Smith and he was bad. It wasn't all his fault, he was never shown much love as a child and he got into a lot of trouble with the police. Just as you are doing now. You have to believe me, Jacob. If you're aware of what's happened, then perhaps you can stop yourself doing more bad things and change your future. I came here tonight on purpose to make sure Rosie was safe. I'm worried sick you could harm her like you did Eloise. Please Jacob, I beg you, think about what I'm saying. Remember the person you were and how you've changed.' She paused, willing him to understand and accept what she was saying.

'Bullshit!' he said. 'You've made all this up to save your own skin.'

'No!' she cried, grabbing his arm again. 'It's true, Jacob. I can show you evidence if you let me.'

'Liar!' he cried, moving away. 'You're making excuses for the way you treated me.'

'Jacob! Not only are you behaving as Shane would have done but you're living with his girlfriend – Rosie.' She hadn't intended to blurt this out but she needed to make him understand.

'You're mad!' he said, taking another step away. 'It just shows how evil you are, making all this up.'

'No. It's true, really. Shane lived here with Rosie right up until he died. His mother told me.'

He was furious now; rage had replaced disbelief. She could see it in his face and the way he held his body. He was reacting just as Shane would have done, she was sure. All-consuming anger and bitterness were replacing rational thought. She jumped as he grabbed the glass of water and hurled it against the wall. It shattered into a cascade of splintered glass and liquid. 'I'll kill her, the two-timing bitch! I'll fucking kill you both.' His eyes were glazed and bloodshot, blazing with anger. He turned and went into the kitchen, coming back with a carving knife.

'No, Jacob!' she screamed and backed away. 'You don't have to hurt anyone any more. Put the knife down. Try to remember who you are – Jacob, my son. Andrew is your father. He lives with us. We both love you.'

He continued towards her as she backed into the hall. 'You're a lying bitch!' he shouted. 'I'll make you pay for what you've done to me.' Then suddenly he was gasping for breath, and his hand shot to his chest as the colour drained from his face. She watched in horror as his knees buckled and he crumpled in a heap, the knife falling from his hand and clattering onto the wooden floor.

'Jacob!' She rushed to his side and dropped to her knees. 'Jacob?' His eyes were closed; he was unconscious but breathing. She ran to fetch her phone, pressing 999 for the emergency services as she returned to his side. 'Ambulance,' she said, dropping to her knees as the call connected, 'Quickly. My son has collapsed. Flat seventeen, Hill Court, Highland Grove. Yes, he's unconscious but still breathing. He had a heart transplant a year ago.'

Then as she waited for the ambulance, praying that despite everything Jacob, her son, would live, a noise sounded from somewhere close by. Like a door opening. She instinctively looked towards the front door but it remained closed. A figure appeared at the other end of the hall.

'Rosie!' Her face was swollen and her lip was bleeding but worse than that was the fear in her eyes. Elizabeth went to her, opened her arms and held her close. 'It's all right,' she soothed. 'You're safe now. I'll look after you.'

'Shane?' Rosie asked quietly.

'You heard?'

'Yes.'

'I'm so sorry, I should have told you sooner.'

'But I didn't even know he was dead.'

Elizabeth pulled back in surprise. 'You didn't know? Oh Rosie, he died in hospital three days after the accident. It was sudden. A blood clot to his brain. Didn't you see it in the newspaper? His organs were used for transplant.'

'No, I was in such a state that I shut myself away and tried to get over what had happened. I didn't want to know anything about Shane any more. I've always been terrified of him finding me again.' She took a deep breath. 'So this wasn't my fault?' she said, looking at Jacob.

'No, love. It wasn't. But there's no need for us to mention any of this to anyone, ever. It can be our secret.'

Chapter Fifty-Three

One month later, DC Pamela Small sat at her office desk, going over the list of contacts in Oliver Cambridge's mobile phone. There'd been a handful of contacts who for various reasons they hadn't been able to speak to on their first trawl through, and as they were no nearer finding out who was responsible for Cambridge's murder they were having a last-ditch attempt before the active investigation was closed. Pamela now crossed off Jacob Wilson's name, having just spoken to his mother. Like most of the contacts in Cambridge's phone Jacob's number was there because he'd been supplying him with cannabis. Jacob's mother had just confirmed her son had been a regular user – buying it from Chez – and he'd been with her on the night of the attack. She'd said Jacob was now in hospital, fighting for his life. That poor family, Pamela thought. Some people had more than their fair share of ill luck. Bad enough to have a son born with a congenital heart disease but to have a heart transplant fail and require another one was something else.

Jaded, and in need of a change from going through the contact list again – 'Repeat everything before we put this to bed,' the boss had said – she set aside the list and looked again at the forensic report. Perhaps something would strike her afresh, open up a new line of inquiry, although she doubted it. Forensics had been very thorough as usual but they hadn't been able to lift much of use from Cambridge's possessions. He hadn't regained consciousness before his death so hadn't been able to give them a description of his attackers, and lying in the rain for a whole weekend had washed away any useful forensic evidence. They knew from the footprints on his body and clothes that there'd been more than one assailant, and he'd died from multiple internal injuries and pneumonia. For a while they thought they might have one decent fingerprint, on the metal buckle of Cambridge's belt, but when they'd run it through the police computer it had come out as a match for Shane Smith, who'd died in a car accident the year before. So either the belt had once belonged to Shane or he'd come into contact with it at some time before he'd died, or the fingerprint had been smudged after all, for not even identical twins shared the same fingerprints.

She continued reading the report, going over what she and the team already knew, then with a small sigh put it aside and returned to the list of phone contacts. She had a hunch Cambridge knew his attackers – possibly thugs he'd crossed; the drug world was merciless and brutal. She'd spoken to his supplier who was more ruthless and brutal than most, even offering him sweeteners if he could help identify the attackers, but he claimed to know nothing of the attack, which was highly doubtful. Likewise, Cambridge's so-called mates had been 'unable' – which Pamela took to mean unwilling – to tell her what they knew, obviously fearing reprisals. So it was looking increasingly likely that this case would join the hundred or so other unsolved murders that were filed away each year in the UK. Cold cases as they were known, no longer being actively investigated but left open in case a new lead came up.

Chapter Fifty-Four

Jacob was in a different room but the same ward and hospital as before. Many of the nurses were the same too; transplant centres tended to keep their specialist nurses. They'd begun joking with him as soon as he was out of intensive care and off the danger list – 'Couldn't keep away from us, could you?' 'You must like it here.' And now he was beginning to feel a bit better he could laugh and joke with them too, as well as thanking them and the doctors for all they were doing.

'I'm so grateful,' he said whenever he had the chance. 'I promise I won't mess up this time.' For most of the staff knew that had he gone for his regular check-ups the infection that had caused his heart to reject would have been picked up sooner and treated.

Jacob couldn't believe his good fortune; not many got the second chance of a transplant when the first failed.

He was aware many patients died while on the transplant list waiting for a suitable organ. It was his lucky break, and doubtless the prayers of his parents and the whole village had helped. True, the organ wasn't as perfect a match as the first one. It had come from a 44-year-old woman who'd died of a brain tumour. The doctors had said that while they were as confident as they could be that her cancer hadn't spread to other parts of her body they had a duty to tell him as cancer cells could be transplanted with an organ. At the time he'd been too ill to make the decision and was now grateful to his parents for deciding to go ahead, for without this new heart he would certainly have been dead by now. They visited most days and he appreciated the huge sacrifices they were having to make while he was so ill.

Get-well cards festooned every available surface in his room and a large helium 'get well soon' balloon was tethered to a chair in one corner. Before it was anchored down it had wandered around in the air from the opening and closing door, giving the appearance of someone being in the room if he caught sight of it out of the corner of his eye. It had given him a shock and frightened him, especially at night when it lurked menacingly in the shadows, so he'd asked a nurse to tie it to the chair.

It was a pity he couldn't tie down his thoughts in the same way. They were strange thoughts, dreams, hallucinations, which the doctor had reassured him were due to the high level of medication he was on. They would gradually ease and disappear, he said. But it was unsettling to see and hear things so real he was convinced they had actually happened, and indeed some of them had, which made it more confusing. Illogical, out of character situations that made no sense at all. Why, for example, had he split from Eloise and gone to live with Rosie, whom he hardly knew? When he'd asked his mother she'd become evasive and had changed the subject. When he'd said he was thinking of phoning Eloise to try to patch things up she'd said, 'No! Definitely not. And don't try to contact Rosie either.' She'd been so adamant and fervent that he hadn't liked to question her further. She said she'd explain more when he was completely better, and also possibly introduce him to someone called David who could help him come to terms with 'what had happened'. Meanwhile his father, pragmatic as usual, had said he was just pleased to have his son back and to concentrate on getting better and look to the future.

Easier said than done, Jacob thought. Alone in his room when his visitors had gone, he couldn't stop his thoughts wandering and some of them were disturbing. On the day he learnt that Mary Hutchins, had died, he'd been convinced her death was his fault. That he'd gone to her cottage in the middle of the night and had hit her over the head with a candlestick. It was so vivid and real he couldn't get the thought out of his head and had eventually told his mother. She'd reassured him that Mary had died as a result of a fall, although there'd been some speculation in the village at the time that her cottage had been broken into and she'd been robbed, but that had never been proven. As his mother had said, he would have known this, and the drugs had fuelled his imagination. It would be better once the medication was reduced and he was home again. Relieved, he'd seen she was right. He was looking forward to going home, his mother's cooking, taking Mitsy for walks, and eating a big bowl of chocolate-chip ice cream. She'd laughed at this and promised to buy some in specially as he'd never liked ice cream before; that and the Earl Grey tea he was also asking for. Tastes can change, she'd said.

Epilogue

Summer turned to autumn. The leaves changed colour and fell from the trees in the wind that whipped around Maybury village. Brian Roberts, whose family had been farming the land next to Acorn Cottage for generations, was on his tractor ploughing the field ready to plant wheat as he did every year. The soil was perfect for ploughing, moist but not waterlogged. He hummed a tune to himself as he went up and down the field, the old 500 hp diesel engine chugging happily, and a flock of birds in his wake. He was making good time and would be finished soon and home for lunch. As he slowed to pull round the top end of the field and make another turn he caught sight of something glinting in the hedgerow. Something large enough to pique his interest. A metal can? He didn't think so. Wrong shape.

He drew the tractor to a halt and applied the handbrake.

Leaving the engine running he jumped down and trod over the freshly turned earth to the grassy verge for a closer look. A silver candlestick, half covered by grass and leaves. He picked it up and brushed off the dirt and detritus of autumn. Was it worth anything? Probably only to its owner. It clearly hadn't been here for very long as it was only partly tarnished. He turned it over, wiping away the dirt, and an inscription appeared. He rubbed it on his fleece. *To Mr and Mrs Hutchins on your wedding day. 6th May, 1944.*

Mary Hutchins. It had been a wedding present to her and her husband all those years ago. But how on earth did it get here and what should he do with it? When she'd died she'd left no surviving relatives and had bequeathed all her possessions to the church. He couldn't just throw it back in the hedgerow now he'd found it, and neither did he feel comfortable keeping it. Perhaps he should take it to a charity shop as they'd done with all the other items from her cottage that couldn't be auctioned. Or perhaps he should take it to the rectory and give it to Andrew? Yes, that would be like fulfilling her wishes of leaving her possessions to the church, and Andrew would know what to do with it. He returned to his tractor and placed the candlestick in the storage compartment next to his flask. But on the other hand, a while ago now there'd been a lot of talk about Acorn Cottage being broken into and money stolen. Had a candlestick been stolen too? He couldn't remember it ever being mentioned, and Mary had died soon after returning home from hospital. Perhaps he should take it into the police station next time he was in town? Yes, that seemed the best course of action. He'd do it as soon as he could.

Author's note

While this story is fiction, I find the subject matter of cellular memory fascinating, and also the fact that so many people experience inexplicable personality changes after a transplant.

To learn more about Lisa Stone and her books please visit www.lisastonebooks.co.uk

Suggested topics for reading group discussion

1. The opening chapters of *The Darkness Within* are from Shane's perspective. What do we learn about Rosie and how much of this could be said to be true?

2. Later when history repeats itself and Rosie is blaming herself for forming another abusive relationship, Eva says there is nothing wrong with her other than she is 'too trusting'. How far do you think this is true?

3. Transplanting organs has become commonplace. What are the ethical dilemmas? Are these increased if we accept the cellular memory theory?

4. Setting aside cellular memory being responsible, why might Rosie have been attracted to Jacob? Is there anything in his manner or conversation that should have alerted her sooner?

5. The author juxtaposes Jacob's decline into depravity with life at the rectory. How far are his parents prepared to go to make allowances for him? Is this reasonable?

6. Is there anything his parents could have done differently to prevent Jacob's decline?

7. Elizabeth is devastated by Eloise's claims but believes her. Why?

8. If we accept cellular memory exists in humans, as it does in plants and lower life forms, then it throws into question our uniqueness as individuals. Discuss.

9. When Elizabeth realizes why Jacob is behaving as he is, she goes to Rosie's flat. Discuss possible outcomes if Jacob hadn't collapsed when he had.

10. When Jacob is recovering in hospital after his second transplant he experiences strange thoughts and dreams. What might they be traced to? Why is Elizabeth adamant he must not contact either Rosie or Eloise?

11. When DC Pamela Small is reviewing the evidence in Chez's death near the end of the book she says: '*For a while they thought they might have one decent fingerprint, on the metal buckle of Cambridge's belt, but when they'd*

run it through the police computer it had come out as a match for Shane Smith who'd died in a car accident the year before. So either the belt had once belonged to Shane or he'd come into contact with it at some time before he'd died, or the fingerprint had been smudged after all, for not even identical twins had the same fingerprint.' Why is she wrong? Could the real explanation ever be proven?

Can I Let You Go?

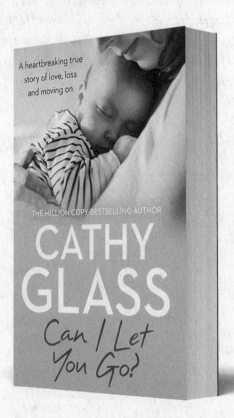

A heartbreaking true story of love, loss and moving on

THE MILLION COPY BESTSELLING AUTHOR

CATHY GLASS

Can I Let You Go?

Faye is 24 and pregnant, and has learning difficulties as a result of her mother's alcoholism

Can Cathy help Faye learn enough to parent her child?

The Silent Cry

A mother battling depression. A family in denial

Cathy is desperate to help before something terrible happens.

Girl Alone

An angry, traumatized young girl on a path to self-destruction

Can Cathy discover the truth behind Joss's dangerous behaviour before it's too late?

Saving Danny

Danny's parents can no longer cope with his challenging behaviour

Calling on all her expertise, Cathy discovers a frightened little boy who just wants to be loved.

The Child Bride

**A girl blamed and
abused for dishonouring
her community**

Cathy discovers the
devastating truth.

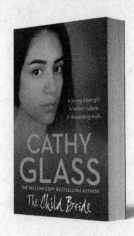

Daddy's
Little Princess

**A sweet-natured girl with
a complicated past**

Cathy picks up the
pieces after events take
a dramatic turn.

Will You Love Me?

**A broken child desperate
for a loving home**

The true story of Cathy's
adopted daughter Lucy.

Please Don't Take My Baby

Seventeen-year-old Jade is pregnant, homeless and alone

Cathy has room in her heart for two.

Another Forgotten Child

Eight-year-old Aimee was on the child-protection register at birth

Cathy is determined to give her the happy home she deserves.

A Baby's Cry

A newborn, only hours old, taken into care

Cathy protects tiny Harrison from the potentially fatal secrets that surround his existence.

The Night the
Angels Came

A little boy on the
brink of bereavement

Cathy and her family
make sure Michael is
never alone.

Mummy Told Me
Not to Tell

A troubled boy
sworn to secrecy

After his dark past has
been revealed, Cathy helps
Reece to rebuild his life.

I Miss Mummy

Four-year-old Alice
doesn't understand why
she's in care

Cathy fights for her
to have the happy home
she deserves.

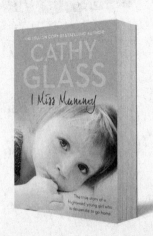

The Saddest Girl in the World

A haunted child who refuses to speak

Do Donna's scars run too deep for Cathy to help?

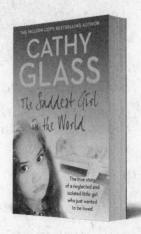

Cut

Dawn is desperate to be loved

Abused and abandoned, this vulnerable child pushes Cathy and her family to their limits.

Hidden

The boy with no past

Can Cathy help Tayo to feel like he belongs again?

Damaged

A forgotten child

Cathy is Jodie's last hope.
For the first time, this
abused young girl has
found someone
she can trust.

Inspired by Cathy's own experiences...

Run, Mummy, Run

The gripping story of a
woman caught in a horrific
cycle of abuse, and the
desperate measures she
must take to escape.

My Dad's a
Policeman

The dramatic short story
about a young boy's
desperate bid to keep his
family together.

The Girl in the Mirror

Trying to piece together her past, Mandy uncovers a dreadful family secret that has been blanked from her memory for years.

Sharing her expertise...

About Writing and How to Publish

A clear and concise, practical guide on writing and the best ways to get published.

Happy Mealtimes for Kids

A guide to healthy eating with simple recipes that children love.

Happy Adults

A practical guide to achieving lasting happiness, contentment and success. The essential manual for getting the best out of life.

Happy Kids

A clear and concise guide to raising confident, well-behaved and happy children.